OUR PEOPLE
MORE STORIES OF THE SOUTH

George Spain

Ideas into Books® WESTVIEW
Kingston Springs, Tennessee

ii

Ideas into Books®
W E S T V I E W
P.O. Box 605
Kingston Springs, TN 37082
www.publishedbywestview.com

ISBN 978-1-62880-100-2

Cover and album design by Peg Fredi.

First edition, March 2016

Printed in the United States of America on acid free paper.

.

ALSO BY GEORGE SPAIN

Delightful Suthun Madnesses
Our People: Stories of the South
Lost Cove
Come Sit With Me
The Last Giant

DEDICATION

to

Jackie and Our People

ACKNOWLEDGEMENTS

Thanks to Jackie's and my ancestors for providing me with an excess of extraordinary people and events around which to weave my characters and stories.

TABLE OF CONTENTS

FOREWORD

FOR THE READER AND TO WRITERS TO BE

I was raised on classic comics and various other kinds of books, and began writing poetry in the mid-nineteen sixties. Early on, one of my poems was published in *Soviet Life,* a Russian magazine, another in the first edition of *Cumberland Poetry Review.* Heady stuff! It fueled my fire. Kind people said kind things, which helped me persevere through the long dry years that followed.

My early poetry was influenced by Dylan Thomas, James Dickey and Walt Whitman. In hindsight, most of my poems were not very good, but one of my English professors whom I admired kindly agreed to read them. After doing so, he said, "George, you can write, so keep at it and keep on reading lots of the best poets." His words spurred me to keep going.

My professor's advice to READ - READ - READ was the best I could have received. If a person aspires to write historical fiction, then my advice is to read good historians, biographers and writers of historical fiction. Let them be your primary teachers, more than technical books on, "How To Write Historical Fiction". And as you begin your own writing, don't be afraid to let them help you with one of their wonderful phrases or a lightning word.

Think about what makes certain writers exceptional; writers such as Faulkner, Twain, Poe, Melville, Steinbeck, Eudora Welty, Harper Lee, Larry McMurtry, Cormac McCarthy and John Grisham. I personally would advise reading Edward P. Jones, author of the Pulitzer Prize winning *The Known World*; he is one of my favorites. And then think about what you have written. Look at the words; the sentences. Can any be improved; can any be eliminated? Think about your audience. Who are you writing for? However, a writer must realize that to be successful, ultimately, he must write for his own satisfaction.

What is historical fiction? It is a fictional story around a historical person or event; one where the reader might gain a new understanding or appreciation of such person or event; the writer is not presenting pure history but creating a story that mixes historical characters, places and events with those of his imagination. Truman Capote's novel, *In Cold Blood,* was a pioneer in studying history as much as possible, and then, since no one was present at the time of the event to report it, adding as much fiction as needed to make the story believable; Robert E. Lee and Jerome Lawrence's *Inherit the Wind* is a perfect example of this technique being applied successfully. Although I personally follow the rule, "A fact should never stand in the way of a good story," a writer should use fiction to fill in the gaps.

I'm often asked, "Where do you get your ideas for stories?" From personal history, family history or, sometimes, they just pop into my head. From everywhere, though some seem to come from nowhere.

My Russian poem came from a simple photograph: a child's body on a sled, being dragged through the snow during the siege of Leningrad in 1941-42. An idea might come from a fragment of family history that is so intriguing it will not leave me; slowly it evolves into a story. One morning, at about four o'clock, an idea came as a question: *Could I write a ghost story about my wife who died in 2009?* That thought became one of my books, *Come Sit With Me.* In this particular story, there's enough factual history that made several who know me well assume that it really happened. Almost all my stories are taken from bits and pieces of my ancestors' lives or from southern history.

Once a writer has settled on an idea for a story the real work begins. Ernest Hemingway was once asked if writing was hard. He answered, "No, you just sit down at the typewriter and bleed." That's a tad dramatic, but I agree, "It ain't easy."

Good stories set a hook with the first sentence and first paragraph, snaring the attention so tightly that the reader doesn't want to stop. My *Death of a Confederate Captain* begins:

> They said Captain Robert Taggert hanged himself in Lady's stall on June 27, 1874, because she had been his son, Bob's, favorite saddle horse. Bob had died on that exact same day, ten years before. Years later, Aunt Sally, the Taggerts' cook, told me that the rope broke after the Captain was dead and that his body fell into the straw but the mare never stepped on him. Though he didn't

leave a note, I knew why the "Captain",
for that's what everybody called him, did
what he did.

A huge amount of research may be required to set the
stage for a story. In my short story, *The Searcher*, which
occurs two days after the Battle of Nashville on
December, 15-16, 1864, I offer a detailed description of
the city and the battlefield, attempting to make the reader
see it, smell it, hear it, taste it and touch it:

It is early morning of the second day
after the Confederates have retreated
southward. The shell-torn hills and fields
are covered with debris. Bodies and parts
of bodies are still being found and
buried. It stinks with a moldy odor: the
Confederate dead in their shallow graves,
buried where they have fallen; parts of
men and horses scattered in the mud and
litter; the blood of the wounded; the dead
and the sick filling the hospitals,
churches, homes and schools; the stench
of the unwashed thousands of prisoners
packed into abandoned buildings and
warehouses; the burning of dead horses
and the wreckage of battle; the piles of
rubbish, the piss, the shit and decay of all
the living and the dead. It is the odor of
war rising from a city of 30,000, now
filled with 70,000 Yankee soldiers and
thousands of Rebel prisoners and hordes
of refugees, freed slaves, laborers, team-

sters, gamblers, drummers, prostitutes
and herds of cattle and horses and mules.

Then, out onto this stage walks the major character,
Katrine O'Conner, an Irish woman searching the city and
battlefield for the father of her son, a black soldier, who
has fought in the battle with the 13th United States
Colored Troop Regiment.

Of utmost importance, the writer has an obligation to
be true to the characters he creates: let them speak as
they would have spoken; Let them do as they would have
done, even if, at times, they are disturbingly violent.
Remember, all the bad language and bad behavior must
fit the character; they are not going to make "a silk purse
out of a sow's ear". If the story is no good, it won't be
made better by injecting obscenities or throat cuttings.

If you want characters to come alive, infuse their veins
with emotional and psychological blood; don't write what
makes the reader feel good; write what makes the reader
know that what they are reading *is, or could be,* real. I
have never known an all-good or all-bad person.
Therefore, in order to give more reality to primary
characters, avoid their being one-dimensional. In my
short story, *God's Punishment,* a kindhearted, strong
mountain woman takes in two young Confederate
deserters for the night, and while they are sleeping kills
them with an ax in revenge for Confederate guerillas
killing her husband and son. I have known many
preachers, politicians, physicians, a few killers and some
drug dealers; not one was totally good or totally bad.

Much of what a reader understands about a character is told by what that character does and says. But a description by the writer can be extremely helpful.

Another of my stories, *Lucy Taggert's Six Letters,* begins with a description of a woman that intertwines her outer and inner beauty and strength.

My Lord, Lucy Gaunt Taggert was a stunningly beautiful woman! Every small bit of her body, every small bit of her mind and soul and all of her spirit was a woman's—a woman second to none and certainly second to no man.

Her long straight neck was crowned by a finely shaped head with a face so strong and striking that men, and even women, could not help but stare at her. Her head was always held high with her slightly curly, soft-gray hair drawn tightly back in a bun. Her face toned with pride; her eyes ash-colored, intelligent, reserved, almost cold, seldom blinked as they saw the lies and fears beneath the masks of others; her lips, full and pink, pursed slightly as might a young woman's who was about to kiss her lover. She was sixty-three—

Her beauty was sensual, not like that of a rose or a sunset; it was the beauty of the bed. Her flesh, touched with light and shadows, spread over her body like smooth white milk. Men sought her but never once did she seek them. Many men, including her minister, Reverend Thomas Dark of the Estill Springs Baptist Church, could barely control the lust in their faces or voices when they were near her. She treated these men, even if they were among the gentry, with the same coldness she might use when dealing with ill-mannered white trash. When she saw sex in the eyes of Reverend Dark the day he came to her house to comfort her and pray with her after Bob's death, she told him to take his Bible and hat and go home and go to bed with his wife. After that, she never set foot in church again. Men saw her beauty, her aloofness, her perseverance; what they did not see was her anger, an anger that eventually turned into hatred when death came to her home.

I believe characters—fictional children—should think and talk as they would have in their day and place. Field hands didn't talk like house servants; an uneducated man from deep in the mountains of east Tennessee didn't talk like a plantation owner from west Tennessee; the words and sounds of a woman who has just arrived from Ireland differ from those of a third generation Irish Bostonian. I don't talk like my far-back-in-time ancestors. Some of their sayings are no longer used. Some are extinct. Some of the words we now use have only recently been put into *Webster's*.

Some writers and readers don't care for dialect. An example from *The Hunters* shows my love of dialect:

> Ye say hit's down thar?
>
> Uh huh.
>
> Neath them bluffs?
>
> Uh huh. That's whar hit kilt her an I seen hits tracks.
>
> Ye say hit et her?
>
> Uh huh, an hit drug her leavins back in tha cave.
>
> Lord, Pa, you reckon hit's still thar?
>
> Aye, God, if hit is I aims to kill hit.
>
> Well, I shore don't want to git kilt.

Research in dialect is as important as in other areas. It is what gives life to 'dem dry bones'. If you are writing about an old former slave who, after the war, became a preacher and about an old former Confederate talking to one another as they sit, side by side on a wagon seat riding toward Winchester, Tennessee, on June 3, 1898, for the annual Confederate Decoration Day, research should be done concerning the weather for the day, what crops were in the field, what flowers and shrubs were growing beside the road, what birds called from the fields and hedgerows, what the names were of the mules pulling the wagon, what sounds their hoofs and snorts made, what the air smelled of, what wood the wagon was made of and if it was painted, how they knew one another, what they looked like, how they were dressed, how they felt toward one another, and what you want them to tell about life. While doing all that research, the writer mustn't forget to study their language habits.

"You know, Colonel, you nevah ask me what it was like bein a slave an I's nevah said a thing til now...folks look at me an they sees a kind-lookin, ole white haired colored preacher who likes to help people, an that's pretty much true now, but I hadn't always been this way. A long time ago, tha Lawd an Liza change me. I wants to kill people...wants to kill white people fo what they done to us...I'd wanted to kill you I's so full of hate. Bein a slave is a bad thing, so bad you can't nevah know it, we wadn't much mo than a bunch of two-legged animals worth lots of money...the Major an his wife, they was church goin people who said the blessin at all their meals an always talkin bout Jesus an how someday they's goin to heaven, an look at what they did...they's made me hate Jesus an tha Lawd God. But all tha while I nevah lets on, I's covered it all up, all my sadness an hate, even when they's sold my Liza an Hattie away, I's didn't show nothin cause I's promised her I wouldn't kill someone or do somethin awful, an one day I'd come an find em an we'd be togethah again...an thas what I did...an tha Lawd was good to me an forgive my sinful heart an answered my prayers, an so Him an Liza, they's teach me to want to be good an to help others an He move my heart to

preach His word an help sinners like me
to find Him..."

During the Great Depression of the 1930s, the Federal Writers' Project sent out hundreds of jobless writers to interview former slaves about their lives in slavery. Two thousand slave narratives came from this, many were written in dialect, a resource available in several publications.

We are the creators of our characters and the worlds they live in, the air they breathe, the earth they walk upon, the words they speak. Your primary obligation is to them, not the reader. To paraphrase Hemingway, "Bleed your blood—and theirs—into the words you write."

George Spain
Nashville, Tennessee
2015

A 31

Levi Thomas Crossley, "Granddaddy," holding me on his mule, "Beck," in Shohoh, Kentuck

My mother's grandparents, Jeremiah and Sarah
Turner. Jeremiah fought with the 7th Tennessee
and Robert E. Lee in the Civil War.

Crossleys: at family farm in Schochoh, Kentucky. Farm remains in the family. Back row, L-R L.S., Billy, my mother Fannie Elizabeth, seated are my grandparents, Levi Thomas and Lillie Jane ad Collie stock dog.

Four George Spains, L-R: George Edward Spain,
George Stainback Spain, "Papa" holding, George
Bradford Spain, and George Joseph Spain.

L. B.: My wife, Jacqulyn Katrine Buxton Spain "Jackie," Leah Pearson Lynch, Katrine Leah Lynch Buxton "Tinie," and Elizabeth Katrine Spain Flynn "Tina."

Jackie's grandparents, H.M. and Lillie Armstrong, Burton with their grandchildren on the front porch of their house and farm "Seven Hills" in Nashville, Tennessee. The home is gone and the land renamed, "Burton Hills." Jackie is the cute little girl on the left front corner.

A gathering of pains

My grandparents, George "Papa" and Olevia "Mama" pain are in the center. My father is behind Papa. The rest are aunts and uncles. They were smart and loved to laugh.

A Gathering of Burtons

Jackie's father, Nelson Burton, is to the left in suit and tie. I am kneeling in the center holding our grandson, Leland. Jackie is on the right with the red vest.

Jackie's great grandmother, Leah Holmein
Pearson; with her sons at the Pearson home
In Franklin County, Tennessee

The Lynch brothers from Winchester,
M: L: B Lafayette, Francis and William
(Jackie's great grandfather). They joined the
1st Tennessee together and fought through
most of the Civil War. Francis was killed
at the Battle of Kennesaw Mt., Georgia.

Wedding of Jackie's parents: Katrine "Trinie" Lynch and Nelson Buston. Wedding party in front of Lynch home in Winchester, TN. The wedding was paid for with money from the sale of a coal mine that Trinie's mother owned on Sewanee Mountain.

Seven Hills

Jackie's grandparents (Burtons) home in
Nashville, TN. This house stood near the
Middle of the battlefield of the Battle of
Nashville. We were married in the gardens
to the left of the house.

Our Marriage

In the gardens of "Seven Hills,"

June 22, 1956

Our Family

For fifteen years we went to Big
South Fork in Tennessee and rode
horseback. Our son Adam, in the
back at right, was killed in
Afghanistan in 2010.

FAMILY MEMBERS ON
PREVIOUS PAGE

Front row, left to right:

> Darwin Spain (son)
> Zoe Spain
> Creed Spain
> Pearson Flynn
> Jesse Spain
> Lillie Flynn
> Lealand Spain
> Anna Spain
> Leah Flynn
> Shane Spain
> Shane's friend
> Jackie Burton Spain
> George Edward Spain (me)

Back row, left to right:

> Lorie Spain (Darwin's wife)
> Lynch Spain (son)
> Sara Spain (Lynch's wife)
> Brad Spain (son)
> Trina Flynn (daughter)
> Pat Flynn (Trina's husband)
> Angie Spain (Adam's wife)
> Adam Spain (son, killed in Afghanistan, 2010)

Our People

More Stories of the South

How We Helped Win World War II

Cast of Characters

Billy Bob............(12) The oldest of our group, our heavily freckled leader ruled over us with his fast fists.

TC ....(11) When it came to creating disgusting deformities, he was the master with his eyelids turned inside out.

Bush..................(11) My best buddy, whose devout Catholic family—who drank all kinds of alcohol openly—saved me from many prejudices.

Double M ....(11) Living all the way over on the next street, he was not quite a full member but he had the best climbing trees and a barn.

GE ....(10) I was the youngest, the chubbiest and the quickest to come up with ideas for devilment.

I don't remember if what I'm about to tell happened at the beginning, middle or end of that glorious summer of 1946 when I got a whipping almost every week for something I did that was so wonderful I can still hear it, smell it and feel every speck of it sixty-five years later.

* * * * *

World War II—more than God—cast its shadow around my world and the worlds of my four boyhood friends while barely touching the edge of our day-to-day lives. Not one of our fathers was in the service. Not one of our mothers was a "Rosie the Riveter". The heavy droning of bombers, the thundering of artillery and the screams of wounded and dying were oceans away. Fire and falling walls, the stench of blood and decay, the gaunt faces of hunger, the gaping mouths and crushed bodies were the lives of other boys. Our war—the war we saw—was in *Life* and *Movietone* newsreels; in newspapers and the happy faces of soldiers and sailors on our streets; in the occasional jeeps and trucks on our streets and the planes and gliders that flew over us. There were ration stamps, Victory Gardens and Uncle Sam posters. And there was Mr. Wright who lived two houses down from us, our volunteer Air Raid Warden, who wore a helmet and sometimes let us walk with him when he checked on "blackout nights" to be sure curtains and shutters were drawn and closed so that no light would guide German or Jap bombers to our homes. The shadow of war was so far away it never nightmared our sleep. It was not real. Our world was summertime and Christmas and laughter and the adventures of our play.

Finally, the war ended.

But not for us.

* * * * *

All of my uncles had come home safely from the war. Nobody I knew had been killed. Though I've never breathed a word of this to anyone until now, inside my head I was more than slightly disappointed that not one relative—even if only a second, third, or fourth cousin—had given his life on the field of battle, and then, after several rounds of rifle fire and bugle notes, had been buried with full military honors in a national cemetery. It was an early lesson in life: You don't always get everything you dream about.

Johnny Banner, the only brother of Betty Banner—the prettiest girl on our street or, for that matter, on any street for miles around—had returned home from Europe. He'd been all over France and Germany reporting for the *Stars and Stripes*. It's still hard to believe that he came home loaded with all kinds of neat Nazi German war stuff, which he gave to my buddies and me. Bush and TC each got a German army raincoat that snapped together to make a two-man pup tent, Billy Bob got a mess-kit, and Double M got an ammunition belt. But I think it was because he knew I was madly in love with his sister—even though she was twelve, and two years older than me—that he gave me the absolutely, positively, most perfectly splendid thing an American boy could get: a German helmet with a bullet hole smack dab in the middle of the front and, to add to its splendor, what looked like real blood stains inside around the hole.

In my mind, what Johnny Banner did ranked him right up there with Tom Mix, the Green Hornet and Superman as one of my heroes. And Betty? Well, she was the first and only crush of my young heart, a heart that—except for mothers and aunts, who didn't count—had not yet known the feeling that comes from loving a real woman.

Then there was TC's uncle. We all wished he had been ours. Whether he was trying to or not, with his clipped mustache, dimpled chin and wide grin he looked a lot like Clark Gable, except he didn't have Gable's big ears. He was a real "Flying Tiger" Ace in China where he had flown P-40s with a shark's face and big teeth painted on their front. He knocked down fourteen Jap Zeroes from the sky. You'd think killing Japs the way he did, the furthest thing from his mind would have been a young nephew back in Tennessee. I met him only once and then only for a few minutes. He tousled my hair and I felt like I had received a blessing. He must have been another out of the ordinary kind of man like Johnny Banner for he brought back something for TC that was extra special, but still didn't compare to my helmet with German blood around the bullet hole.

When he gave TC a Chinese warrior's bow and a quiver full of arrows with sharp iron arrowheads, I thought TC's eyes were going to pop out of his head. Inside of the bow, near the handle, was a Zen saying written in Chinese. Though it didn't look like real writing to me, his uncle could read the stuff. First, he read it in Chinese, which sounded a lot like metal clanging together. Then, he read it in American, *In the case of archery, the hitter and the hit are no longer the opposing objects, but one reality.* That made absolutely no sense to me or any of the others. No one asked, "What's that mean?" We just squinted our eyes seriously at it and nodded like we knew.

TC was an absolute archery fiend. He was good at it. All five of us had bows but his was a "Bear", a real Fred Bear bow. As soon as he got it he wanted to show it off. It was the real thing. He took it to the backyard to try it out. I couldn't even bend it. Billy Bob's arms shook so hard he let go and the bow string smacked him on his forearm so hard he let out a "Dadgum it!" and almost swore but caught himself because TC's mother was hanging out clothes. The arrows had long feathers. You could kill a deer with them, or a Jap, or a Nazi. The bows the rest of us had were either homemade or cheap ones made for shooting at paper targets. They could make a dog yelp but that was about all.

* * * * *

We were at the Cussin' Tree. We'd just finished the Camels that Bush had stolen from his sister's hiding place. It was mid-morning. A breezy day. We stood there wishing we had more Camels. And thinking. Trying to come up with the day's adventure. Then, out of the blue, Double M who was not known for coming up with masterful plots and brainy plans said, "Let's paint our kites like Stuka dive bombers an' shoot the Huns from the sky...let's use our bows an' arrows and BB guns like artillery and machine guns." He called the Germans "Huns" because that's what his grandfather who had fought in World War I called them.

Still no one spoke. Our brains were turning over what he said, slowly at first. Then, quickly, it began to take shape and there it was—Double M's blazing idea shooting straight up into the sky.

With a slight hint of admiration, Billy Bob said, "Well, I'll be damned, Double M! I didn't even think you had a brain. Let's get those Nazis."

The rest of us followed up with our "I'll be damns".

"Let's kill those Krauts!" chimed TC.

"Shoot their heinies from the sky!" Bush and I said together and burst out laughing. We loved the word "heinie."

We knew we had the day by the tail. And to top it off, the wind was picking up.

"Well, I'll be damned!" Billy Bob repeated.

"That's a bully of an idea," Bush said, whose father was always quoting Theodore Roosevelt.

"A real bully of an idea," I echoed. Next to mine, Bush's father was my favorite of my friends' fathers.

"Ok, everybody, go get your bows an' arrows an' BB guns. I'll bring my kite. Who else has got one?" asked Billy Bob.

"I have," said Double M, raising his hand.

"Me, too," chimed TC.

"An' me, too," I said.

"And I'll bring some paint an' brushes from my dad's shop so we can paint 'em. I'll see y'all back here. Everybody hurry like hell," said Billy Bob as he bent down and crawled through the secret passageway we had cut in the hedge that surrounded our refuge from our parents.

"Alright, men," Billy Bob commanded, "Get your weapons an' hurry back to your battle stations. Double-time it!"

* * * * *

The summer before, we had sworn to our parents that we would only shoot our bows in our backyards when an adult was present. We made lots of promises to our parents during those years, but the "backyard promise" we halfway meant after TC almost killed me.

It started out as a pleasant afternoon in my backyard. My parents were away. We decided to play "Chicken". The idea was that we would lie on our backs in the grass and not move. TC would shoot a steel-tipped arrow straight up in the air; as the arrow returned, anyone who jumped or rolled away was a "Chicken". And anyone who didn't move was either a hero, a wounded hero, or a dead hero. Three times the arrow shot skyward. Three times we were all Chicken. Then, on the fourth, I didn't move. I squeezed my eyes shut and said a quick prayer: *Dear God, my mother loves me and she loves you, too. Save me!* There was a thud. *The arrow has struck me in the heart. I have only one more breath, only one more thought left in me, 'Mama!' There was a scream far back in my head, but it wouldn't come out. Why would my mouth not scream? I am dead. That's why. I am dead!*

Then came a scream. A real scream.

"EEEEEEEEEEEE!!!"

But, it wasn't my scream leaving my head; it was Cornelia, our maid's scream: "Oh, my dear Lord Jesus! EEEEEEEEEEEE!!!"

I could hear her pounding feet, her heavy breathing coming closer and closer. I still hadn't opened my eyes. I couldn't. I was afraid of what I would see sticking out of me.

The last tremor of the scream and the last deep gasp for air was ten inches above my face. Then, strong hands gripped me by the shoulders and I was lifted from the ground and hugged so tightly against Cornelia's big bosoms I thought I was going to die, not from an arrow but from bosom suffocation.

The only time Cornelia ever whipped me was on that day as she was dragging me by my hand back to the house, all the while declaring, "You done scared me ta death...you done scared me ta death...you get in that house now an' you ain't goin' out ag'in 'til yo mama an' daddy gets back." Then came the three blows; they were more like the pats you give someone you love who needs comforting.

But that night, when my parents returned, my mother's laying on of hands was not a patting. And, as always, she honored that perverse pact of our mothers and called the others to report our most recent act of savagery. So, once again, before we could have our suppers, each of us had to add another promise to our long list of promises, "I swear to never ever again...."

* * * * *

We were out of breath when we got back to the Cussin' Tree with our weapons. God had heard our prayers. We had gotten away with our bows and BB guns and kites without being seen.

With his bow and quiver over his shoulders, Billy Bob stooped low as he came through the hedge that surrounded the Cussin' Tree. He carried a large, well-made, bright-red kite; two cans of paint and a dried-out paintbrush gripped between his teeth.

We were waiting for him with three kites, four BB guns and five bows. TC had wrapped cloth around the heads of two of his arrows. Sticking above his back pocket I could see the spout of a lighter fluid can. The time for all out war had come. We were going to save our nation and the good people of the world. But first—

"Holy Jerusalem, Billy Bob! Where'd you get that?" asked Bush pointing at the red kite. "It's a beaut!"

"Uh-huh," said Double M, without his lips moving.

Billy Bob put the cans and brush on the ground and held the kite up, turning it slowly for us to admire and long for.

"Mama got her for me for my being so good. Today, it'll be flown by Red Baron the Second, son of the legendary Red Baron, Germany's greatest World War I ace."

"Did you say you got it for being good?" asked Double M.

"Man, you pulled one over on your mama." I said.

We all laughed.

Billy Bob's eyes got hard and his fists doubled up. We shut up. "OK, let's get 'em painted and in the air," he hissed.

He opened the cans. One contained a putrid green paint; the other, black. Three kites lay beside the buckets.

Most Nazi planes were painted that exact same putrid green; with black crosses on their wings. Billy Bob went to work. In no time the kites were painted. They were ready to lift from the earth and rain death and destruction on civilization and the people we were sworn to defend.

With weapons and Stukas in hand, we went to the field beyond the hedge. It was covered with weeds and scrub brush, once part of a long-gone golf course. It was sided by three streets that, except for mornings and afternoons, had little traffic. Only a few houses looked down through a screen of trees onto the field. The battle we were about to unleash would not be interrupted by the real enemy—grown ups.

"Bush, you and GE fly the planes and the rest of us 'ul do the shootin'"

"Damn, Billy Bob, I wantta shoot, too," I said.

"Well, somebody's gotta fly the planes...tell you what, y'all do the flyin' an' I've got two extra cigarettes I'll give you."

"Now?"

"No, not now dummy! After the battle."

"Well, how 'bout a half one now?"

"Damnit, GE, you'll get it when it's over. Now, get the planes up in the air."

Their motors roaring, the Stukas hurtled down the airfield and soared into the air. The blitz-krieg had begun. Explosion after explosion came nearer and nearer. Smoke rose in the distance. We could hear them approaching. Billy Bob shouted, "Are you ready, men?" And then—there they were against the blue sky, the black crosses like the markings of death. They rolled from the sky, one after another, shrieking downward, their machine guns flashing fire like sparklers. "Give 'em hell!"

Pffit-pffit-pffit, the bullets whipped past our ears, striking all around us, kicking up dust, cutting through small saplings, ricocheting off rocks. "Fire-fire-fire!" They opened up with their rifles. They had no effect. The roar of the diving planes and machine guns was deafening. Everyone was yelling.

The dive-bombers rose from their first strafing run; then they turned and came straight back.

Bush pointed at the lead Stuka, "Get 'im! Get 'im!" Side by side, they fired as fast as they could cock them and pull the triggers. It zoomed right over their heads. We could see the bullets striking but nothing happened. It rose with the others and began to make another turn.

"Load the artillery...we got to get those Krauts!"

They laid the BB guns down, picked up the bows and quickly strung arrows.

"Here they come again," Double M hollered.

The first one zipped over untouched. The second one got by. But, as the third Stuka started to stoop, TC fired and, suddenly, the bomber came to a halt in midair; the arrow struck its cross frame breaking it in two. It shuddered to a stop and then, shaking back and forth fell to the earth.

"Well, I'll be damned!" said Billy Bob.

And the rest of us followed up with our "I'll be damns".

They reloaded. And waited.

TC brought the second one down with an artillery shell through the tail.

We began to chant, "TC, TC, TC!"

But the last Stuka was piloted by Nazi ace Red Baron the Second. It came roaring down, dodging and twisting, its machine guns firing and firing, spewing death and destruction. As it zoomed over, Red Baron the Second leaned out of the cockpit and shot a finger at his enemies.

"Shoot the son-of-a-bitch, shoot the son-of-a-bitch, TC!" shouted Billy Bob as he shot a finger back at the bright red dive-bomber as he made the turn; the roar of the engines became a high-pitched scream as it bore down with guns spitting fire.

At that moment, out of the corner of my eye, I saw a red flash. I turned. Six feet away stood TC. He looked like Robin Hood. His left arm straight out, his hand gripping the bow's handle; his right arm crooked back, his fingers pulling the taut bowstring all the way to its maximum, the arrow's feathers touching his fingers, the front of the arrow's shaft resting on the top of his left hand, the cloth-covered arrow head extended a few inches beyond the front of the bow—the cloth was engulfed in flame. TC's face was set in stone, as grim as death; his unblinking eyes fixed on the shrieking Stuka. He held...and held...and held...until I thought he had been hit and was standing there dead.

And then...and then...his fingers twitched and released the string, the arrow shot forward, the flames on its head swept backward as bits of burning cloth flickered in the air. Like a fiery rocket, the thin arrow's trajectory streaked upward in a diagonal line that struck the plane, breaking it into pieces of fire. But that was not the end; the arrow streaked onward, higher and higher, until it came to the end of its arch where its flame curved downward and downward, falling into dry brush and sedge. Oh, how glorious it was. It burst into a conflagration of fire, the leaping flames and smoke rising higher and higher, with the wind spreading it quickly across the field toward the tree line and the street beyond.

No one spoke or moved.

Then, Bush spoke, "Well, I'll be damn!"

"Well, I'll be a double-dog damn!" said Billy Bob.

"Damn...damn...damn...damn!" I couldn't stop saying, "Damn."

TC's eyes stretched wide like he was seeing the end of the world.

And maybe he was, for in the very next moment people came running out of their houses. Women were standing with their hands over their mouths. Men were running toward the fire with rakes and shovels. There was shouting and a few screams and many curses.

I'd heard preachers preach that the world would end in fire, that everything was going to be burnt to a crisp. Maybe this was it. Maybe we were seeing it start. Maybe we had started it. Nobody seemed to notice us. For the moment, we pyromaniacs were invisible. People and dogs were running back and forth, a cat was stepped on, there was yowling and howling and over and over, a crusty old voice tried its best to shout, "Call the fire department...call the fire department...call the police...call everybody!"

Suddenly, between all the pandemonium and clamor there was a split-second of silence, and in that split-second, there was a high-pitched whimper, "I've got to hide." I looked to my side. TC was pirouetting in a tight circle, his face was the face of terror, "Oh, my Lord, oh, my Lord, they're gonna hang me for sure!"

Above his whimpering; above the yelling, barking and screeching; above the weeping and gnashing of teeth; above the flames and billowing smoke; from far away, there came the strident sirens of fire engines and police cars racing nearer and nearer.

And then they arrived.

* * * * *

It is the anticipation of death that is more feared than the actuality. So it was with us. The horrors of torture to extract our confessions, the horrors of coming punishments, the horrors of eternal damnation in hell; these horrors pressed our eyes open in the darkness of our nights. Yes, we would one day be found out, and if, on that day, we were not killed outright, we would likely be put to the rack. However, it needs to be said that—

No matter our pain.
No matter our tears.
No matter our penance.
We were the heroes who shot down Red Baron the Second.
We were the heroes who helped win World War II.
We were the heroes who helped save the earth.

To this day it is glorious.

APACHES

(TELEGRAM)

MESCALERO AGENCY TO COMMISSIONER, INDIAN AFFAIRS, WASHINGTON, D.C., 21 AUGUST 1879, WARM SPRING. ALL INDIANS HAVE LEFT THIS RESERVATION GOING WEST. WILL INTERCEPT THOSE SUPPOSED TO BE ON THE WAY FROM SAN CARLOS. HAVE INFORMED THE MILITARY.

RUSSELL, AGENT

"These hills are full of Apaches. They've burned every ranch in sight. He had a brush with them last night. Says they're stirred up by Geronimo."

The first words in the movie "Stagecoach" - 1939

"They are the keenest and shrewdest animals in the world, with the added intelligence of being human beings."

Major Wirt Davis - 1885

When they scalped an enemy they sang one song over it, a special song. The song goes on, "I will get a piece of the enemy's ribs, and I will get a piece of the enemy's backbone for me."

Western Apache Raiding and Warfare - 1971

*"I was born on the prairie where the wind blew free
and there was nothing to break the light of the sun. I was
born where there were no enclosures."*
Geronimo

"I have killed ten white men for every Indian slain."
Cochise

"This could be good land without the Apaches."
From the movie "Chatto's Land" - 1972

*On the hottest day of summer, when the sun was
directly overhead and scorching the earth, heat waves
created images of distant lakes. Everyone was asleep,
even the soldiers; no one saw us or heard us; we broke
away from our reservation and moved across the earth
like the wind.*

Of course, our mothers—the reservation agents—knew
we were gone, for we had to have their permission to go
out and play. Once outside, we became our true selves:
wholly irreclaimable, savage killers; marauding; pillaging;
burning. Filled with the power of the grizzly and the
cunning of coyotes we were five bloodthirsty Apaches on
the warpath.

We ran as fast as our legs would carry us to our camp
beneath a large mock orange tree. A thick wild shrub
hedge encircled the camp. It shielded us from any
"White Eyes" that might be in pursuit. Normally, we
called the tree the "Cussin' Tree", but on this day, Billy
Bob said it was to be the "Sacred Tree". He was twelve
and the oldest. He could probably have beat up any two

of us together at one time. As always, he assumed leadership without any discussion or hint of dissent.

There was one problem about Billy Bob. And it was a big one. He had no eyebrows. They still hadn't grown back since they were burned off the month before when he had convinced us to steer our Red Rider wagons through a cardboard wall of fire. Having no eyebrows took away some of his ferocity. But only some because even though it made his face look a little like an owl I knew he could still kill me with his bare hands.

We sat cross-legged in a circle. Billy Bob stood above us. He began by giving us our names—

"Of course, I'm the only one who can be Geronimo.

"TC, you'll be Cochise.

"Double M, you're Chatto.

"Bush, you're Victorio.

"An', Spain, you'll be Loco."

"I don't want that name," I said.

"Well, since you're the craziest one of us...it fits," smirked Billy Bob.

Double M, who didn't even live on our street, sniggered and I kicked him and we both drew back and likely would have gotten into it if Billy Bob hadn't ordered, "Damnit, you two, cut it out!"

"Well, I still don't like it," I said.

With that, Billy Bob, who was a good head taller than me, stepped over, leaned down and stuck his freckled face into mine, and in a voice that had a fist in it, said, "Did you hear what I said? You're Loco an' I'm Geronimo, an' I'm tellin' you to quit whinin'! Loco killed a grizzly with a knife an' was a chief, too, just not nearly as famous as Geronimo. You're Loco...got it?"

"Uh-huh."

"One more thing, every time y'all talk to someone, use your Apache name. OK, that's settled...now get your stuff out."

One by one, we reached into our pockets and paper bags and pulled out what we had pillaged from our homes. We set our loot on the ground in front of us.

"Cochise, did you get the paint?"

"Yea, my sister's toothpaste."

"Chatto, what about the tobacco?"

"Yea, five of my granma's Lucky Strikes."

"Victorio, since your folks are the only ones that drink a lot, did you get the firewater?"

"I got it, but sure as hell my Daddy's gonna know 'cause I had to put an awful lot of water back in the bottles so he wouldn't see how much was gone."

"OK, Loco, what about you?"

I reached into the brown paper bag and pulled out a big handful of white feathers.

There was silence.

"Damn! Was white all you could get?" rasped Billy Bob.

"Well, White Leghorns are all we've got in the pen, an' I almost couldn't get them 'cause the rooster like to'ave spurred me to death while I's pullin' his tail feathers out."

"Well, dad blast it, if you couldn't get some Rhode Island Reds it seems the least you could have come up with was some Dominickers...somethin' with color! Ah, hell! Pass out the Leghorns...give me that big one." He stuck it between the bandana and the back of his head. The rest of us did the same.

"Okay, y'all, look at these pictures I tore out of *National Geographic* at the library, an' do your faces with a white streak across your noses an' cheekbones."

Billy Bob was crazy about Apaches and when it came to Geronimo he was a certified nut. He'd read everything he could get his hands on in libraries, the *National Geographic* and comic books. He had seen every movie that had an Apache in it. And he had a photographic memory of everything he had read or seen about them.

"Listen, y'all! Geronimo was a Chiricahua Apache, so that's what we are. We're Chiricahuas. We're the fiercest of all Injuns."

I leaned over to Bush who was sitting beside me, "Did you hear what he just said we are?" I whispered the word in his ear.

Bush began giggling loudly and couldn't stop.

"So what's so funny, Victorio?" hissed Billy Bob.

"Well, Spain, uh...I mean, Loco, uh, said you just said a dirty word."

"What'n hell are you talkin' about?

"He said, you said we are Cheer-we-ca-cas."

With that TC fell over sideways on the ground and Double M started slapping his thighs and we all burst out laughing like hyenas—except for Billy Bob, whose neck was blood-red with anger. He was so angry he was about to start bleeding from his nose. Then he was silent. And when he got silent, we got nervous. His jaw muscles twitched. His mouth was tight as a knife blade. His voice shook. "Loco, I'm very near to scalping you!" As he spoke his eyes became slits. His hand went down to the boy scout knife scabbarded on his belt.

"Okay, okay," I said. "Loco speaks with forked tongue." I think it helped saying, "forked tongue" because the red in his neck went from bloody red to faint pink. The hand on the knife reached into a leather satchel that hung from his left shoulder. He took out a pipe. It was beautiful. The bowl was small and simple. It was made of red stone. The wooden stem was as long as my forearm; two redbird feathers tied to a short leather strap hung from the stem.

He took the satchel off, laid it on the ground, placed the pipe on it and said, "This is our war pipe. It will give us power. Now, the White Eyes have come. They spread across our land like locusts. They kill us. We will not let this happen for we are Apaches. After we have smoked the pipe we will drive them back. Follow me. I will paint your faces for war. I will sharpen your weapons. I will gather horses an' guns. Then, they cannot stand against us."

At that moment, as the words came from his mouth, Billy Bob turned fully into Geronimo. As he called us to join him in driving the White Eyes from our land, we answered with war whoops.

We were barefoot and wearing only shorts in front of which we had tucked white dishtowels so that they hung down like breechclouts. In those days, in the summer, the bottoms of kids' feet were tough as horses' hooves. We all had red bandanas tied around our foreheads.

Billy Bob pulled a black and white photograph from the satchel and held it up. We leaned forward. There were five Indians in a line: one was a baby; the other four were men; two of the men were in the center on horseback. "I'm the cruel lookin' one on the horse with a blaze. See those white stripes across their noses an' cheeks? That's lightnin'. Cochise, gimme the paint." TC handed him the tube of toothpaste. "Now, I'm goin' to get y'all ready for war. Chatto, lean over toward me."

One at a time, Billy Bob put a streak of white toothpaste across our faces. When he finished, we looked at one another. "Hell, Billy...I mean, Geronimo, that's not half bad," said Double M. As he talked he squnched his face up trying to look mean. "How do I look?"

"Bad...real bad, like a Cherry...what is it we are?" asked Bush.

"CHIRICHAUA! Can't y'all remember anything?" slashed Billy Bob.

I looked around. Everyone's face had hardened, hair was longer and black; mouths were thin lines, eyes showed no mercy, skins were dark and tough as leather; we were transformed by another of Billy Bob's heroic visions. But more had to happen before we swept down out of the hills without warning to raid the unsuspecting ranchers. There were more ceremonies to perform: the sharing of blood...and the smoking of the war pipe.

"Chirichauas, you are my people. We are of one blood!" As he spoke he pulled the knife from the scabbard, touched its point to his thumb; then, in a voice I had never heard before, except in movies when something serious was about to happen, something so serious it made you hold your breath, he said, "We will share our blood." And with that he began making a small cut on his thumb, and then on the others, each time pressing his thumb against theirs.

When he came to me I looked away as he cut my thumb. Then I fainted. I fell over sideways. Someone splashed water on my face and pulled me upright.

I shook my head. "Damn, that hurt like a son-of-a-bitch." But I was proud. We had mixed our blood. Truly, we were now "Blood Brothers".

Then, Billy Bob bowed his head to the pipe and picked it up with both hands, raising it up to the sun. "Sun Father, bless Your sacred war pipe. We will breathe its breath in and blow it upward to You. Chatto, give me the sacred tobacco." Double M handed over the five cigarettes, and Billy Bob slit one after the other with his knife and pushed the tobacco down into the bowl. When he finished, he held the pipe toward the sun. "Now, Chatto, give me the sacred fire." Double M reached in the pocket of his shorts and took out two wooden kitchen matches and handed them to Billy Bob. We watched in silence. He lit a match, put it to the bowl and took three deep breaths. Immediately, smoke rose. He turned slowly and blew smoke in the six directions.

He passed the pipe around the circle; each of us blew smoke toward the sun. It came to me. I have asthma. I took a deep breath. For a second, I thought I was going to pass out again. I coughed hard enough for my insides to come out. Bush began to pound my back; TC took a slug of water from his canteen and spit in my face.

Billy Bob looked at me with disgust. We were no longer boys playing a game. We were Apache warriors following our leader, the great Geronimo. *We were the rulers of our world.* Geronimo rose on his toes, "Hear me now. All this land an' all that is in it is ours. Today, we will sweep across it. First, we must take up our weapons. They are in the 'Sacred Wickiup'. I will bring them to you an' place them in your hands."

He turned, bent down and entered the low opening of an oval shaped brush hut that stood beside the "Sacred Tree". In a moment, he came out with his arms wrapped around a gosh awful armful of what he called "weapons". Mostly they looked like a bunch of sticks. "As War Chief, I will take the largest bow, four arrows, an' one of the tomahawks." He laid the rest at his feet.

"Cochise, since you are the best shot next to me, you shall have this strong bow an' three arrows.

"Chatto, the third bow is yours with two arrows.

"Victorio, you get the longest spear an' the other tomahawk.

"Loco, this will be your spear."

"Damn, Geronimo...is that all I'm gettin'. That little thing ain't even got a point on it. It wouldn't kill a chipmunk much less a human being...damn!"

"Well, you're the littlest an' that's all that's left."

I was about to cry. He could see it. "Okay, Loco, remember you're a warrior. I'll let you choose where we're going to raid."

"Really...me?"

"Yeah."

Oh my gosh! My mind raced. Who had something we wanted? What could we get away with and not get caught and killed by our parents? Who in the neighborhood did we dislike the most? Who did I dislike the most? The words jumped from my mouth.

" BROTHER BLACK!"

A few weeks before, Brother Black, a Church of Christ preacher, had embarrassed me terribly in front of Bush and Double M, both Catholics. TC, Billy Bob and I were Church of Christers. We went to Lipscomb, a Church of Christ school where Brother Black taught. He knew us, especially me, since he sometimes preached at our church. Next to his house, which was only two streets away from where I lived, he owned a large field where he boarded horses.

On the day of my humiliation we had caught a lost pony and needed somewhere to keep her until we found the owner. I was certain Brother Black would help us out so I volunteered to go to the front door and ask him. Being as he was a preacher, I knew he would say, "Absolutely, boys, turn her loose in the field and come ride her anytime you want until you find her owner. I've got a pony saddle and bridle you can use. Is there anything else you need?"

But on that hot summer day, with a big smile on his beaming, righteous face, that Man of God looked down on us, and in his best preacher-voice, said, "A dollar a day, boys, a dollar a day. That's what I charge everybody, and to be fair to everybody that's what I'll have to charge you."

I stumbled away, my head hanging down, muttering, "No, thanks...no thanks." We didn't have a dollar a week among us. Sixty-five years later, the bitter taste of that rejection remains fresh in my mouth. But on the day it happened my mind was saying as my feet drug me away, *'I'll get you back, Brother Butt Hole!'*

Now, my time had come.

"So, what's this about Brother Black?" asked Geronimo.

I jumped to my feet and shook my spear in the air. "Ha-ya! We'll set his horses free to run with the wind. We'll take revenge on that White Eye for shaming us. Ha-ya! Blood for Blood! Ha-ya!"

"Well, damn, Loco!" Geronimo stepped back and stared at me like I was someone else. *I was.* Apache blood burned in my veins. I was ready to strike our enemy. I could see in Billy Bob's eyes that he was seeing that day again and was hearing that preacher say, '*A dollar a day, boys, a dollar a day.*' His eyes narrowed then expanded red with blood. He stared straight up into the sun. He seemed to grow taller and stronger. He began to stomp the ground hard, first with one foot then the other. His voice chanted –

> *Ha-ya Ha-ya Ha-ya Ha-ya Ha-ya*
> *The sun's horse is a yellow stallion;*
> *His nose, the place above his nose, is*
> *of haze,*
> *His ears, of the small lightning, are*
> *moving back and forth,*
> *He has come to us.*
> *The sun's horse is a yellow stallion,*
> *A blue stallion, a black stallion;*
> *The sun's horse has come to us.*

When he said, "The sun's horse has come to us" the first time, we came alive with his vision. We jumped to our feet and began stomping the ground, turning in circles, shaking our weapons above our heads, repeating with him the second time, "The sun's horse has come to us. We are ready. We are Apache. Hear Geronimo. He speaks!"

"Cochise, Victorio, Chatto, you will drive them toward us. Go to the far end of the pasture. Loco and I will slip up to the house to see if any White Eyes are there. If none are, I will signal you with the cry of the hawk three times, 'EEEEEEEEEEE!' When you hear it, climb the fence, spread out an' run screaming at the horses an' drive them toward the house. We will open the gate."

Except for the hawk screech, which was more like a girl being strangled, it sounded like a good plan.

We ran from tree trunk to tree trunk toward Brother Black's house. Both of us were now calling him "Brother Butt Hole". There was no car in the driveway or garage. Geronimo signaled me to stay behind a tree. Stooping as low as he could, he ran across the lawn and peered over one windowsill after another. Then—and I couldn't believe he was doing it—he stepped up onto the front porch and knocked on the door, not once but twice. No one came.

With that, he motioned to me and we walked out into the side yard, which sloped to the pasture below. We could see the horses—there were eleven of them. At the far end of the field was the fence where the other warriors awaited Geronimo's signal. The signal came—

"EEEEEEEEEEE!" "EEEEEEEEEEE!" "EEEEEEEEEEE!"

With a final screeching scream, Geronimo began to cough, wheeze and...damn, he sounded like me having an asthma attack. I slapped him on the back. He wheeled around, "Damn you, Loco, cut that out!"

From below, we heard war cries. Running across the pasture like devils, three warriors rushed toward the grazing horses, leaping, whooping, shouting and shaking their weapons. The horses threw their heads up, snorted, reared and wheeled in the air and broke into a gallop straight toward us. Before they reached the slope, Geronimo threw the gate open and yelled to the top of his voice, " Ha-ya Ha-ya Ha-ya! The sun's horse has come to us!"

And there was another voice mixed with Geronimo's, "Ha-ya! Ha-ya! Ha-ya! The sun's horse has come to us!" At first, I couldn't tell where it was coming from; then I realized it was coming from me.

Pounding the earth, the horses came thundering up the slope. In a cloud of dust they galloped through the open gate and out onto the street. Not far behind, running harder than I had ever seen them, were Cochise, Victorio and Chatto, their faces unrecognizable with wildness, the white toothpaste melting down their cheeks. They passed me, racing behind the horses whose hooves on the asphalt street cracked like rifle shots.

We were transformed back in time and space. Our feet did not touch the earth. Our minds, our bodies enlarged with blood. No human, no animal could stop us. Like wolves we veered in and out of scrub brush, cactuses, boulders, mesas and canyons; all was desert and air and the black stallions and blue stallions and yellow stallions blew and snorted ahead of us, their manes and tails streaming in the air behind them. We ran on and on,

hollering and yelling—the horses—the Apaches—the sun—
all together as one.

Then came a jolt of horns, a screeching of brakes and
angry shouts. And in an instant we were all back in the
real world.

All but one...

Billy Bob was standing in the middle of Granny White
Pike jumping up and down and hollering, "I was born on
the prairie where the wind blows free. I was born where
there were no enclosures. I was born..." He stopped,
looked around; his face flushed. He was confused, "Where
am I...where is everybody?" His mouth clamped shut. For a
moment he stood still as a statue, you could see reality
returning horribly to him. He shuddered but didn't move
from where he stood. He was lost. We looked at him...then
we walked side by side out into the street as though the cars
and horns and people and shouts were not there. We
closed around our leader and friend and without a word led
him across the street onto the Lipscomb campus, where the
horses were now quietly grazing.

Exhausted, we plopped down on the grass near the
horses. Bush and TC had their canteens. They poured
water on Billy Bob's face and head. As he sputtered and
cooled he gradually became himself again—almost, but
not completely. His normal domineering voice and
manner were completely gone. If you had not known him
in the fullness of his normality you would say, "Damn,
that boy's awfully low on spunk, ain't he?" Mostly, he just
stared into the distance. When we asked him if he was

okay he just shrugged or said a word or two so low you couldn't understand him.

Finally, TC pointed at him, "Golly, guys, look at Billy Bob's eyes, they've got that 'thousand-yard stare' just like the ones you see in soldiers eyes in *Life*. Sure as hell, he's shell-shocked. We better get him home to his mama before he starts runnin' in circles an' screamin'."

But nobody moved. We were sitting there remembering the day Billy Bob went home with his eyebrows burned off. That night's punishment was stuck in our minds forever. That night, our mothers called one another and shared their child's confession. By suppertime we had all been whipped with hands, switches, belts and anything that didn't break bones or permanently mar flesh or soul for life.

What were we to do? Our leader had turned to mush.

And then...and then, like the Day of Judgment, Brother Black stood above us with the Wrath of God on his face. Behind him stood several men in suits who looked like God's avenging angels.

I do not want to tell you what happened to us.

GOD'S PUNISHMENT

Hear the word of the Lord God as it is written in
Numbers 14:18, *The Lord is longsuffering, and of great
mercy, forgiving iniquity and transgression; and by no
means clearing the guilty, visiting the iniquity of the
fathers upon the children into the third and fourth
generations.*

My name is Nancy Mae Pearson. My grandchildren
call me "Nanny". I am eighty years old. Every night before
I get into bed I ease down on my knees and ask the Lord
for forgiveness and for His mercy to take away my sins
from those who come after me. Guilt weighs heavy on me
for what I did long ago: things I have never told to
anyone, things that brought terrible suffering upon my
family. Now, I have decided I must tell them before I die
so that they all will be warned and may have the strength I
did not, and the Lord willing, will avoid bringing pain
upon their own.

Of my nine children, only Lillie Jane, my daughter,
and Jeremiah, her husband, and I remain here in Lost
Cove where it all happened. Everyone else is dead.
Nathaniel Pearson, my husband, and six of our babies are
buried in the cemetery a little ways back of the house on
the lower slope of the mountain. One day, I will lie there
beside Nathaniel and near my babies: Tennessee, who,
like my first, never drew a breath of life; James, who we
called "Brother", our first live-born, who was killed with
his father; Patty, a straight-laced old maid school teacher;

Lafe, our second son, though strange and sometimes scary, may have had within himself the most love of us all; and our little one, "Angel", who we thought of as sent down from above. Jane Ann is buried with her husband in Nashville in the Catholic cemetery and Betty Sue disappeared with her husband somewhere, far out on the plains in Indian country.

I could not write my name until I was sixty-eight. Lillie Jane had said it was time for me to learn and she would teach me. She was a good teacher and every night, after supper, I was her student. She taught me to read and write and spell. I have practiced all that I learned, over and over and over for years and, now, in my old age, I have confidence in myself that what I write will be as it should be and that my confession will make clear why we must heed God's warnings and, if we do not, how His punishment can descend upon those we love.

Before I married I was a Wagner. Mama and Daddy and the ten of us children lived on Crow Creek, a mile or so down from Buggy Top Cave. We came from North Carolina in 1839, the year after Jackson rounded up the Cherokee and sent them west. Mama said I was born when they were halfway here. She said they were on top of a mountain when her water broke and they had to stop for three hours while she had me in the midst of a thunderstorm. I wonder if that is what marked me. For truth be known, I was an ugly baby and never got any better. As long as I can remember seeing myself in a mirror I have seen someone looking back at me who is as ugly as homemade sin. But then, thank God, I was born tough and I was born smart, at least, smart most of the time.

When we finally got to our eighty acres on Crow Creek, Mama said Daddy swore terribly bad, for a good bit better than half of our land was a steep mountain slope and the rest, more rock than dirt. As the old saying goes, "We were as poor as Job's turkey," and could barely make a go of it. Six of us were girls. I was the youngest. As soon as one of us turned twelve, Daddy began to look for any man, no matter his age, who would take us off his hands. Mama never argued against him on this or, for that matter, on anything else. So, one after the other, my sisters were taken off. When I turned twelve I was the only one left.

For me, twelve turned to twenty and I was still there. My leaving took eight more years. I guess it was being as ugly as I was that caused no one to want me. But my time finally came. I have always believed it came about because Daddy gave Nathaniel Garner real money to marry me. The day we walked out of church I saw Daddy give Nathaniel a ten-dollar gold piece.

We married in the summer of 1859. I did not love Nathaniel. I loved his wild brother Silas and, though Silas was married, I lay with him one last time in Buggy Top Cave the week before my wedding, while Nathaniel was away in Winchester for a mule sale.

No matter my face and the money, I could tell that Nathaniel was truly taken with me the morning after our first night together. I knew I was good at making love; Silas had told me so four times. Poor Nathaniel, he never suspicioned the baby girl born dead eight months after we married was not his. She was not fully formed. We never named her. It will be on my heart until I die. That poor little thing bore the retribution for my sin of fornication.

But she did not bear it away forever, for it returned two-fold the next year when Angel and Lafe were born. Both were born alive but each one, in its own way, was not created whole.

We all liked to say that Angel came to us made of love. You could see it in her face and hear it in her sounds even though she could not speak or take a step because her body was so small and twisted. She loved us, as we loved her, every day of her fourteen years.

At first, Lafe seemed normal but then, when he had just turned four, God sent more retribution on us. On November 17, 1864, John Gaunt and his band of Rebel Bushwhackers rode down the mountain into the cove and tortured and hanged Nathaniel and Brother for hiding runaway slaves. They slaughtered them like hogs. And, oh, God, Lafe was forced to watch and hear it all. The horror of it never left him; as the years passed, his soul became twisted more than Angel's body.

The loss of my baby and my husband who I had grown to love...my Lord, the pain has never left me; I know now that it never will leave me. As I washed and dressed their bodies, hatred came slowly into me until it filled me. I swore to God that when the time was at hand, I would, as He had with me, take my vengeance, even though He had said, "Vengeance is Mine." There was no forgiveness left in me. Every night I lay in bed seeing what I would do. I know I may be damned to hell forever for the hatred that consumed me. I did not try to stop it. I did not pray, "Father, forgive them, for they know not what they do." I prayed for their deaths. So, I waited for the time the Cherokee called, "The taking of blood for blood," to come. Then I would take my revenge.

And the time did come. On December 23, 1864, a week after the Battle of Nashville, the cold fell so hard across the mountains, icicles hung from the nostrils and lips of mules and cows; water froze in buckets beside the fire; snow lay knee-deep on the ground; tree limbs popped like rifle shots. The clouds hung low and dark above the cove all that day. Night came. The children were asleep in the loft. I was sitting in my rocker in front of the fireplace mending the girls' dresses when there was a knock at the door. Quietly, I got up and took Nathaniel's loaded rifle down from above the fireplace and went to the door and asked who was there. A boy's voice answered.

Standing there in the dim light were two boys, both dressed in ragged butternut uniforms, their dirty, gaunt faces and deep-set eyes showing their fear; they had no weapons; they were just two freezing, starving boys who had fought and lost with Hood in Franklin and Nashville and now, tired of fighting, they had slipped away from the Confederate Army and were headed home to their mamas and papas and sisters and brothers in Georgia.

They had lost their way. With no food and no heavy coats or blankets they were slowly freezing to death. Then, they came upon the natural bridge at the north end of the cove; they walked out on it and saw far below smoke rising from our chimney. They followed it to our house.

They were polite boys; holding their hats in their hands, saying "Yes, ma'am" and "No, ma'am." You could tell their mamas had taught them good manners. Neither one was more than four or five years older than Brother when John Gaunt killed him. All they asked for was for permission to sleep in the barn. They did not ask for food.

I brought them inside, warmed them by the fire and fed them. When they were full, I gave them heavy wool blankets; lit the coal-oil lantern and led them to the barn; put fresh straw in a stall and told them to come to the house in the morning for breakfast. The smaller had tears in his eyes as he thanked me. He said I reminded him of his mama.

I waited two hours to be sure they were asleep, then I got the ax from behind the wood box and went straight to the barn and killed them both. I put their bodies in the wagon and covered them with hay. The next morning I told the children I was going to the Big Sink to get more dead limbs for firewood. When I got there I dumped the bodies into the Sink.

Killing them did not take away my pain. It brought more.

God's punishment came upon me again and on my family for the hatred in my heart and for the killing of those two innocent boys. Lafe, my only living son, was chosen once more. In the winter of 1878, John Gaunt shot him to death on the road between Sherwood and Sewanee. Moments later, Lafe's fourteen-year-old friend, Jeremiah Vann, killed John Gaunt.

Long years later, Jeremiah married Lillie Jane. He has become a son to me. They have five children. In my nightly prayer I plead with God to not hurt them for my sins and to be merciful unto them and that my death, when it comes, will be sufficient to remove my iniquities from my grandchildren and great grandchildren forever. Amen.

Nancy Mae Pearson
Lost Cove
January 1919

Codicil to My Will
OF
May 1, 1861

To Benjamin Pearson Magruder, my beloved son "Ben", I am attaching this codicil to my will so you will understand that you are not to blame for any of the horrors that have come to our family. What I have done is for one purpose only—to protect you. I love you more than life itself. Know this from me: There is no demon in you; there is only goodness. May God bless you and keep you.

Be it known to all, what I write here of our family is true. I swear it on my mother's Bible, which lies before me, so help me God!

* * * * *

On June 10, 1865, in Maury County Tennessee, one month after the war ended, Ben discovered my father's body in the boxwood garden behind Father's house. The force of the pistol ball to his head had knocked him backward against the iron bench beneath an arbor of pink roses. The arbor stands at the far end of a long brick walkway sided by two rows of dark green boxwoods. Father's derringer lay on the ground beside him. Though he left no note, everyone assumed he had killed himself because of grief over the death of his sons—my brothers—Robert and John; and because of the loss of all of his wealth, his hundreds of slaves, crops, cattle, sheep, hogs and all of his money. All that was left were two houses, a few barns, three horses and thousands of acres of untilled fields in Tennessee and Mississippi that were being steadily overgrown in weeds, briars and scrub pines.

* * * * *

My father, Benjamin Lucretius Magruder, was sixty-six when he died. He died on his birthday.

Though five months have passed since Ben found his grandfather's body, he still cries out in his sleep. Ben is only ten. He is my only child.

No one anticipated that my father would commit suicide. With our surrender he was openly bitter and worried about the future, but that was true of all of us. Mama told everyone she had not had the slightest worry about leaving him alone. That morning she had walked across the pike to our house to help Mary, my wife, prepare the dinner and cake for his birthday party. Our homes are four miles south of Columbia, on opposite sides of Pulaski Pike, his on the east side, mine on the west. Our entrances face one another. The houses set back over two hundred yards from the pike. Together, the two places cover over three thousand acres of the best land in Maury County. He brought us here from Charleston in 1840. The houses are nearly identical: Georgian style, two-story red brick with plain fronts. Kitchens extend to the rear. The old slave quarters are a hundred yards behind the house, the barns beyond. Oaks, maples, tulip poplars shade the houses and lawns. Like the houses, the flower gardens are almost identical in design and planting. Now, uncared for, they, like the fields, are rapidly turning to weeds.

* * * * *

The morning of Father's birthday, I saddled my horse and told Mary I was going to Columbia on business but would be back in time to help her and Mama set up for the party. Since a few neighbors had been invited, Father was to be there by five o'clock to greet the guests.

He did not come. At five thirty, guests started arriving. Still he had not come. Everything was ready.

Mama was pacing back and forth in the front hall, ushering everyone into the front parlor to have a glass of dandelion wine. Then she would return to the front door to look down the long, narrow lane to the pike. I could see the wide look growing in her eyes, the look she got when she was starting to get upset. She began to rapidly pat her right thigh—another sign. I watched her out of the corners of my eyes.

She had once been a beautiful woman who loved life. But years of sadness and disappointment had taken their toll. With the deaths of six of her children, her love of life died. When her "people", as she called the slaves, walked away as soon as the Yankees showed up, she could not believe they left her. She had thought they all loved her. Only Old Moll and two or three older ones stayed.

She never looked happy. Even when she smiled it wasn't really a smile; it was little more than a twitch of her lips and cheeks. When anyone spoke to her, she tended to look down or to the side. As I am remembering her, I think of rain clouds or ashes. And there were times when she frightened me. The beginning of her spells had started long ago when we lived in Charleston.

* * * * *

By five forty-five all the guests had arrived.

Mama was standing in the opened entrance looking down the lane. "Sometimes he's so un..." Her voice trailed off. Beads of sweat were on her forehead. The pitch of her voice was changing. Her eyes were getting larger. Wisps of hair worked loose onto her forehead. She was rapidly patting her thigh. Since the deaths of my sisters I had seen these signs come upon her, only for days sometimes, but then there were times when she wasn't her real self for a month. My father had no patience with her when she was like this. After loud threats he would order Old Moll—who had been Mama's maidservant since she was a little girl—to take her to the little room at the rear of the house; its walls were thick and the door heavy. It had no window.

Mama looked at the hall clock again, leaned forward, peered into the parlor. Everyone was drinking and talking. She turned and looked at me. Her large eyes stared into mine. They did not blink. "Edmund, you need to go over there and get him," she whispered. Her voice had deepened, as it always did when one of her spells was about to come on her.

But just as she spoke, Mary came out of the parlor and, hearing her, said, "No need to, I've already sent Ben."

And it was at that instant we heard his screams, growing louder and louder, as he came running toward the house, "Mama...Mama...Granpa's shot hisself... Granpa's shot hisself!"

* * * * *

My father never talked about his parents. Only once did Mama mention them. I don't recall why or when she did. It may have been when I was sitting with her in the little room. I only remember her suddenly saying, "Your father's mother was cruel." That was all.

All I know of his early life is that he was from Scotland and in 1818 shipped from Liverpool to Charleston where he started a sugar store. In a few years he made enough money to become a slave trader though he always referred to himself as a "broker". Selling Negroes made him wealthy.

In 1825 he built a fine house on the harbor and married Rachael Bondurant, the only daughter of a prominent French Hugenot family in Charleston. She brought him more wealth.

I was born in 1831. Before I was born my father named me Benjamin Edmund Magruder. He was certain I would be a boy. I was to be called "Edmund", the name of his father's father. But when I came, and he saw me as I was, I know he wished I had been stillborn, for he detested all things imperfect and I was more than imperfect. A large red birthmark covers the left side of my forehead, spreading down across my cheek and ear. My left leg is two inches shorter than my right so that I have to wear a built-up shoe and walk with a jerky motion. My speech is slow and hesitant; when I become anxious I stammer so that I appear dull of wit. Nothing about me resembles my father. I am short with small bones and have curly black hair and facial features similar to my mother's. Except for my impairments and her spells, I have always felt that she and I were almost the same person.

Ten months after my birth, mother had another boy but he was dead. Four years later my twin sisters were born and after them in the next five years my brothers, Robert and John came.

Death lives with our family. In 1841, a yellow fever epidemic killed my pretty little sisters, just as they turned six. Their dying was horrible. I wasn't allowed to go near them so I didn't see it, but Mama told me about it during one of her spells: "My precious little babies were all healthy and happy one day and then they had sweats and headaches and their skin was reddish. Then they turned yellow and vomited, over an' over, and I couldn't stop it and, oh, God, Edmund, streaks of blood ran out of the corners of their eyes and mouths. They suffered continuously for seven days and nights. I didn't leave their sides: cooling them with wet cloths, changing their soiled nightdresses and sheets, reading their favorite stories and praying and begging God to save them. But He didn't...I couldn't understand why He didn't save them. My love for Him should have saved them. And then they died and were buried in the city cemetery.

"Then it came to me—what killed them. I had seen it. The night before my babies first came down with the fever, it came to their room in the dark and stood in the doorway looking into where they lay. It stared at them. It stood there for the longest time with its mouth opening wide, then closing over and over. It was saying something

I couldn't hear. It just stood there, staring and moving its lips. I could almost see its face in the candlelight. It was strong looking, tall, straight, and well dressed like a gentleman. For an instant, as it turned from the doorway, its face was clear. I saw that which called itself *Benjamin Lucretius Magruder*. Now, I know it for what it truly is. I know what killed my babies."

* * * * *

I never saw a tear in Father's eyes when my sisters died, nor one when they were buried. You would have thought nothing had happened. His face, his voice, his words were as always, empty of sadness or concern for Mama, much less for me.

I could not stop crying, yet he never dried my tears, never hugged or kissed me. He never said a word. Tears were streaming down Mama's face and he never took her hand. He did not touch us. He did not like to touch or be touched, not even by Mama. He never struck me and I am certain he never struck her. If a slave needed to be whipped, the whipping was given by one of his overseers. While I know of no one, white or Negro, he ever physically hurt, he was the cruelest man I have ever known.

He and Mama slept in separate rooms. Every morning, exactly at four o'clock, he got out of bed. By five o'clock, he had shaved, washed, combed and neatly parted his reddish-brown hair and dressed in one of his dark suits and weskits tailored in London. The slightest speck of lint was brushed away. His shoes gleamed. He was fastidious in all things: appearance, speech, behavior and, most especially, in his business dealings.

He was taller than other men, straight and broad-shouldered, with large hands. His body was strong. But it was his cold, deep-set, dark brown eyes, heavy brows, thin lips and sharp-boned face that intimidated anyone who came near him. When he stood before you with his eyes on yours, you did not oppose him—ever.

Once, long ago, as I looked at him, all I saw was darkness and so I have thought of him ever since as darkness.

In public, he presented himself as he wished to be seen. Not as a vulgar, uneducated dealer in human flesh with tobacco juice dripping from the corners of his mouth; but rather, as a man of substance, refined and well-mannered, a man of honor who tithed to the church and was a gentleman of the first order.

His belief was not in God, but in the one who was cast out. I am certain that if he ever prayed it was to that one. As with many things, he deceived others into believing that he was a man of faith. Soon after we arrived in Maury County in 1842, he became a communicant at St. John's Episcopal Church. Religious practices meant nothing to him. He came to church only on Easter and Christmas and then he usually slept through half the service. Once, after an Easter service, I heard Reverend Carpenter ask him, "Mister Magruder, since my sermon today was on the eternal blessings of God upon man, I am interested in your opinion, sir."

Father's face flushed and turned to stone. His eyes narrowed. He looked at Reverend Carpenter for a long moment, as though not comprehending what the reverend had asked, or as if he was looking at a fool. Then he said, "My opinion, sir...my opinion to your exceedingly prolonged sermon about what you call 'the eternal blessings of God'...my opinion, sir, is that I am starving and must get home to eat."

* * * * *

After the burial of my sisters, Father left immediately for Savannah with a large coffle of slaves for the market.

The next morning, Mama called me into her bedroom. She was looking into the mirror on her dressing table. She pointed to her right eye.

"Edmund, does this eye look higher than the other one?"

"What?"

"Pay attention! Look at my eyes! Does the right one look higher than the left?"

I leaned forward and looked. "No, ma'am, they both look the same."

"Oh! Well...well, you go on and eat something. I'm not hungry."

I did not see her again until that night at the dinner table. She said nothing when she came in and sat down across from me. She laid her Bible beside her napkin. I was so hungry I wasn't paying any attention to her. Then Old Moll brought in a plate of biscuits but didn't set them down. She just stood beside Mama looking down at her. I was reaching for the molasses when I realized something was wrong and looked over at Mama. Her forehead was shimmering with sweat. She was staring into the candle flames. At first, I thought the flickering flames were making her eyes tremble. Then, I saw they were flitting back and forth at each of the candles then down at her

Bible so quickly that they seemed separate from her. Her lips were moving as though she were speaking but there was no sound.

"Miss Rachael, what's the matter with you, baby?" asked Old Moll.

Mama didn't respond. Her eyes continued their rapid movements.

"Mama, look at me! What's wrong?" I asked loudly.

This time her eyes fixed on mine. For an instant, she did not seem to recognize me. Then, she shook her head and said, "Oh, Edmund, honey, pass me the greens."

The next day, I was out in the front yard watching ants eat a sparrow I had killed, when she hollered through the open parlor window, "Edmund, come in here for a minute and help me."

As I ran into the room, Old Moll was standing off to the side shaking her head, with her face all knit up as though she was about to cry. Mama was sitting in her rocker, in front of the fireplace, staring into a hand mirror, turning her head, first one way then the other. "Come over here next to me, Edmund...Old Moll keeps telling me I'm wrong, but she can't see worth a hoot anymore. Now, get right up close here and look at my nose."

I leaned against her. She smelled good. She always did. I loved to feel her body touching mine. Some nights, when Father was away, she would let me sleep with her. I would always press myself against her.

She held the mirror closer and touched the right side of her nose. "See how it's bent to the right and looks like it's broken. It makes me look strange...see it right there?"

I squinted and peered at her nose and saw nothing. I stepped back, "Mama, your nose looks just like it always has."

Instantly, her eyes turned angry. She threw the mirror in the fireplace, breaking it to pieces and without a word left the room. That night she did not come down to eat. The next day she seemed herself again. But her face was unhappy.

As the years passed, her "spells" came only once or twice a year. But when they came, they always scared me. During one, she stuffed herself with food. She ate and ate and ate saying, "Oh, I'm so thin." Twice, I saw her stick her fingers down her throat until she vomited. Then, she might fast for days. If I came into her bedroom in the evening, she would turn to me and say, "My precious boy, do you think I'm still a little beauty?"

* * * * *

Before my sisters died Mama was called a "petite belle" by her Charleston friends. She was a little bit of a thing, more girl than woman in size. Her face sparkled. Her high voice and smile made everyone but Father smile. Tiny, coal-black curls lay all around her face. When I was a boy I thought of her as a girl. I loved her. As I grew older I loved her more.

But, Ben, you've seen how she was. Unhappiness never left her face, always staring as though she was somewhere else; seldom speaking to any of us; barely attending to her appearance; wandering the house at night, quoting scriptures and praying out loud. Only when she went to church or a funeral would she fix herself up and put on a front as though all was well.

* * * * *

In April 1861, Robert and John joined the First Tennessee and left home, never to return. I was given an exemption since I oversaw so many Negroes that were raising cotton and food. There was lots of money to be made during the war. If it hadn't been that he needed me to keep the plantations producing, Father probably would have gotten the army to take me, even with my limp, hoping I would be killed.

A year later, almost to the day of my brothers entering the army, word arrived that John had been killed at Shiloh. The Yankees buried him in a mass grave on the battlefield. My God, the grief that came to Mama and Old Moll. Father was away in Memphis where he was half owner of *Magruder and Powell,* the largest slave brokerage company in Tennessee. Once he was there he usually took a coffle of slaves down to replace those who had died or were worn out on his two plantations in Mississippi. He was gone for three months

The day after we learned of John's death, Mama came into the library where I was updating Father's account book. Suddenly, she walked over to the desk, closed the book and said, "Edmund, the Devil is doing this to try to get me to curse God."

"What's that, Mama?"

"Taking all my babies away."

I got up and hugged her. "No, Mama, don't say that. It wasn't the Devil; John was killed by the Yankees." I gave her a kiss on the cheek and sat back down. "Now, while I finish up, why don't you go lie down and get some rest."

She reached down and opened the account book, bent over it, squinting her eyes at what was written there. Her eyes moved from left to right, as though she were reading. For a moment, I looked away. When I looked back, she was gone.

* * * * *

My brothers were more like Father than Mama. They were handsome, strong and reserved. Early on, Father took them with him to slave sales and to his plantations in Mississippi. They had little to do with me. To them, I was the same as I was to our father, little more than the smartest Negro he owned. I was tutored with them at the house for one year, but come the day of my twelfth birthday, he put me to work in the fields.

When John turned sixteen, he and Robert left for Harvard and I stayed home. If not for Mama's teaching me at night, I would never have learned to read and write or known mathematics well enough to keep the plantation accounts. Though Father instructed her to teach me all I was able to learn, I am certain he did not believe it would be much for he was convinced I was unable to understand anything complicated.

Except for my ability to drive Negroes in the field and make them work and make money, I was a pariah to him as, increasingly, I was to my brothers who were becoming more and more like him.

Mama was my only refuge. As I grew older, I became more like her, seldom smiling, wondering why God let us be hurt. She began to share her hidden thoughts with me. As I heard them I felt her coming into me. As it grew stronger I began to see and smell and hear and know all that she saw and smelled and heard and knew. One day, as we sat on the bench under the rose arbor, she took my hand and said, "All of this is God's providence to test me as He did Job; He put Satan here, in my house, under my roof."

* * * * *

On planting day in the spring of 1844, Father gave me a whip and made me a driver of fifty Negroes. He had been preparing me for this since he first sent me to the fields. For five years, I had worked beside them from dawn until the horn was blown at dusk; I sweated and was dirty and stank like they did. But the day the whip was put in my hand and I was made a driver, it came as easy for me to whip a Negro as it was to whip a mule.

Then, on a sunny summer day on my eighteenth birthday, I was given a chestnut saddle horse to ride beside the overseer, so I could learn his ways: how he worked the fields; cared for the stock; kept the Negroes fit; and oversaw everything necessary to till and plant the land, then harvest it for money.

In 1855, when I was twenty-eight and married, with a new baby—you, Ben—Father named me overseer of all three thousand acres and two hundred and sixty-seven slaves. His giving me that responsibility caused me to believe that one day part of it would be mine. But, I should have known that while I gave orders to all those Negroes, I did not own the shadow of a single one of them. Not one thing of all that my father owned would ever be mine; not a house, not a barn, not a horse, cow, or one boll of cotton, not even one small clod of all the clods of dirt that held my sweat.

I discovered this soon after Robert was killed at Nashville in December 1864. Father was away delivering slaves to a plantation outside Montgomery. I had gone to his office to write in the *Slave Birth Register* the names of three children born during the past week. Lying there, on top of the desk, was his will. It was open, as though he wanted me to read it.

And I did. Only then was I convinced that what Mama had been telling me was true. I picked it up and read:

"Be it known that all of my lands, including my two plantations, Glenhaven and Glenmor in Maury County Tennessee, and my two plantations, Glenfernate and Glenbarr in Issaquena County Mississippi, and all of my livestock, farm machinery, crops in the fields and those harvested to be sold; and all of my Negroes; and my half of the brokerage company, Magruder & Powell, in Memphis; and all of my stocks, bonds and money shall go in equal portions to my sons, Robert Disharoon Magruder and John Hamilton Magruder; and that they shall dutifully see to the paying of any and all of my outstanding debts; and that they shall care for my wife, their mother, Rachael Bondurant Magruder, until her death; and that my son, Benjamin Edmund Magruder, and his family shall be allowed to live rent-free in the old overseer's house at Glenmor and that he shall be paid commensurate to his work so long as he faithfully executes his duties.

Written by my hand and witnessed by the two signatories below my name on this May 17, 1861.

Benjamin Lucretius Magruder
Witnessed by:
Thomas Finch
James Syler

Below this, in his hand writing, is the following addition:

Be it known now that as my sons Robert Disharoon Magruder and John Hamilton Magruder have both died in the war, I now by this addendum to my will make it known that it is my wish that Robert Edward Magruder, son of Robert Disharoon Magruder, and that James Calhoun Magruder, son of John Hamilton Magruder, shall receive all of my land, slaves, houses, livestock, and all other of my possessions in the same equal portions as their fathers would have had they lived; and that they shall see to the care of my wife, Rachael Bondurant Magruder, and son, Benjamin Edmund Magruder, as defined in my will of May 17, 1861.

So written by my hand on January 24, 1865.

Benjamin Lucretius Magruder
Witnessed by:
Thomas Finch
James Syler

As I read, I smelled the sulphur from his mouth. It rose from the paper. I blew my nose and spat on the floor. I had never believed in demons for I did not believe one word of the Bible; it was all superstition, made up by men who made their living creating tales to explain the awfulness of life and how the next life would be better if you gave them money. But Mama taught me I was wrong, for she had seen a demon, had touched it, smelled it and taken it into herself. And over time, as I listened to her, there came into me images and sounds like those within her. As I reread the will I realized that all that she had been telling me was true—and that a demon was living among us.

*****

The day after she learned John had been killed at Shiloh, Mama began taking laudanum morning, noon and night, Mostly, it calmed her. But when Robert was killed in Nashville two years later, it was little better than water. She wandered from room to room, praying loudly, over and over, "Dear God, protect me from the evil one, cast him out into the fire, save me from the roaring lion...slay the serpent." Some days this went on for hours. Afterwards, she slept half a day, sometimes the entire day.

The old Negroes, still on the place after Robert's death, were so scared of her they avoided coming to the house; if they had to, they never looked at her face, especially her eyes. Only Old Moll could comfort her. If Father happened to be here, he had her give Mama laudanum until she passed out. He couldn't tolerate her spells. A few weeks before his birthday, he had a doctor come from Columbia to examine her. The doctor said she had *religious monomania* and should be put in the asylum in Nashville, but as it was occupied by the Yankees the only thing that could be done was to increase the laudanum when she became too excited. And if she became uncontrollable, he told Father to lock her up somewhere where she couldn't hurt herself or escape.

Three nights after Robert's death, Father sent a Negro over to tell me to come quick and help him with Mama.

He was standing in the open front door when I tied my horse to the post by the porch. As I limped up the steps he snapped, "Damnit, boy, can't you move any faster than that?" Without answering, I stepped inside the entrance hall as he continued, "She's in the parlor and has wrapped her arms around my Grandfather clock and says she'll pull it over if I try to take her out...Dr. Lester's right, she's crazy as she can be and needs to be put away but, until we can, I want her locked up in that back room. Now you get in here and help Old Moll!"

I did. I gently gripped Mama's arms. She resisted for a moment, then gave way to Old Moll and me patting her and telling her we loved her and that everything would be all right. We took her to the small room off the kitchen. The thick walls and door muffled her loud praying and pleading. When we were finished, Father gave the keys to Old Moll and said, "If she gets out you'll be sorry."

* * * * *

Every night after that, when I left the fields, I went to see Mama. Usually, toward nightfall she calmed. We would talk. Then, in that little cramped room on a steamy August night, she suddenly said, "He sleeps with Negroes. He's done it since the day we were married." She told it matter-of-factly, as though she were talking about something she had read in a novel. But she was speaking of her husband, my father. For a moment I couldn't comprehend it but then I knew, as she touched my cheek, that it was true for she never lied to me. I felt such a terrible sadness for her and—after the sadness—there came a great hatred for my father.

A few evenings later, as I entered her room, her eyes were wide and her hand was rapidly patting her thigh. She jumped from her bed and gripped my hands and said, "Edmund, do you know there are demons in him? Do you want to know how they got into him?" The words rushed from her, as she struck her thigh as fast as her hand would go. "They came from all those Negroes he's laid with. You know how they worship demons from where they come from. And...and...you know how he hates to get dirt on himself...well, he'd come in with dirt on his hands and knees from where he'd been laying on one of them out in the fields. I've seen it...I've seen it...I've seen the dirt as black as they were on his knees and hands, and I could smell their stink on him...Lord God, the stink. You know those people aren't human like us, they've got demons inside of them. That's how they got in him. They entered him when he was on top of them. They came up in his thing. No telling how many he's got in him."

As she talked, I could see what she saw; I could see what had been beyond my understanding. As I listened, her words came into me and became part of me; all that had been was revealed—all those years since the ones I could first remember—when my father shunned me, when he had not loved me and would never love me. All those years, I had been able to believe it was only because I was not made right, that all of me was an ugliness he could not bear. And because of what was revealed, I knew that nothing that was his would ever be mine. Nothing. Nothing. Especially his love.

To protect himself, he would have put Mother away from sight forever—for she knew who he really was.

*****

Ben, you probably wonder why I have not said more about your mother. I can only say it is because I know little about her other than she is a good woman and keeps God's commandments. We are so different. The only thing we share is our love for you. I am comforted knowing she will raise you to be a good man.

I had hoped that killing my father would have killed the demons and protected you, but it is not yet dead. This morning when I was shaving, I saw in the mirror that my birthmark is gone and my hair has turned reddish-brown. I spoke to the mirror. My stammer is gone. That which was in my father is growing in me. It will soon become me, as it did with Mama. I have killed that one in her. Now, my dear mother will never be locked away. I am sorry Old Moll tried to stop me. I no longer trust myself. Father's derringer lies on the desk in front of me. It will now destroy the last one.

Goodbye, Ben,
I love you.
Benjamin Edmund Magruder
November 17, 1865

YA-NU

I know not how the truth may be
I tell the truth as 'twas told to me.

James Mooney

From 1887 to 1890, ethnologist James Mooney made several field trips to the Cherokee, gathering material he later published in a series of papers "relating to the history, archeology, geographic nomenclature, personal names, botany, medicine, arts, home life, religion, songs, ceremonies, and language of the tribe...[these writings are] the largest body of aboriginal American literature in existence. They were eventually gathered together into a single volume, *MYTHS OF THE CHEROKEE AND SACRED FORMULAS OF THE CHEROKEES*. One myth told of Ya-nu Asga-ya, the Bear Man.

During the "Winter of Popping Trees" in 1786, a full-blood Cherokee boy was born in northern Georgia. As his mother looked into his eyes she saw goodness. She named him Astu.

Four years later, smallpox came among the Cherokee. It killed Astu's entire family, his father first, then his two brothers, finally his mother. The night she died her father, Yan-egwa, took Astu to his cabin.

Among his people, Yan-egwa was revered as a medicine man for his wisdom. Whites called him, "Big Bear". A member of the Paint Clan, he knew all things of life, birth, death and regeneration. He had kind brown eyes. He lived alone. His cabin stood beside a narrow river. Born with a second sight, he could see into the beyond.

The morning after his daughter's death, Yan-egwa woke Astu and said, "Come with me." He took his grandson's hand and led him down from the cabin into the river. He immersed Astu six times. Each time he lifted the boy up into the air and pointed him toward one of the six directions. Then he held him as high as he could reach above his head and said, "You are no longer Astu; you are now Ya-nu. Bear is your medicine. From this day on I will teach you the ways of healing and of seeing."

And so it came to be.

* * * * *

Many years passed. Then came a cold morning when Yan-egwa could barely rise from his bed. Now old and frail, he could feel his spirit beginning to slip from his body. When that day's darkness came and Ya-nu was deep in sleep, Yan-egwa covered himself with his bearskin so he might see into the beyond.

He saw Death sitting cross-legged by the river staring at him and whispering, "It is time...it is time." There was no sound as he rose from his bed; the air did not move as he left the cabin and walked through the grass toward the river. Death was standing and waiting for him with outstretched hands. He steadied Yan-egwa as they entered the water together. He washed his old friend's body one last time. Then they lay down side-by-side in the soft grass beside the river. And there, just as the sun was rising, Yan-egwa's spirit left him.

* * * * *

I was almost a man when Grandfather died. I could not stop the tears from my heart as I painted his face the white color of his clan and combed his iron-gray hair. I cried aloud as I lifted his shrunken body from the ground and cradled him in my arms. I carried him deep into the forest to the grove of sacred beeches. There, as he had told me to, I laid him on the ground beneath the trees and covered him with leaves.

Winter was near. The leaves were dry and brown; they crackled under my feet as I returned to the cabin. I gathered Grandfather's medicines together: the dried plants and roots in baskets, the powders and salves in clay jars, clothes, blankets, the bearskin, everything. It took many trips to carry it all to a cave Grandfather had taken me to years before. The cave was at the bottom of a high stone cliff. He said this was where the four-leggeds and the little people had come from when the world was created. The swimming things had come from the creek that flowed out of its mouth. The water ran downward to the river. It gave fresh life. I lived there for eight winters.

From the cave, it was a day's fast walk to Diamond Hill, the home and plantation of Chief James Vann. Grandfather had been his medicine man.

James Vann was a wealthy half-Scot, half-Cherokee alcoholic, feared by many and loved by few. He tortured and killed his enemies and thieves; no matter if they were Indians, Negroes or whites, he shot them, hung them and burned them alive. Though he could be unbelievably vicious, it was he, over the objection of other chiefs, who brought Moravian missionaries to the Cherokee. He knew that to survive, his people must learn the white man's language and ways. And yet it was he who, until he was killed, was one of the greatest protectors of the Cherokee lands.

After I covered Grandfather's body with leaves I took his place as James Vann's medicine man.

Every night, before sleep overtook me, my grandfather would come and talk to me and I would talk to him.

"Oh, Grandfather, it is you who saved me from the darkening land when I was a child. You fed me, clothed me. You immersed me in the waters. You gave me my name. You loved me. You taught me your wisdom. It was you who said. 'Ya-nu, one day you will become a Bear Man like me.' Oh, Grandfather, you are deep in my heart. I hear your voice telling of the bear who did not die, the bear who became a man. And, as I listen I become him, walking upright, walking on all fours, eating his food; the hair grows thick and long over my flesh. I hear him in your voice—I hear him speak."

A man was hunting in the mountains and came across a black bear, which he wounded with an arrow. The bear turned and started to run the other way, and the hunter followed, shooting one arrow after another into it without bringing it down. Now this was a medicine bear, and could talk and read the thoughts of people without their saying a word. At last, he stopped and pulled the arrows out of his side and gave them to the man, saying, "It is of no use for you to shoot me, for you cannot kill me. Come to my house and let us live together." The hunter thought to himself, "He may kill me," but the bear read his thoughts and said, "No, I won't hurt you." The man thought again, "How can I get anything to eat?" but the bear knew his thoughts, and said, "There shall be plenty to eat." So the hunter went with the bear.

They went on until they came to a hole in the side of the mountain, and the bear said, "This is where I live," and they went in. By this time the hunter was very hungry and was wondering how he could get something to eat. The other knew his thoughts, and sitting up on his hind legs, he rubbed his stomach with his forepaws and at once he had both paws full of chestnuts and rubbed again and his paws were full of blackberries, and he gave them to the man. He rubbed again and had his paws full of acorns, but the hunter said he was full and could not eat them, that he had eaten enough already.

The hunter lived in the cave with the bear all winter, until long hair like that of a bear began to grow all over his body and he began to act like a bear; but he still walked like a man. One day in early spring the bear said to him, "Your people down in the village are getting ready for a grand hunt in these mountains, and they will come to this cave and kill me and take my skin from me, but they will not hurt you and will take you home with them." The bear knew what the people were doing in the village just as he always knew what the man was thinking. Some days passed and the bear said again, "This is the day they will come to kill me. When they have killed me they will drag me outside the cave and take my clothes off and cut me to pieces. You must cover the blood with leaves, and when they are taking you away, look back after you have gone a piece and you will see something."

Soon they heard the hunters coming up the mountain and then the dogs found the cave and began to bark. The hunters looked inside and saw the bear and killed him with their arrows. Then they dragged him outside the cave and skinned the body and cut it in quarters to carry home. The dogs kept on barking until the hunters thought there must be another bear in the cave. They looked in again and saw the man at the farther end. At first, they thought it was another bear on account of his long hair, but they soon saw it was the hunter who had been lost the year before, so they went in and brought him out. Then each hunter took a load of the bear meat and they started home again, bringing the man and the skin with them. Before they left, the man piled

*leaves over the spot where they had cut up
the bear, and when they had gone a little
way he looked and saw the bear rise up
out of the leaves, shake himself, and go
back into the woods.*

* * * * *

The sun stood straight up in the sky. The sky was as
blue as the blue of a Jay. White light poured down onto
Diamond Hill. Heat rose in waves from the ground. I was
under the shade of a tree bleeding a slave's leg when
Vann came around the corner of the house; with him
were three or four Indians. He was drunk. He stumbled,
cursed and kicked one man on the ankle. The color of
his flesh—the color of a white man—flushed red with
whiskey. I was kneeling on the ground with a flint knife,
about to cut into the Negro's swollen leg when Vann
tapped me lightly on the back with his riding crop, "Leave
him...get up...I've got something to show you!"

I followed him up the slope and around the side of his
house to a long log shed where he stored his trade skins.
The logs had no chinking.

"Look inside! Tell me what you see."

I pressed against the shed wall, next to the door, and
peered through an opening. Slats of light and dark spread
across the inner walls and floor. At first there was
nothing. Then, in the far corner, I saw a large still form.
The rest of the room was empty. I cupped my hands on
each side of my eyes and squinted to see the shape more
clearly. I saw a mound of skins.

"You mean those skins?" I asked.

"Goddamn, boy, you can't see worth a damn, can you? Your grandfather would see it...he could even see things that weren't there."

The others were laughing at me; they were as drunk as Vann. One dropped down on his hands and knees, another jumped on his back and began to ride him around shouting and laughing, "Ya-nu – Ya-nu – Ya-nu!"

Vann whirled around and shouted, "Shut your damn mouths!" and struck them with the crop. He shoved me aside and threw the door open, whistled and called, "Bonnie Boy, come...Bonnie Boy, come!"

The others became silent. They moved away from the door and stood sideways as though preparing to run. I stepped back not knowing what to expect. Vann's face was aflame with anger and whiskey. Except for an almost imperceptible sound of shuffling in the shed, there was silence. No one moved. Everyone stared at the door. We waited.

For a moment there was nothing. Then the doorway filled with blackness and through it came the largest bear I had ever seen. Its glossy black coat glistened as it lumbered into the sunlight, its brown eyes blinking from the sudden brightness. When it was fully outside it stopped and began to turn its head back and forth; its snout held upward, sniffing the air, making heavy huffing sounds. It turned and fixed its eyes on Vann. They looked at one another, then Vann lifted his right arm into the air and said, "Up, Bonnie Boy."

The bear rose like a man onto its hind legs, its front legs extended before it, paws turned downward. It was taller than the tallest Indian. A white crescent blazed its chest. It walked toward Vann who began to chant:

He! In Rabbit place you were conceived—Yoho!
He! In Mulberry place you were conceived—Yoho!
He! In High place you were conceived—Yoho!
He! In Great swamp place you were conceived—Yoho!
And now, surely, we and the good black things, the best of
all, shall see each other—Yoho!

When he finished, he took the bear's right paw in his hand and looked at me, "Ya-nu, when I am away you are to see to Bonnie Boy's care...let nothing happen to him that should not happen. Do you understand?" I nodded. Then, he ordered the bear back into the shed, closed the door and said, as he walked away, "Go back to your bleeding."

Five years before, Vann had killed the bear's mother while hunting. Inside a hollow log behind her body, he found her two-week old cub. He lifted it out by the scruff of its neck and held it squirming and squalling above his head. Turning in a circle, he showed it to the others whose knives had already commenced skinning and cutting up the mother. "This is my son, Bonnie Boy, in whom I am well pleased!" he shouted, mocking the missionaries whose Jesus stories he did not believe. He mounted his horse and with the cub held tightly across the front of his saddle, he rode to the cabin of an elderly slave couple who watched over a small herd of his cattle six miles from Diamond Hill. He left it with them to raise and train.

When the last of the bear's caretakers died, Bonnie Boy was brought to Diamond Hill. Trained to walk upright, to wave, to clap and blow a horn, he was a great showpiece for Vann to use to impress his many white visitors, and as further proof of his power to his followers and slaves. Within a year the bear's newness wore off.

* * * * *

Only when I made my weekly visit was he let out of the cage. I hated the cage. As the hate grew in me, I began to hate Vann. Except for me the only other contact the bear had was with the slave Vann had ordered to feed and water him. The man was terrified of the bear. He did his work quickly, silently. He never went inside the shed. He never spoke. He dumped the food and water through a wide opening between the logs into troughs and fled.

Bonnie Boy slowly began to waste away from lack of sunshine and exercise and, most of all, from not being touched or loved. His beauty and power were disappearing. His thick, gleaming fur was dry and dull; his muscles weakened—his movements slowed—his head lowered—his snout was barely above the ground.

When I unlocked and opened the cage door he shambled out and leaned against my legs, reaching out with one paw pulling me close to him, pressing his head upward for me to stroke him. He could barely stand. His head turned away when I tried to get him to do a trick.

We sat for long periods staring into one another's eyes: his small, round, brown eyes; mine, brown like his, only larger. At first, he would not fix on mine, but looked away. But then he began to stare back. And as he did, and as I stared into his, I was certain he was seeing my thoughts. And I realized I was seeing his. And then...and then...in my mind, I heard him speak my name and I saw—Yan-egwa, my grandfather.

* * * * *

Three months later, in the time of the ripening of the first corn, I set him free.

The Indians and most of the slaves were at Estanally for the Green Corn Dance. They would be gone for days, celebrating the harvest of our sacred food. And Vann was four-days' walk away trading for skins with the Creek. He would not return for weeks. And if he drank with them, as he always did, he would be gone a month.

I took Grandfather to the cave. I knew that we would be found and that I would be killed. But there was no fear in me. My grandfather had given me many years of life; he had loved me as I loved him. Now, I must give him life if only for a little while. Now, we were together again talking and eating chestnuts and blackberries and acorns. We sat on our haunches; he patting me and comforting me with words, "Ya-nu, do not be afraid, you will not die. You will live forever with me."

I had no awareness of time passing. We were there for days, I do not know how many. Then one evening, just outside the cave's entrance, there came the baying of hounds; the sound of splashing, the clacking of rocks and the voices of Chul-e-oa, No Fire, Kittichi and Falling—and they were on me. They beat me with clubs and dragged me from the cave. They tied my hands, put a lead-strap around Grandfather's neck and took us back to Diamond Hill. They locked Grandfather in the shed. They took me to the house and chained me to the wall in the cellar. As they climbed the steps to leave, Chul-e-oa said over his shoulder, "Chief Vann will deal with you when he returns."

Days, nights passed, but there was no awareness of them. There was no food, no water, no light, only black. All was silence but for broken bits of sound above me: muffled voices, laughter, a loud curse, chanting, once a gunshot, a scream, silence, more laughter, then the silence returned and did not leave.

I slept.

I do not know if I was dreaming or awake when there came the sound of shuffling in the dark.

"Grandfather?"

The shuffling stopped.

"Grandfather, are you there?"

"Grandfather?"

For a moment there was nothing...then before me was Grandfather's voice,

> *Hah! I rise from the earth!*
> *Hah! I shake myself!*
> *Hah! I walk upright before you!*
> *Hah! I walk as a man!*
> *Hah! I come for you!*
> *Hah! You are my son!*
> *Hah! Follow me into the woods!*
> *Hah! We will live there forever!*

The cellar door opened, a shaft of light slanted down the steps.

"It is time."

How My Father Captured (with a Little Help) the Notorious Car Thief and Escape Artist "Road Runner" Rigsby

For more than twenty years "Road Runner" Rigsby was the premier car thief and escape artist in Middle Tennessee. Toward the end of Road Runner's career a reporter, interviewing him in the Davidson County Jail, asked how many cars he had stolen. He answered, "Well, that's sorta hard to put an exact number to, let's just say it was quite a few dozen over a hundred. Ya know when we're born tha good Lord gives us all a gift an I guess I was just lucky cause He gave me two: stealin cars an fast feet."

It was the latter gift that led to the police and newspapers nicknaming him, "Road Runner." Police Chief Jesse Rhett, a close friend to my father, said, "Houdini didn't hold a candle to him. One minute he'd been standing beside you and the next he'd vanished. Our fastest officers couldn't catch him on foot; even the young ones running him in relay couldn't lay a hand on him. Damn, that man could run! I came on him stealing a 1969 Corvette out on Murfreesboro Road near the Asylum. When he saw me he took off running in the grass beside the road. I clocked him for a stretch and I'll be damn if he didn't just about hit twenty-five miles per hour; then he jumped the fence over into a cornfield and was gone. If he hadn't smoked like a chimney he could have hit thirty flat out. I'll tell you one damn thing...he'd have played hell with the Gold Medals in the Olympics.

His real name was Nathan Bedford Forrest Rigsby. He grew up poor in "The Barrens", a heavily forested, sparsely populated part of Williamson County that stretched for miles along Backbone Ridge and the Natchez Trace. It was a semi-lawless area known for producing good whiskey, for cock fighting and, on occasion, for a killing or two. Independence, not book law, was the rule that guided those who lived there. Road Runner told my father, "Livin in Tha Barrens had hits good points an hits bad, but after tha Revenuers tried to stop my truck an shot at me an like to have kilt me when I was headed to Nashville one night with a load of shine...I said to hell with this! I'm goin into a new line of work. So I said a prayer an left tha hills, an tha Lord directed me to my callin.

"He was a man of good disposition. I doubt he had a mean bone in his body. I never heard of him hurting anyone and I never heard an ugly word come out of his mouth. Stealing cars was just what he did to get by and had some fun doing it." I heard Chief Rhett tell all this about Road Runner in Daddy's office. It stuck with me, as did most of the things that were part and parcel of my life with my father, like wrestling and boxing matches, going to Sulpher Dell to baseball games, riding proudly beside him a little before Christmas to deliver Wild Turkey to his best customers, and hunting rabbits with him and his fine pack of beagle hounds every cold fall and winter.

Before proceeding on with Road Runner's exploits, some background regarding my father is essential to fully understand the events that occurred the afternoon my father captured him. For me, my father was a man far beyond other fathers I knew. Like Road Runner, he started out poor. He was the oldest son of a proud, intelligent and funny family that lived in the hills beyond Bordeaux, northwest of Nashville. George Stainback Spain, his father, whom we all called "Papa" was one-eighth Cherokee; he had olive skin and definitely looked like an American Indian. He was a tinsmith, a still maker, whiskey maker and foxhunter who never paid one cent of sales tax, which he considered to be illegal. "Mama" Spain was a redheaded daughter of a wandering Irish tinker. She dipped snuff, had fire in her eyes and laughter and love in her heart. They had ten children, most of whom were as comical as any people I've ever known.

Though my father only completed the eighth grade he, like his parents, had a first class brain and world-class ambition to raise himself and his family upward, which he did by being the best new and used car dealer in Nashville. This ambition allowed me to be the first Spain to graduate from college.

George Joseph Spain, my father, was big. He wore expensive suits, fine shoes, gold watches and rings, had manicured nails and his hair oiled close to his scalp. He could have passed for a successful gangster. Known as "The Cadillac Man", he sold fine cars at George Spain Motor Company. and those he drove glowed like the diamonds on his fingers. He liked drinking and gambling, policemen, politicians and people who lived on the edge, some of whom were in the numbers racket.

While not especially tall, he was heavy and looked like he could be tough. And he could be! One Saturday night he took me to a "street fighter" boxing match on the top floor of a downtown hotel. In the midst of the shouting, a man sitting behind us began hollering obscenities; instantly, Daddy turned in his chair and told the man to stop cursing. The man made a bad mistake: he told my father to "go to hell!" With that Daddy jumped up, turned, grabbed the man by his shirt, yanked him to his feet and pressed his fist tight against the man's cheek. Slowly, in one clear word at a time, he said, "If you cuss one more time I'm going to beat your face so bad no one's going to know you...you got it?" The man's eyes got big; he nodded rapidly as he was shoved back into his seat. I don't remember a thing about the boxing match, but every detail of what my father said and did I see, as it was, seventy years later. Yes, he could be tough, but it was his love of his family and his thoughtful- ness to his friends that made him the good man that he was.

My father's capture of Road Runner Rigsby took place on a hot early afternoon in July 1961. I was at the car lot to pick up a red and white 1957 Chevy station wagon. He had gotten it for me on a trade-in with a black undertaker. Joe and Parks, two black men who worked for Daddy, had it filled with gas and shining like it was brand new. Daddy and I were in his office signing some papers, when there was a loud roaring of a car motor and shouting from Joe and Parks. Through the office plate glass window we could see the Chevy just starting to move as Joe ran up to the driver's door brandishing a broom in one hand and a crowbar in the other, while Parks was on the other side whirling a hammer above his head, both yelling loud enough to wake the dead. It was like watching a movie in slow motion: Joe, tall and strong, leaning forward, thrusting the broom handle like a spear through the driver's open window into the steering wheel so it couldn't be turned. The car came to a shuddering stop. Then the film sped up as Daddy rushed past me with a silver, snub-nosed pistol in his right hand calling, "George Edward, get the handcuffs out of the bottom drawer an bring em to me."

The thief was captured without a struggle and brought back into the office where Daddy pushed him down into a heavy chair and handcuffed him to its arm. Outside, Joe and Parks waited with their weapons.

While the rest of us sweated like pigs, the thief was as cool as a cucumber. He looked at my father and politely asked, "Mr. Spain, I'd be much obliged to you for a smoke." With a touch of a smile, Daddy took a pack of Camels out of his coat pocket, shook a cigarette out, leaned over and put it in the man's mouth and lit it with his gold lighter. He walked around the desk, sat down in his swivel chair and began to slowly study the slender, well-mannered man whose dark hair was oiled and slicked down just like my father's. Cleanly shaven and neatly dressed he could have passed for your next door neighbor. The only thing odd about him was the red and yellow track shoes on his feet. For a long moment no one spoke, then Daddy, who knew who the thief was the second he saw his face, said, "Well, Road Runner, you've sure got yourself in a pickle this time." He turned to me, "George Edward, meet the famous Road Runner Rigsby, Tennessee's number one car thief and escape artist...Road Runner, meet my son, George Edward Spain."

Road Runner smiled, nodded to me and looked back at Daddy. "Mr. Spain, thanks for the cigarette. Camels are my smokes too." He took a deep drag on the cigarette, blew three smoke rings out and said, "Well, fellows, you caught me dead to rights. Sorry there ain't no reward for catchin me...when's the police comin?"

This time the silence was longer. I could see Daddy thinking. Finally, he said, "No need for any hurry on that. We've got plenty of time. Let's talk awhile. I know a lot about you from my police friends, and you know what? You and I have a whole lot in common. Both of us were born and reared in the hills, you're from a wild and whiskey-making part of Williamson County and I'm from a wild and whiskey-making part of Davidson. I bet you only went as far as the eighth grade. And I bet you had a good mama and daddy. Right?"

Road Runner grinned like a possum. "Well, I'll be doggone, you've pretty much nailed me down. So, I hope you won't be offended if I was to ask if your daddy made whiskey like mine?"

And so it began. What an afternoon it turned out to be! Daddy got two glasses and a half-full bottle of Wild Turkey out of a desk drawer and poured two tall ones for Road Runner and himself. In those days I didn't drink; I was underage and, besides, my mother wouldn't have abided Daddy giving me a thimble full of alcohol. (The truth be known, Daddy's drinking got out of hand now and then, and he'd have to go "dry out" for a few weeks at the Seventh Day Adventist Sanatorium in Madison,

Tennessee.) Well, Daddy sent Joe and Parks to Brown's Barbecue for some sandwiches and fries. Now, tale telling took over as one story after another was told with laughter and the slapping of thighs and, as they tried to one-up each other, the bourbon dropped lower and lower in the bottle until...it was gone.

As the evening approached and it began to grow dark, I started to think Daddy was going to invite Road Runner home for supper. And then the phone rang. The moment my father picked up the phone and said, "Hello, this is George Spain..." the smile left his face and his jovial tone subdued. "Oh, hi, honey...I'm just about to leave...George Edward is here and we're finishing up on his...OK, OK...We'll be home in a minute." He hung up and looked at Road Runner, "Well, old buddy, all good things must come to an end." He pulled the top drawer open and took out some keys, stood up, came around the desk, bent down and unlocked the handcuff on Road Runner's wrist, reached in his coat and pulled out his pack of Camels and handed them to Road Runner. "Keep em...you know it crossed my mind when we were talking: a little more one way or the other, you could have been me and I could have been you. So, my friend, go and steal no more...at least, not from me. Let's go outside; I want to watch you run.

I swear when we stepped outside and the lot's bright lights hit Road Runner's face, I saw his eyes glistening, like when you have tears in them. He turned to my father, took his right hand in both of his, held it for a moment, then let it go and whirled around like a top on his red and yellow track shoes and in two strides, disappeared.

Three days before Christmas that year, Daddy got a letter from the Williamson County Jail. It was from Road Runner. It read, "Well, they finally caught me, Mr. Spain. Two Highway Patrol officers on motorcycles ran me down in a cow pasture when I slipped on a cow patty and went down. I hope this finds you well and your family well and wish you all a Merry Christmas. When I get out I plan to come by and bring you a fresh pack of Camels. Mr. Spain, if ever I was to buy a car I'd sure enough buy it from you, but as you well know, all kinds of folks just keep on letting me have theirs for free. Tell George Edward that his friend Road Runner said, 'Hi.'"

LULU'S
TIME OUT CAFÉ

BLACK BOTTOM

"Black Bottom was notable as a Negro neighborhood in downtown Nashville [Tennessee] until the 1950s. The area was nicknamed 'Black Bottom' because of periodic river floods that left muddy residue on the streets.

This area existed since 1832 as the Sixth Ward. On Nashville maps, the Sixth Ward had Broad Street as the north boundary and stretched from Summer Street (Fifth Avenue North) east to the Cumberland River. Proximity to the river suited workers engaging the river trade, Irishmen working on bridges, and Negroes working boats. Black Bottom attracted many houses of prostitution, gambling joints and saloons."

Tennessee Encyclopedia of History and Culture,
pub. 1998

Fred was an orphan, but he didn't look like one. He looked more like the favored son of the first family in Belle Meade, the wealthiest neighborhood in Nashville, Tennessee. His silky, blonde-white hair suggested descent from Saxon aristocracy. His fine-boned, handsome face and innocent looking bright-blue eyes were quick to laugh at the absurdities of life. He was medium-sized and well-proportioned with movements as smooth and coordinated as an athlete's. Upon first meeting him, it didn't take long to recognize his intelligence and that just a skin sliver beneath his charm lay bits and pieces of the devil. The longer I knew him the more I thought he would end up either a politician or in prison.

We first met in 1957; my senior year at David Lipscomb College, a Church of Christ school in Nashville. Back then most Church of Christers believed their way was the only way to heaven; everyone else was going to hell. Beyond the old-timey sins listed in the Ten Commandments and the Sermon on the Mount, C of C preachers multiplied "sins of the flesh" like politicians did laws. The list of sins that would send you to hell stretched into infinity: dancing, gambling, drinking, mixed swimming, sex before marriage, swearing, girls wearing pants and on and on and on. For the most part, acceptable ways for having fun were about as exciting as watching plums dry and wrinkle on hot concrete in the dead of summer.

Fred transferred to Lipscomb as a junior from a hard-core conservative, two-year C of C college in Georgia. The only photo I can find of him in the school annual is the year he enrolled. In the photo you can see his slightly hooded upper eyelids and "devil-may-care" smile. Here was someone who walked into our sphincter-tight world ready to open us up, but with charm—always with charm. I took to him immediately, as did my wife, Jackie, and, like almost everyone else, Fred loved and admired Jackie.

Though he had the glint of wickedness in his eyes, we were drawn to him. Mixed in with his devilment was so much goodness; you could see it in his face and hear it in his laughter. Fred taught me much about having fun and enjoying life during our short time on this earth.

If it was not for an assignment to write a major paper for my minor in sociology, I would likely have never gone to the Time Out Cafe. I badly needed an A to boost my grades for I had mostly played at studying my first three years; my Ds, Cs, and few Bs were stark evidence of it. Now, that I was married, and married above myself, it was time to put away childish things and get a little more serious about my responsibilities in life. While sociology tended to be deadly boring, and the teacher as exciting as a coffin nail, I wanted to let my wife's parents see that her future was not entirely ruined. And I needed to show my father, who had only completed the eighth grade, that his faith and financial investment in me, the first Spain to go to college, was not going to be flushed down the toilet.

My life, my future happiness, my faith in prayer (for I prayed without ceasing for an A) depended on that coffin nail giving me an A. The subject of my paper required something so special no one else would write about, something no one at Lipscomb had ever written about. I prayed to be given a sign that revealed the subject.

And, lo and behold, the good Lord answered my prayer with the sinning of two of my classmates. Cain and Abel, as we shall call them, had gone to a house of prostitution, the Time Out Café, in downtown Nashville. The day after my prayer, Abel bragged about it to a girlfriend, who told her C of C church-elder daddy, who called the President of Lipscomb, who then hauled Cain and Abel in before a tribunal which convinced them to confess. The next day, their sins spread like greased lightning through the school.

Most of us know that bragging about personal iniquities, especially really big ones, is first off, dumb and second off, can end up coming back to bite you on your ass. It's hard to wrap your mind around Cain's stupidity. But I guess I owe him some gratitude for being the Lord's instrument in providing me with the subject for my paper.

Prostitution!

Prostitution in Nashville, Tennessee. Prostitution in the deep, red heart of the Buckle of the Bible Belt. This was an A+ subject made in heaven. And the clincher would be that I would base my paper on live, first-hand, in-the-field research—at the Time Out Cafe.

But there was one hurdle I had to get over. I had to have Jackie's approval. And, to have any chance of getting that, I had to get Fred to agree to go with me, to protect me from getting into trouble—to protect me from myself.

Convincing him took less than a minute, maybe less than that.

But even with Fred and me together, it took us both a solid half an hour of fast talk to convince Jackie we would do nothing wrong. It ended up with me swearing, on the very Bible used to marry us seven months before, that all we were going to do was go inside and talk. After I swore, she took the Bible and gave it to Fred and made him swear. Her eyes looked at us like the openings of a double-barreled shotgun. Finally, she nodded her approval. Then, she turned to Fred and in her slow, southern voice, threatened to kill him if anything else went on. She was petite and looked a tad like Scarlet O'Hara, but she could be as tough as a railroad spike. She shot a twelve-gauge shotgun and, later on, became the Tennessee State Women's Skeet Champion for four years.

She gave me a big kiss and said, "I love you."

April 15, 1957. The weather was perfect. Under the cover of darkness, Fred and I were on our way. I was silent. But as soon as he got in the car Fred started cracking jokes. I tried to laugh but couldn't. I was scared to death.

Three days before, I had driven to the cafe to be absolutely sure I knew where it was; but more importantly, to double-check the streets and neighborhood to find the quickest escape route in case we had to flee. Empty lots, deteriorating antebellum and Victorian homes, small businesses, tenements, warehouses, repair shops. Where houses once stood, there were empty lots of bricks; alleys were littered with broken beer bottles, rusty cans and shreds of paper. From them rose the smell of decay. It was the beginning of Black Bottom. All in all, it looked like a part of town where you could get your throat cut, or catch some awful kind of disease.

Now, in the dim light of the street lamps, all I had seen in my reconnaissance was in shadow or blackness.

Then, we were there. We could see it: 302 Sixth Avenue South. Two buildings to its left was a house of God, a place that cared for the Spirit: a Greek Orthodox Church. Next door was a place that cared for the body, the Davidson County Welfare Office, where once a month the poor got money to stay alive. On the right was a vacant lot, a place barren of all the lives that had once lived there. But even from the outside, I knew that inside 302 was a place that gave sustenance to the very creation of life and to our secret pleasures. I looked up at the red neon sign: Time Out Cafe. I had to will myself not to push the gas pedal through the floorboard and speed away. Inside were women; women who knew things I did not know, things I might never know; women who, for money, gave to men one of the greatest pleasures of life; women who brought momentary joy beyond reckoning.

I turned down the next side street and parked in the darkest shadows I could find. I slid my wedding ring off and put it in my wallet. We got out of the car. Fred had quit talking. We walked up to Sixth Avenue and turned toward the Time Out. Dressed in jeans, short-sleeved buttoned-down collar summer shirts and loafers, one quick look and anyone would have known we were not of the working classes; we were privileged college students. Fred's name for the night was Fleetwood Rumsey; mine was Marlon Dean.

The cafe was a streetcar stuck onto the front of a Victorian, two-story brick townhouse. The letters on the neon sign above the entrance glowed like flames; for an instant they flickered and read The Gates of Hell. I squeezed my eyes closed, then opened them and read Time Out Cafe. One stiff-legged step after another, I followed Fred, then he turned and we were climbing steps that seemed to never end. My head was woozy; shaking it didn't help. Then I realized I had stopped breathing. I gulped air. With the third deep gulp, a door opened before me, a bell tinkled above my head, I took one last step—and was inside. For a moment the light was blinding; the smell of cigarettes, perfume, the greasy odor of French fries and hamburgers sucked my breath away and I had a fleeting horror that my asthma had closed my airways and I might drop dead between the bar stools.

A narrow counter lined with twelve round bar stools ran down the middle of the diner. Behind the counter were two grills, a deep fat fryer, coffee pots, a refrigerator, a large cooler chest for cold drinks and beer; above it were two shelves stocked with buns, pickles, Tabasco Sauce and Heinz Ketchup. Everything was shining. It looked as clean as my mother's kitchen. An A health certificate hung above the cash register. To the left, at the far end where the counter ended, was a doorway covered with a beaded curtain of bright green, gold, blue and red beads—they glimmered in the dim light that shone down upon them. No one was in the room. We eased down on the bar stools farthest from the beads.

"Hello, fellas! I'm Lulu; what can I get ya?"

A voice, gentle and happy, came through the beaded curtain followed by a woman like none I had ever seen. OH...MY...Lord! She was...she was stunning!

Her hips swayed as she came toward us and her ponytail swayed with her hips. Her hair was as long as the tail of a show horse and as red as fire, a streak of bright yellow ran all the way through the center; like the wand of a hypnotist it waved back and forth to the movement of her well formed body. Her eyes were the eyes of a cat: almond shaped, emerald green with long black lashes. They were half closed as though she was studying us or had just awakened. Her full lips were the exact same red as her hair. Her mouth was partly open showing perfect white teeth; from between them her pink tongue flicked out twice and touched her upper lip.

As she stepped before us she gave one last swivel, turned and was only two feet away, so close I could smell her. Her scent was a mixture of flowers and honey, the same I had smelled when we first came in. Her gold sleeveless sweater was cut low in front. I could not take my eyes off the smooth skin of cleavage between her two heaping breasts. I could not move.

As sometimes happens to me when I am overwhelmed by intensity, a part of me separates and rises upward in the air, from where I look down on all that is going on below. At that moment, I was suspended in the night air above the diner looking down through the roof at my statue sitting there as Lulu and Fred shook hands and began talking. I was leaning toward her, trying to see more, when, all at once, a hard elbow hit my ribs and Fred's voice barked in my ear and—I was back in my body.

"Damnit, Marlon, quit staring; it's rude. Lulu wants to know what you want."

I looked up into her face, "S'cuse me, ma'am, did you ask what I want?"

"Yes, sir."

"Well, I guess I'll take two of those." In a daze, I nodded to her breasts.

"Damnit, Marlon, wake up! She wants to know what you want to drink."

"Oh...okay, she means...what do I want to drink?"

"Yeah, big boy, we've got whatever you want." Her green eyes opened wide. She laughed.

"Well, uh, ma'am, do you have a coke?"

"Sure we do, silly!" She turned her back to me, slid the cooler door back, bent over, pushed ice around and came up with a coke.

She wore green skin-tight pants; they were the same color as her eyes. The more I examined her, the more I could see. There was not an angle anywhere on her; she was all curves. At that moment she was the most magnificent creature I had ever seen.

I glanced down at my left hand, the white circle where my ring had been glared up in condemnation. I put my hand in my lap under the counter.

Through the thick fog of fear and lust that filled my brain came Lulu's siren call, "Come with me, boys, I've really got something special to show you." She walked to the far end of the counter, turned, crooked her finger and said, "Follow me." In a trance, I obeyed her command and climbed down from the bar stool and followed Fred, who followed Lulu through the sparkling curtain of beads.

I took one step, two steps, three steps forward and was on the other side in a large room. The room had a high ceiling. Three sofas and several cushioned chairs surrounded an oriental rug. A black coffee table stood in the middle of the rug. On the table was a silver tray with cut-glass decanters of whiskey, sherry and wine. A large brass chandelier with eight glistening amber globes hung above the table. Against the far wall, a stairway led upward.

Across the room, a grayish cloud of smoke rose above a big bosomed woman who looked to be in her sixties. Draped in a purple silk robe with a white fur collar and a silver sash she was half reclined across the largest sofa in the room. Asleep in the crook of her left arm was a fawn colored Pomeranian, with a green rhinestone collar. The woman stared at us through large glasses with green rhinestone rims. Her eyes were like those of a hawk watching its prey; they pierced the smoke of the cigarette that dangled from the left side of her mouth.

"Gentlemen, this is my sweet mama, Mama Lulu. Mama, these gentlemen have come for a little relaxation. If you'll take care of them I'm going back out front." With that, Lulu's wonderful bottom and ponytail swiveled around and disappeared through the sparkling beads.

Mama Lulu was her daughter grown old: the same green eyes, the same long, red hair though faded and streaked with gray and coiled in a bun; her once firm body now wrinkles and folds; the skin of her face cracked a thousand times from long years of cigarette smoke that had dried up every speck of smoothness. Yet you could still see she had once been as stunning as her daughter. While time had taken its toll on her youth and beauty, it had not weakened her spirit. Here was a woman awed by no man. She tilted her chin upward and followed us with her eyes as she gestured with her right hand for us to take a seat in the two chairs directly across from her. She was the Madam of this house; yielding to no man's laws, nor to the laws of God.

We sat down.

"Are you boys old enough to drink?" Her husky voice was made of ashes.

"Yes, ma'am," said Fred.

My brain, my mouth, neither would work.

"You wanna drink?"

"No, ma'am; not me," said Fred.

She turned and looked at me. "Well, how 'bout you, quiet one?"

I couldn't make a sound. I was afraid that if I opened my mouth dust would come out.

She looked at Fred, "Is your friend a dummie?"

"No, ma'am. Marlon's just sort of exhausted. He's been staying up too late at night studying all kinds of things. He's just wore completely out...so we decided to come down here for a little relaxation." With that he poked me hard in the ribs. "Isn't that right, Marlon?"

"Uh, huh, Fleetwood."

"Fleetwood!" she laughed, "Who'n hell ever had a name like Fleetwood?"

"Well, ma'am, my daddy was named Fleetwood, an his daddy was named Fleetwood, an his daddy was named Fleetwood, which, I guess, makes me Fleetwood the fourth."

A lot of what Fred said was full of crap and, of course, he was the one who had come up with our stupid names. But who was I to complain since I sat there like a stump with my jaws locked up and my mouth unable to open.

"Okay, boys, do you wantta see some of tha girls?"

"Yes, 'um," said Fred.

With that, "Yes, 'um" she turned her head toward the steps and yelled, "Okay, y'all come on down!"

The Pomeranian's eyes flickered open, then closed again.

They came down the steps like exotic birds. There were seven of them; all in silk, their nightgowns, pajamas, negligees rippled: pink, purple, midnight blue, yellow and every shade of red; hips undulating, the swishing silk catching the light from the chandelier; four with long, lustrous hair, the three youngest with pageboys; their eyes and lips glowed as they stepped down onto the floor and began to glide around the room in front of and behind us; their perfumes mixing in the air; brushing our cheeks and hair with their fingertips, cooing, cheeping and chirping to one another, "Aren't they cute...look at that pretty blonde hair...I bet that one's got muscles...uuumm me, which one do you want?" My eyes closed as I felt myself being drawn to their touch and to their calls.

Oh, my gosh...oh, my gosh!!

Then it was that something, some thing, some part of me, began to rise upward. I thought I was beginning to separate again...then I realized, no, this is...oh, my gosh...I knew what it was, what was rising and, in that instant, I heard Jackie's voice: *George Edward, you get up out of there right now and get yourself home!*

As I fled, my ears were filled with the raucous laughter of the nine women, the tinkling of the bell, the door slamming, the gulping of air, the pounding of feet all the way down the street to the car and with Fred, far behind, crying, "Don't leave me, George! Please don't leave me!" The racing of the car's motor, the screeching of tires almost drowned my unceasing whimpering as I stomped the accelerator with every muscle in my body; the car shuttered and leapt forward, faster and faster, straight on; and then, there was a loud shout in my ear—I didn't even know Fred was in the car—"Hot damnit, Spain, you're gonna kill us if you don't slow down!"

But I didn't slow down. We hurtled onward through space and time, as fast as the car would go, as fast as it and God could take me away from the Madam, and from the birds, and from Lulu, and from the Time Out Café and, at least, for that night— from Sin.

"Prostitution in Nashville, Tennessee" made an A+.

And Fred? Well, Fred went west never to be seen or heard from again. Except for once—and that once was filled with laughter.

COLONEL BENJAMIN STAINBACK AND REVEREND BILLY HIGHFIELD

ON THEIR WAY TO THE JUNE 3, 1898, CONFEDERATE DECORATION DAY CELEBRATION IN WINCHESTER, TENNESSEE

"Reverend, they should uv hung that son-of-a-bitch Davis an dug up Calhoun an hung im too an then lined up an shot all uv them sons-of-bitches politicians that got us in that Goddamn war with the Goddamn Yankees, an then we should have lined up half ir gen'als, with Hood smack dab in front, and shot them too...I'm tellin you, Reverend, killin six hundred thousand people just to hold onto a bunch of niggers wus a slop jar full of shit...an as to States' Rights, that's another crock of shit!"

Benjamin Lafayette Stainback
Confederate Colonel

"Lawd have mercy, Colonel, yo sho a booguh man today, but yo tellin the Gospel now, fo the good Lawd knows all about them dark days...you want anothuh drink outuh this jug fo I put it back unduh the seat way from the sun? Yes, suh, Colonel, the Lawd knows, He knows...get on, mules, we ain't got all day, time's awastin!"

Reverend Billy Highfield
Minister and Former Slave

THE COLONEL

Seventy-two-year-old Confederate Colonel Benjamin Lafayette Stainback was a banty-sized man, only five-foot, five inches tall and getting shorter every year. But he was still tough as a railroad spike and so stern-faced and bad-mouthed that people thought he was taller. He'd been around tough-talking, bad-cursing men since he was eighteen when he went to work for the Nashville, Chattanooga and St. Louis Railway. Then, during the four years he fought with the First Tennessee, the toughness and cursing got worse, and as soon as the war was over he went back among the railroad toughs as an engineer for fifty years. By the time he retired, he could say every curse word the Devil had come up with; and "Goddamn" had become another word like 'the' for him. But he never used any "blackguards", as Miss Lillie called them, when children or women were around. He was as thin as a fence rail. The Colonel's uniform fit him as well as it did when he had first put it on just three weeks before Johnson surrendered him along with the few that remained of the Army of Tennessee over in North Carolina in the Spring of '65.

"Miss Lillie" Jane Wagner, The Colonel's wife of fifty-four years, thought he still looked smart when he was all dressed up in his outfit, especially when he wore his sword that he had not surrendered to the Yankees. She liked to brag to the women at the Estill Springs Baptist Church that he was still the fittest man she had ever seen, "Why, honey, he don't have a slice of pie anywhere on him even though he sho eats like a field hand." And, of course, hearing such bragging, the Church ladies just had to whisper behind their hands to one another about the men who Miss Lillie might have been checking over for pie slices.

She and The Colonel had one child, a boy named Marcus "Mark" Aurelius Stainback. The Colonel had named him. He was so filled with pride to have a son to carry on the Stainback name— a name of no certain origin—that he wanted his given name to be something special. And it was. Whenever anyone would ask, "Where in the world did you come up with that odd name?" red splotches would break out on his neck and he would stare into their eyes like they were fools and after a moment would hiss, "Well, I'll Goddamn tell ye where...as sure as hell my boy's goin to be a great man, so I named him after a great man." Then if they asked him who Marcus Aurelius was he would shake his head and hiss almost as if he was about to strike, "I ain't got time to educate halfwits, so go look it up on your own damn time." Other than himself, Miss Lillie and the Reverend, there were eleven other people in Franklin County who knew that Marcus Aurelius was one of Rome's greatest emperors: an old Jewish clock repairer, six professors at the University of the South, three lawyers and one doctor.

Eighteen years after his father named him, Mark was killed on the beautiful morning of October 8, 1862, at the Battle of Perryville. Long years after he died, when Miss Lillie had lady visitors for lunch, at some point she would pick up one of the four framed tin-type photographs of him she had placed around the house and hold it up with his face toward the others and say, "Our Mark would have made such a good daddy if he'd lived, he so loved little children."

The Colonel never got over his son's death. Afterward he never talked about him. He never let anyone see that his heart was broken; he just became more irascible and rough-mouthed. People avoided him when he came to town. Some whispered that he was the one who should have been killed at Perryville instead of his boy, but they were careful who they said it to so it didn't get back to him for he always carried a derringer in his coat pocket and always seemed on the edge of dangerous.

You only had to look at his scarred and purple-splotched hands and muscled forearms to tell that he was old and had worked hard with his body all his life. But his watery eyes were not the eyes of most old people; they could still see as clearly as when he was a boy. They had a haunting, dove-gray color that matched exactly the color of his uniform and were tiny and quick as a mink's, never seeming to rest as they scanned for something far off, or the face of the person standing right in front of him, or the magnificent words of his beloved Shakespeare.

Shakespeare was his Bible. He went to the Bard nightly for wisdom and comfort. There were nights when he was reading a play or sonnet while Miss Lillie was sitting on the other side of the coal-oil lamp reading her Bible that were like heaven. He would look up from his reading and see her looking over her glasses smiling at him, and for a moment his heart would leap and his eyes would mist from loving her so much.

Other than her, there were only a few things in life that gave him much pleasure or rested his unyielding spirit: eating milk gravy mixed with crumbled biscuits—his dessert at every meal; walking with his dog Shep through the fields and woods of his forty-seven acres beside Elk River; reading Shakespeare and memorizing his soliloquies and Sonnets—he was now on number thirty-four—and not having to be around "fools rampant" which included everybody but Miss Lillie and the Reverend.

For thirty years The Colonel and the Reverend had worked together as engineer and fireman in a sometimes burning hot, sometimes freezing cold locomotive cab of the Nashville, Chattanooga & St. Louis Railway. During those years they had grown to totally trust and respect one another and once or twice they had saved each other's life. They knew they were each other's friend though neither had ever said it. They also knew that they were the two most intelligent people they knew with the exception of Miss Lillie whose practical wisdom outranked them both. They were mostly self-taught and, loving books as they did, owned well-stocked libraries of history, philosophy, science, literature and theology. Their brains forgot nothing they read or heard. In the Reverend's monthly visit to the Stainbacks for supper and conversation, the two of them sprinkled every kind of quotation into their discussions which would grow louder and louder when they were debating fine points of theology or Aristotelian logic and had had too much of Reverend Billy's homemade cider of which The Colonel bought three barrels every year and fermented with molasses. But no matter how much they enjoyed their brilliance, when they were in Miss Lillie's house, her word was law. When they became too loud and too swollen with themselves, she could settle them down with a loud clearing of her throat or with three or four firm words, "Y'all calm down!" or

"Y'all, that's enough now!" They would immediately get quiet and, usually, the Reverend would say it was about time for him to be getting back home.

Early on in her marriage to The Colonel, Miss Lillie had realized that she was going to have to keep the bit in "Mr. Stainback's" mouth or someone was going to kill him before he reached thirty—and it might be her. Lillie Jane Wagner was the only creature on earth that The Colonel was scared of.

THE REVEREND

Except for The Colonel and Miss Lillie, most white people called Reverend Billy Highfield, "Uncle Billy". He was born a slave on Samuel Highfield's plantation in Greene County Alabama in 1836. He was a big, light-colored baby and grew into a light-colored, big-muscled man, standing a little over six-foot-three in his broad bare feet that didn't wear shoes until they were ten years old. Because of his color and high cheekbones, some thought his daddy must have been an Indian.

But it wasn't his size or appearance that made him special to people when he came to live near Tullahoma; it was his kindness to others, poor or rich, black or white, righteous or sinner. When people needed him, no matter how bad a sinner they were, he went quickly and prayed for God's help and always left them comforted. The same prayer he prayed for the righteous. Those who knew him well, both black and white, thought he was one of the best people God had put on this earth. He was a happy man with a face that seemed to keep a slight smile as though he was thinking something good. No one could imagine that he ever had a troubled thought. And he loved to laugh, most especially at The Colonel's colorful condemnations of mankind, though he wished he could make them without saying "Goddamn" so much.

Reverend Billy Highfield was a great preacher. He was known afar for being able to quote all of the Bible and for his sermons on "The Day Christ Died" and "We are All God's Children". Though he sometimes used words that few in the congregation of the Mt. Zion African Methodist Church understood, they were never troubled since they knew he would never speak a falsehood even with a single strange word. Every Sunday his deep bass voice rolled mercy and forgiveness over them like ocean waves, bringing hope and comfort as did the waters of baptism and the Supper of the Lord.

While he was kind to everyone and was an ordained gospel minister, Billy Highfield made some white men uneasy when they were around him, not so much because of his size but their instinctive recognition that he was far smarter than they were. Only in a whisper did any of them ever say he was an "uppity nigger", and that only when they were certain that the person they were talking to would not pass it along to The Colonel. No man or woman who knew The Colonel wanted those words passed on to him as they knew there was a good possibility of his coming after them with his gun or a knife.

In the fifteenth year of Billy Highfield's life he had been a prime field hand worth over a thousand dollars. However, instead of putting him into the fields, Samuel made him his groom with responsibility for caring for his two fine saddle horses and four brood mares. Three years later he brought him into his own house as his body servant and that same year began to teach Billy to read and write.

Samuel Highfield owned three thousand acres, one hundred and twenty slaves and the finest library in Green County Alabama. A year after he was married, his wife Fannie died trying to give birth to a baby boy who was dead inside her. Within one month of Fannie's death, Samuel took her maidservant, a fine-boned woman from East Africa, to his bed. Nine months later Billy was born. Though he was their master and owned them, Samuel loved Mary and Billy; he loved them up to the second he was killed by a Minie ball on the bitter-cold, rainy Friday of December 16, 1864, fighting with the Seventh Alabama Cavalry as part of the rear guard of the destroyed Confederate Army as it began its long retreat southward to Mississippi.

Billy stayed with Samuel all through the war as his body servant. He did not love his father; he obeyed him. Less than ten minutes after he heard that his father had been killed, Billy filled a haversack full of food, hung a bedroll over his shoulder, put on the Major's heavy overcoat and hid in the woods near Franklin. For two days he stayed there until he was certain all of Hood's Army was gone. Then he began to walk through the mud and ice beside the railroad tracks that led to Tullahoma where his only child Hattie lived. Along with Billy's wife, Liza, Hattie had been sold when she was three to a Tullahoma doctor to pay the large debt Samuel Highfield owed on his land. On the evening of the fourth day, covered with mud and freezing, Billy stepped up onto the platform of the Tullahoma Train Station. An hour later he found his wife and daughter living with an old black woman in a green shack on the east side of the railroad tracks. They had been freed in the summer of 1863 by the Federal Army as it moved south through Franklin County.

On a warm Sunday morning in August 1867, Liza died of "the fever". The day after she was buried in Mt. Zion Cemetery, Billy did what she had been praying for: He confessed that Jesus Christ was his Savior and was baptized. As he would tell his congregation years later, "The day after my Liza went home to be with our Lawd, He reached down with His big hand and lifted my old sinful soul up to Him and washed it whiter than snow...yes, suh, that's what He done for me an that's what He can do fo all sinners who wants to be made clean...praise the Lawd!"

Three months after Liza's death, Billy began working as a fireman for the railroad. On the very first day when he climbed up into the cab of a locomotive, there was The Colonel. From that day until thirty years later, they worked side by side. When they retired on the same day, The Colonel took Billy's hand in a tight grip and gave him a fine gold watch that he had just received from the President of the NC&StL Railway and said, loud enough for everyone standing near to hear, "Billy, yo're one helluva man. I'm shore gonna miss yore black ass."

Soon after he retired, Billy went to live with Hattie and her husband, John, at their small place a quarter of a mile south of Tullahoma. He began preaching full time, and it was not long before all black people called him Reverend Billy, and so did some whites.

The Wagon Ride

Today is a perfect day. Decoration Day, June 3, 1898, and Jefferson Davis's birthday is as near perfect as a day can be. The early morning sun is rising in a pure blue sky; the air is easy to breathe, clean and sweet and filled with the smells of earth and new growth; the road is lined with rail fences and wild rose hedges, red sumac, pink fireweed and honeysuckle; from the thickets and fields come the callings of thrushes, quail and meadowlarks; and nearby, to the left of the road where the bank of the Elk River is lined by an old grove of oaks, chestnuts and maples, a flock of crows rises from their roost cawing to one another as they head to the fields to feed. Almost parallel to the road is the railroad track that runs all the way from St. Louis through Nashville and over the mountains to Chattanooga. In the early morning air the dust from the stirrings of the mules' hoofs and wagon wheels hangs close to the ground, and beyond the fences the fields stretch away in their varied shades of green of the young corn and wheat and cotton and of the pastures where cattle and sheep are grazing. It is a splendid day! Even The Colonel feels it for a moment. Then a train whistle from far behind him breaks the splendor, and he suddenly remembers how much he despises this day.

Every third day of June for ten years, The Colonel and the Reverend have made this trip to Winchester for the celebration. They always left Estill after breakfast at The Colonel's, in the Reverend's farm wagon on which he always puts a fresh coat of green paint and red for the wheels. This morning the Reverend left Tullahoma in the dark. He arrived at the Stainbacks a little before daybreak just as Miss Lillie was taking the biscuits out of the oven. After stuffing themselves with ham and eggs and biscuits and gravy and buttermilk, they climbed up on the wooden wagon seat with the woven basket she had filled with fried peach pies and fried chicken and headed up the lane to the main road where they turned left to Winchester.

The wagon bed is packed with clay jugs of the Reverend's cider which he sells on the square every year and gives one fifth of the money to the Church. And every year The Colonel brings his own jug which now sits between their feet under the wagon seat. They go only a quarter of a mile when he reaches down and lifts it up, pulls the cork and takes two long swigs. When he finishes, he breathes out hard, "Damn, that'll make you strut!" and wipes his lips with his sleeve and hands the jug to the Reverend who takes one short swig and breathes out, "Lawd, Colonel, the way you've stoutin it up is mighty fine!" He shifts his bottom into a more comfortable position and undoes the top button of his shirt in preparation for one of The Colonel's soliloquies, which he knows is forthcoming and which he knows will probably last most of the trip to Winchester.

It begins with a hack and a spit, followed by a loud clearing of the throat. His voice is like a rusty saw. "I'll tell ye one damn thing, Reverend, wearin this itchy wool uniform and walkin in a parade alongside a bunch of farty, ole toothless veterans an listenin to them beat their gums about how we could uv won the Goddamn war if such an such had happened or not happened is worse than bein in the Goddamn war, an then sure as hell they'll start on what a drunk Grant was an what a lunatic

Sherman was, an all that stuff is a crock of shit...hellfire
an damnation! Grant an Sherman beat our ass! An I
betcha one of my jugs aginst three of yours that that damn
train from Nashville is gonna unload two or three of
those Nancy-boy reporters and one'll come up to me an
ask that same old stupid-ass question they always ask,
'Colonel, wouldcha mind telling us why you fought in the
war?' That's what they's gonna ask me, why I fought in
the Goddamn war! I tell you, Reverend, if I don't shoot
im with my derringer I'm gonna scare the shit out of im
with my face and voice...'well, sonny boy, I'll tell ye why I
fought in the Goddamn war: cause the Goddamn
Yankees were gonna come down here on my land, where
my house is, an they were going to upset Miss Lillie, an
steal my cows an hogs an whatever else they could lay
their thieving hands on...an they were gonna do all that
just to free all the niggers, an I'd only owned one of em
way back, a no account high-yellar that wasn't worth piss,
an when he ran off I almost fell on my knees an thanked
the Lord, so I sure as hell wasn't fightin' to keep the
niggers...far as I's concerned they could uv had em all
free.'" He paused and took a deep breath. "An one more
thing in case you wanta put something in your little piss
ant paper bout why I waste my good time dressin up in
this monkey suit an comin to these Goddamn things, it's
cause I'm a Goddamn hero since I personally shot an kilt
eleven Yankees an there's some genteel ladies who love
havin a real bonafide hero in the Goddamn parade to
march 'round the square, so's I put up with all this damn
tomfoolery 'cause they pay me to come an dress up an
have my picture made with all the other ole farts.' Then,
Reverend, I'm goin to grab hold of his shoulders an

squeeze down hard an look straight in his eyes an say, 'Now, does that answer yo stupid-ass question about why I fought in the Goddamn war?'" He stops again. This time his neck is flushed all the way around. He licks his lips, "Good Lord, my spit's all dried up I've run my mouth so much." He reaches down and gets the jug and balances it on his knee and pulls the cork out. "Now, Reverend, you take a lick at the talking for awhile while I get my spit back...tell ye what, I wanta hear how ye come up with those milk-sop names, Kate and Beck, for them mules of yores."

The old preacher is looking straight ahead, his face is set like an amber mask with no emotion. He does not speak for a full minute, then begins, "Colonel Benjamin, you wants to know where those names come from...they comes from a long ways back. Member those dark days, when my peoples were owned by yo peoples...they's the names of two of em who was owned...they's the names of a little brothah an sistah, they was twins, they's had faces like sunlight, smiling an laughin...they's little bitty things but even then yo could see in their eyes they's smart as tacks. They lived right next to us with their mama, so near yo could hear em laughin at night an first thing the next monin they's start all over agin." He stops and wets his lips with his tongue an looks down at his hands holding the reins, he turns them palm up as though looking for something, then continues, "Then one monin the Major calls all us people togethah in the front yard an he walks out of the house onto the porch an looks at us sorta sad like an then he begins talkin an tellin us how he's bout to lose the land an if he don't sell some of us we all gonna be split up an sold away...an ever'body gets real quiet an he says he's done the best he can to sell as few uv us as possible an then he stops talkin an he coughs an then he says he's got to go to town tomorrow an settle up with the bank, an Mr. Haddus—he was the overseer—would let those that's been sold know in the monin an'll help 'em get on they ways with their new masters, an then all the rest of us could rest easy an know they's all be stayin with him. Then he closed his eyes an holds his right hand up high an prays, 'Dear God, watch over these my people. Amen.' An then he turns an walks back in the house an there's not a sound or a movement...it seemed like we were gonna never move agin, an then Big Isaac, the driver, claps his hands loud an shouts, 'Les get on to the fields!'" Now his voice is almost a whisper without the slightest inflection. The longer he talks the fainter it becomes, as though he is going farther and farther away, "So he sold off my Liza an my baby girl, Hattie, an some mo people...an he sold off them two little chillun from their mama...an that's where the mules' names come from, those chillun names be Kate an Beck. I still sees their faces right now while I's talkin, I sees em an hears em cryin for their mama an she be pleadin with em white men that were takin em away." He stops...then, "An, O my Lawd God, Colonel, I can still sees my Liza an Hattie cryin an lookin at me an I's beggin Mr. Haddus to take me an not take them an...an none of it kept it from happenin, an they just gone...an...an...." There comes another long silence, and then he speaks in a voice The Colonel has never heard. It is cold and hard, and every word is clear, "Even if it was to send me to burn in hell forevah I'd kill any man—even my daddy, if he was to come back—that'd try to make me or my Hattie a slave agin."

The mules' slow, steady plodding has continued all this while, their movement gently rocking the wagon's seat and the bodies of the two silent old men. Both are looking straight ahead toward the distant bridge that will take them over the river and up the slope to the square and the courthouse where the townspeople and the country people have already begun to gather.

The Reverend turns his head and looks at The Colonel, "You know, Colonel, you nevah ask me what it was like bein a slave an I's nevah said a thing til now...folks look at me an they sees a kind-lookin, ole white-haired colahed preacher who likes to help people, an that's pretty much true now, but I hadn't always been this way. A long time ago, before the Lawd an Liza change me, I wants to kill people...wants to kill white people fo what they done to us...I'd wanted to kill you I was so full of hate. Bein a slave is a bad thing, so bad you can't nevah know it, we wadn't mo than a bunch of two-legged animals worth lots uv money...the Major an his wife, they was church goin people who said the blessin at all their meals an always talking bout Jesus an how someday they's goin to heaven, an look at what they did...they's made me hate Jesus an the Lawd God. But all the while I nevah lets on, I's covered it all up, all my sadness an hate, even when they's sold my Liza an Hattie away, I's didn't show nothin cause I's promised her I wouldn't kill someone or do somethin awful an that one day I'd come an find em an we'd be togethah again...An thas what I did...An the Lawd was good to me an forgive my sinful heart an answered my prayers, an so Him and Liza, they's change me an they's teach me to want to be good and to help others an He move my heart to preach

His word an help sinners like me to find Him. Colonel, there's many a night I thank Him for you bein my bes friend, 'cause spite the ways you talks an Lawd have mercy how you talks, Miss Lillie wouldn't live with no bad man. All those long years we's workin in that hot cab you was lookin out fo me goin up and down them mountains, and you saves me from dyin fo my time."

He took his straw hat off and raised his tear-streaked face to the sky, "Thank you, Lawd God an Jesus, for giv'n me Colonel Benjamin Lafayette Stainback to be my friend, an, Lawd, lay Yo hand on him an Miss Lillie an give them comfort, an a place with You when they leaves this ole world. Amen!"

When he ended, both were quiet. He put his hat back on, pulled a bandanna from his inside coat pocket and blew his nose and wiped his eyes. Then he smiled and gently slapped the reins, "Get on up there, Kate an Beck, times awastin, we gots money to make."

The Colonel reaches out with his hand and gently pats his old friend's knee.

The mules lift their heads and step out faster. Now, in the warmer air, a little dust rises behind their hoofs and the wheels of the wagon, and from beyond the river comes the first sounds of horns and a drum and the high piercing whistle of the train.

REVEREND BILLY HIGHFIELD'S FUNERAL ORATION FOR COLONEL BENJAMIN STAINBACK

AT THE MT. ZION AFRICAN METHODIST EPISCOPAL CHURCH IN TULLAHOMA, TENNESSEE, AT 1:00 PM, SATURDAY, SEPTEMBER 9, 1905

Steal away, steal away,
Steal away to Jesus.
Steal away, steal away home,
I hain't got long to stay here.

My Lord he calls me,
He calls me by the thunder,
The trumpet sounds within-a my soul
I hain't got long to stay here.

The closed casket is made of yellow pine, simple, with black wrought-iron handles. There are no flowers on it, no plaque. Inside—his hands crossed on his chest—is a small gray, wizened man dressed in farm clothes. The clothes are old and tattered by work and wear; the smell of his life is in them, the smell of earth and of war and of perseverance; clothes his wife swore she would bury him in, as she swore she would bury him in the Mount Zion Cemetery in Tullahoma. The casket lies on an oak table at

the front of the chapel of the white-framed Mt. Zion
African Methodist Episcopal Church. Above the casket,
on the stage behind the pulpit, stands a big light-colored,
white-haired Negro man. He is old but still stands straight
and strong. His eyes are kind. They glisten a bit with
sadness as they look out onto the pew-filled church. His
eyes are a comfort to the Negroes who sit before him, and
to the few white mourners who do not know him, the old
man's kind voice is also comforting. Before them stands a
true man of God. For a long moment he looks down on
the casket. Then, he wets his lips, and in a voice that
sounds like God, begins—

"Steal away, steal away, steal away to Jesus...praise be to
Gawd fo the Mount Zion Choir's glorious singin bout our
goin home to be hugged by our Jesus.

"Glory! Glory! Glory to Gawd in the highest!

"Lawd Gawd, an Jesus, an Holy Spirit, hep me lift up
this good man to You in words that give peace to Miss
Lillie who The Colonel loved mo than heaben an earth til
his final breath. Give me words, Lawd, to speak glory, mo
glory even than tha cry uv a baby jus bawn.

"Friends, here befo us lies my dear friend, Colonel
Benjamin Stainback: husband, fathah, soldjah, fahmah, an
chile of Gawd whose spirit has stole away up from us to be
with his Savior, Jesus Christ.

"Today, as we be gathah'd togethah, I wants to talk to
you a while bout love: bout Gawd's love, an bout tha love
uv Jesus who died fo us, an bout the love uv a man an a
woman, an bout the love uv good friends fo one anothah;

we talking bout love so powahful Ole Man Death can't lay his cold, bony hand on it...no, suh, Ole Death can't kill it! Hear me now—

"'*Fo Gawd so loved the world that He gave His only begotten Son that whosoevah shall believeth on Him shall have evahlastin life...*'

"Thas the promise uv the Lawd...life evahlastin. Praise the Lawd!

"Oh, Miss Lillie, an all uv my brothahs an sistahs in Christ, an all uv you who be friends uv Colonel Stainback, heah the holy words of Jesus in the Apostle John's book, '*A new command I give you: Love one anothah. As I've loved you, so you must love one anothah. By this evahone will know you ah my disciples, if you love one anotha.*'

"Next to my sweet Liza an our chillun, I's loved Colonel Benjamin Stainback mo than anyone on this ole earth...praise Gawd fo bringin us togethah...fo friendship tween a man who'd fought fo the Federacy an a man bawn a slave with hate in him was not somethin meant to be, but as we know Gawd's ways be not our ways fo, if they be, I'd nevah have known this good man, much less been his friend.

"I've know'd the Colonel gettin on to mos forty yeahs. We met two yeahs aftah the wah, the year my Liza died. He was tha engineah an I wus tha fahman fo one uv the ole Nashville, Chattanooga an Saint Louis Railway engines goin tween Nashville an Chattanooga.

"Lawd have mercy, let me tell you what happened that first yeuh we togethah. It wus a snowin day in January; we carried a load uv coal ovah to Chattanooga an were headin back home down Sewanee Mountain when, next thing like lightin, we done jump off the tracks an goin straight down the mountain tearin through brush an trees, an befo I could shout fo Gawd to save me I feels the Colonel's arms round me like two pieces uv iron an I heah im cussin an shoutin, 'Hold on Billy...hold on!' An we go flyin through tha air an hits tha groun like two sacks uv cawn so hard I thinks we gonna split open an we rolls an rolls down that mountin til I think, Lawd Gawd, ain't we nevah gonna stop rollin til we ends up at the bottom uv the earth?

"I stand here befo you this very day cause that man lyin there in that pine coffin in his work clothes save me; he saved a po coluhed man he barely knew. An there, not long befo, he'd been fightin with the Federates an I'd had hate in me.

"Listen to me now! Though bad things be in us, Gawd put a good touch uv love in all uv us. I done preach it a thousand times to my flock an I see all y'all out thah noddin yo heads fo you know them Jesus words I'm bout to speak outta Matthew five, forty-three through forty-five—

"'Ye have heard that it hath been said, Thou shalt love thy neighbah, an hate thine enemy. But I say unta you, Love yo enemies, bless them that curse you, do good to them that hate you, an pray fo them which spitefully use you, an persecute you; that ye may be the children uv yo Fathah which is in heaben.'

"Now, thah's somthin else needs sayin bout The Colonel, an Miss Lilly can testify to it cause she an I prayed ovah it till our knees give out. Ain't that right, Miss Lillie? What needs sayin is that...The Colonel didn pay much mind to church goin. Cept fo Christmas an Eastah, he barely evah set foot cross the church dostep. Though I know he was a believah he said to me once, Billy, you Bible thumpin rascal, if I wus evah to see God's face you know who I'd be seein...it'd be Miss Lillie or you sho as...well, I won't say the word he said, bein I's standin right heah at the pulpit with the good book lyin open on it.

"Whooowee! He wus some kind-a stout talkin man. The Lawd have mercy, the words that come outta him on dem trips we made evah yeah togethah in dat ole wagon uv mine, ridin from Estill to Winchestah fo the Decoration Day Celebration. We did'n miss a one cause uv the money. I'd take a load of my cider made from my apple owchawd an sell it all out from the back o de wagun. An dem good ladies who put the Celebration on, they'd pay The Colonel jus to march with the otha ole Federates since they said he wus the onlyst one that wus a sho nuff hero. When he hear all dat talk bout him bein a hero, it'd set him off like a fiuhcrackah cause he hated dat wah. On the way he'd get to fussin bout the wah an tha genals...fact is he'd get to fussin bout mos anythin til finlly he'd say, 'Reverend, I done run out uv spit, now you take ovah the talkin fo a spell.'

"An then come the day, on one uv the trips, I tells him all bout how it wus bein a slave an he don say a word. But when I ends up talkin, I sees tears in his eyes. An, jus bout then, as we starts to cross ova the bridge up ta the gatherin he reaches out an pats me on the knee. Miss Lillie, if I hadn't already know'd it befo it wus right then I know'd dat Colonel Stainback had Gawd all in him, no mattah what he'd sometime say.

"Praise be to Gawd fo this good man!

"Miss Lillie, my ole heart is breakin fo yo hurtin. When my Liza die uv the fevah aftah the wah I thinks, how can I go on? But tha Lawd held me up as He will you. In time, Gawd'll wipe away the tears from yo eyes; fo I believe that when the times come fo sorrow an cryin, when our love ones leave us an steal away ovah Jordan, even then—mos specially then—our Lawd's there fo us to lean on as He leaned on His Fathah when He hung high up there on that cross.

"Hear me preach to you the teachins uv the Lawd! All these thangs are gonna pass away an in the fullness uv time we shall be gathahed togethah again with our love ones. Listen to me now!

"Y'all well know we all made different from one anothah. Look round you. I see it in yo faces. You see it in mine. The Lawd wanted us that way. He mades people not to look like one anothah, so some uv us be white, some uv us be black, some yellah, some red; an He mades women an men, tall uns an short uns, weak an strong, some fas as a rabbit, some slow as an ole turtle. Yet the Lawd, He loves us all jus like mamas an daddies an granmamas an grandaddies love they's chillun an granchillun even tho each an evah one be different.

"Brothahs an sistahs, raise yo eyes upward, fo somewheah up theah in the heabens our brotha Colonel Benjamin Stainback, he's now stealin his way home to rest in the arms uv Jesus an theah, close by, waitin to greet him is his precious boy Mark.

"Ah, Lawd Gawd on high, I sees them through my tears! I's hearin the trumpet sound, loudah an loudah; I's hearin it in my soul, I knows I hain't got long to stay heah. An when I gets theah, aftah I hugs an kisses on my Liza, I'm goin ovah to find my friend, The Colonel, an I'm gonna pull him to me an we both gonna laugh an cry cause we ain't got no color on us an he ain't small an I ain't tall—we both jus right!

"Please bow yo heads.

"Deah Lawd Gawd an Creatah uv the firmaments, an uv all that has been, an all that is, an all that'll evah be. Thou aht the one who sent Yo Son down to die fo us on that ole wooden cross so's we might have a chance uv evahlastin life. Fo that an fo evathin, we love Yo, Lawd. Now, we, Yo chillun, ask that Yo receive into Yo presence the soul uv this good man, Yo child, Colonel Benjamin Stainback...in Jesus Christ's name we pray. Amen.

"Brothahs an sistahs, today, as The Colonel an Miss Lillie wanted it to be, Colonel Stainback goes to rest in the earth near my Liza. Beside him, we leavin a place fo Miss Lillie when it come her time to join him. An, mos likely befo her, I'll join him an my Liza, fo evah night, I prays on my knees fo my Lawd to call me by the thunder so I won't be long to stay heah. Amen."

THE OFFICIAL ONE AND ONLY IMPERIAL WIZARD APPROVED K K K HALL OF FAME GUIDEBOOK

BY

GREEN AND RED PULLEN

Dear Visitor,

*Thank you for choosing to visit the **KKK HALL OF FAME**. We are honored by your presence and are appreciative of your $19.95 entrance fee, half of which pays for the tour and guidebook with the remaining going to the Klan Burn Center for Klansmen burned during cross lighting accidents. At the end of your tour, please visit the Gift Shop, which has wonderful Klan literature, novelties, videos, signed prints and order blanks for those who want some of our big-ticket products. The Gift Shop is the perfect place to do your early Christmas shopping. Again, let me thank you for visiting with us.*

The Imperial Wizard

INTRODUCTION

False teaching is a blight upon history. As the founder of the K. K. Katzenberger Company, Inc., the eminent K. K. Katzenberger III loved to say, "Truth, like Jersey cream, will always rise to the top" or—for the many Latin scholars who are sure to read this history—"*Magna est veritas et praevalebit.*" What follows is the absolute "truth" about the KKK. This book can only be purchased in the gift shop at the Ku Klux Klan Hall of Fame. Copies signed by the authors are also available at a nominal extra cost.

HOW THE KKK REALLY BEGAN

Generally, it has been believed that the Klan—sometimes referred to as the Invisible Empire—was started as a social club by six young former Confederate soldiers in Pulaski, Tennessee, in December 1865. Not so! The truth of its origin is now revealed for the first time. It did indeed begin in 1865. But the location was not Pulaski, Tennessee. The location was Hartford, Connecticut, and it was founded by none other, than K. K. Katzenberger III. "Triple K", as he was known by intimates, was a shrewd carpetbagger and manufacturer of white bed sheets. He sensed there were huge profits to be made in a "reconstructed" South if he could come up with an original marketing idea for Katzenberger Manufacturing Company's bed sheets. This is the story of how that idea became reality and how, to this very day, it continues to pay dividends to Triple K's descendants.

ORIGIN OF THE NAME OF THE KKK

Other than manufacturing white bed sheets and making money Triple K had two other loves: Egyptology and transvestism. Only a few old and trusted servants knew of Triple K's late night glides and twirls through his mansion "TUTME I". Dressed in a flowing sheet, with French lace at the borders, he would glide from room to room, floor to floor, seeking inspiration from the gods of the Pharaohs. On the night of April 15, 1865—one week after Lee's surrender to Grant—as he skipped down the grand stairway he had his ultimate inspiration: He would establish a new society based on a secret Egyptian organization founded in 1421 B.C. during the Tuthmosis IV dynasty. Dedicated to weird eroticisms the society's name, in hieroglyphics (sorry, our keyboard does not include hieroglyphic symbols.) was literally translated in English, *Sissy Koo Koo Klutz-men*. That translation, of course, left much to be desired as the name for the new society so, wily old Triple K took one more whirl through the mansion, and as the blood flowed through his brain, the name came to him—the Ku Klux Klan.

In January 1915, in the midst of a pirouette, Triple K tripped over his sheet and fell forward onto the iron beak of an Ibis statue. His last words were, "Mummify me." Though its exact location is known only by the family, it is said that there is a crypt deep within TUTME I that contains a sarcophagus with the mummy of K. K. Katzenberger III. Lying at its foot are three mummified Irish Wolfhounds: Tut, Tut and Tut, his constant companions.

Three days after Triple K's death, K. K. Katzenberger IV changed the company's name to Nathan Bedford Forrest White Bed Sheet Manufacturing Co. Though born with only a left leg, "Four K", as the company's president was soon nicknamed, continued, with the help of a prosthetic right leg, his father's nightly glides to obtain divine guidance from the gods of the Pharoahs. He later told his son that it was during his second rather jerky glide that he conceived the promotion scheme, which was to result in a resurgence in sales and Klan memberships. Throughout the South, newspapers carried advertisements that read, "Buy Two Nathan Bedford Forrest Bed Sheets and Get One Hood Free". That same night, in his final loop-de-loop, his right leg broke and he fell and struck his head. While semi-conscious, he had an inspired vision of a Klan Hall of Fame, housed in a pure-white semi-trailer truck with a large logo of the fearless face of General Forrest WITH the inscription, "For Fun At Night, Wear Forrest White". Since 1915 the Hall of Fame has constantly toured America.

THE KU KLUX KLAN HALL OF FAME

After entering the Hall of Fame your tour guide will show a brief documentary film that presents the true and glorious history of the Klan. You will see heretofore unpublished photographs of great Ku Kluxers; hear inspiring stories, quotations and such details as how to build and light your own cross at home, the official way to put it in a hole and how to perform the secret handshake in public so no one can see you doing it. You will receive a glossary of Klan lexicon and a list of advertisements of

KKK-approved products. For an additional fifty dollars your guide will provide you with a truly inspirational print of General Forrest to hang in your den at home. The prints are a limited edition, numbered and signed by noted Klan artist Vincent "One Ear" Mullins. For a nominal fee an authentic replica of the General's signature can be indelibly stamped on the lower right or left corner, whichever you prefer. Your attractive memento will be the envy of your friends and neighbors.

The following gives brief vignettes of a few of the great men and women who have been inducted into the Klan Hall of Fame for their lifetime achievements to the Invisible Empire.

General Nathan Bedford Forrest, of course, first, foremost and always is this great general who was the killer of tons of Yankees. It was said, by one who saw him, that in the midst of deadly battle, "His eyes were blazing with the intensity of a panther springing on its prey." He brought that same "intensity" to the birth of the Klan. In the fall of 1866, in room No. 10 of the Maxwell House Hotel in downtown Nashville, Tennessee, he was administered the oath of the Klan. Soon afterward, he was elected first Grand Wizard of the Invisible Empire. In his old age, he admitted that his motivation to join the Klan was simply because he was a poor loser. Be that as it may, it was his former battlefield mantra, "Git thar fustest with tha mostest," that spurred him onward until his panther-like leadership spread the Klan like kudzu across the South. On October 29, 1877, as he lay on his deathbed, General Forrest shouted his final command, "Somebody git tha slop jar quick!"

Reverend Whip LeGree, PPddH, first Grand Kludd, internationally renowned biblical scholar and President of WASATCA, the acronym for the White Anglo Saxon of All Things Christian Association; WASATCA, also happens to be the Cherokee word for "burnt liver." As President and Grand Kludd of the Hoenwald Seminary For White Preachers, Reverend Le Gree wrote and published the scholarly textbook that was to make his name known across the land. In "How God Messed Up When He Got All Wore Down," he brilliantly reveals how God got so fatigued by the sixth day of creation that he blundered terribly on his first try at making man. Then, with flawless logic, Reverend LeGree proves that in the late afternoon of the seventh day, after having had a good rest, God successfully achieved perfection with the making of the first White Anglo-Saxon Protestant.

Colonel Beauregard Q. Calhoun, renowned Grand Cyclops, is a true martyr of the KKK. For the last twenty-seven years of his life, "The Colonel", as he was fondly known, used his own bed to protest the 1954 Supreme Court ruling in *Brown vs. Board of Education,* which resulted in the integration of the nation's schools. The Colonel's resistance to integration became legendary; at the beginning of every school year he crisscrossed the South in his pure-white motor home, pulled up to the front of schools where he rolled his bed up to the entrance, then climbed into the bed and refused to get out until federal marshals arrested him and rolled the bed away with The Colonel shouting words too ugly to put here. Emblazoned on the side of his motor home and on the pamphlets he passed out from his bed was the motto of his home state of Alabama: *Audemus jura nostra defendere,* "We dare defend our rights". In 1982, The Colonel decided to take his demonstration to Massachusetts and has not been heard of since.

Miss Rosebud Peevy, the great and late humorist of Chikenbone, Mississippi, appeared at every Klan barbecue and catfish fry. She brought joy and laughter to Klaverns throughout the South, except for one occasion when she crossed over the line of propriety during a Roast of the Grand Kludd, Reverend Whip LeGree. The audience was roaring with laughter when suddenly she stopped, and with a dead serious look on her face, she hollered, "Well, thank the good Lord, Reverend LeGree, you ain't anything like your fellow preacher, Reverend Billy Love. Last summer, at one of his tent revivals on the outskirts of Stone Mountain, Georgia, he saw me out in the audience and I guess he wanted to get me back for poking a little bit of fun at him a time or two. As he was wrapping up his sermon he pointed his old bony finger at me and shouted, 'A false witness shall not be unpunished and she that speaketh lies shall not escape.'

"Now y'all know I ain't no shrinking violet, so I stood up and shouted back, 'Reverend Love, I ain't never said you was no member of the Ku Klux Klan; all I ever said was that you certainly was a wizard under the sheet!'"

When she finished telling this, Reverend LeGree's face had turned to stone and the room was as silent as a grave. Nobody moved. Then one after the other of the guests got up and slowly excused themselves and left. The roast was over. This came close to ending her career. If you are ever near Chickenbone, go into the filling station there and ask someone to direct you to her memorial site, which is just at the edge of town—the Rosebud Peevy Catfish Pond.

Earl Dee Brightwater*, the Empire's Great Klockard from 1915-1936, remains the most profound thinker and philosopher in Klan history. None has more fearlessly attacked the great questions of morality and life and death. *Earl Dee's Words of Wisdom and Guidance* has become the standard text for the Klan Youth Corps. At monthly Klavern meetings there are group recitations of such profound Earl Dee sayings as:

A bird in the hand is dead!

Since Man is immortal his meat bill will be astronomical!

The ultimate answer lies in the heart of all of us. The answer is twelve!

Belief in an afterlife requires that one is always prepared with an extra change of underwear!

Sex is nobody else's business except the three people involved!*

*To avoid lawsuits against the Hall of Fame and to be true to our dedication to full transparency in all that we say, do and write, we must disclose that charges of plagiarism have been filed against Earl Dee by the President of the London Psychoanalytical Society and Chairman of the Brooklyn Society for the Interpretation of Dreams and by Woody Allen, who has been quoted in the *New York Times* as saying of Earl Dee, "He does not make me make the Ha Ha."

Senator Joe "Thumbscrew" McKlanthy, that truly great American most feared by the former Union of Soviet Socialist Republics. In 1950, he showed his total commitment to catching Commies when he turned his grandmother, parents, youngest sister and several cousins over for investigation to the House Un-American Activities Committee. However, it was in 1979 that he made his lasting mark on our nation's history. That was the year he led the Klan's boycott on Girl Scout cookies and, thereby, saved America! If you lived during those turbulent years you will readily recall the night he appeared on prime-time national television and announced that he had in his possession secret documents* which undeniably proved that the Commies had successfully infiltrated and were in control of the sale of Girl Scout cookies. Who of us can forget the horror felt when he further revealed that the money from the cookie sales was being channeled to Castro for the singularly evil purpose of financing a Cuban invasion of Atlantic City. Of course, these revelations were strongly denied by the C.I.A., F.B.I., secretary of state, the president and the National Council of the Girl Scouts of the United States of America. But we know the truth, and the ultimate proof is incontestable—knowing the Klan was onto him, Castro did not invade Atlantic City.

*These documents were obtained by the Klan Bureau of Investigation (KBI), from a double agent whose code name was KACA (Klan Agent Cuban Agent).

Jimbo "Bighead" Hutto, last, but not least, must be given recognition for his place in Klan history as the designer of the Klan hood. Bighead did indeed have a big head. Shaped almost exactly like a carrot his head extended a full twelve inches above his eyebrows. From 1866 to 1869 he traveled with the Oddities of Mankind Sideshow to every out-of-the-way hamlet in the South. As a skilled tailor he had created a hood that covered his head until—at the end of a drum roll—he jerked the hood off, which caused most of the audience to cover their eyes and several women to faint. It was in the summer of 1869 when the show came to Franklin, Tennessee, that General Forrest and two of his Knighthawk guards attended. As the General observed the fear in the faces of the audience as they stared at the hooded Bighead, he turned to the Knighthawks and pronounced, "Hot damnit, boys, that thar's whut we need!" And it was that very night the General hired Bighead and swore him into the Klan. Two hours later he wired Triple K, telling him he was sending, by the next train going North, a man who would not only expand the Katzenberger Company's reputation and bottom line but would considerably enhance the Klan's appearance. The very next day the General canceled the Klan's contract with the Southern Potato Burlap Sack Company, which had been manufacturing the potato sack hoods Klansmen had been wearing.

EIGHT OR SIX THINGS YOU NEED TO KNOW ABOUT THE KLAN

1. <u>The Secret Handshake</u>: The secret handshake is so secret that if it is done in public, it should be in the largest pants pocket of one of the shakers.

2. <u>How to Build Your Own Cross at Home in Several Easy Steps</u>:

a. Get two boards: one real long, the other not so long.

b.   Lay the real long one on the ground, then lay the not so long one across it about a fourth or a third of the way from the top and with each side sticking out the other side.

c. Next, take four or maybe even nine nails and nail the not so long board to the real long board so it won't fall off.

d. Wrap the whole thing in gunny sacks and tie the sacks on real tight with heavy baling twine.

e. Go to your local Hog Higgins Service Station and get three or five gallons of his best used crank case oil and pour the oil all over the cross.

f. When you've decided where you want to set the cross up, the next step is to dig a hole in the ground. The hole should go straight down.

g. Now here's where a lot of folks get hernias trying to show off by lifting the cross up by themselves and then putting it in the hole. Don't do that! Get three or eight men to help you.

h. Now comes the risky part—lighting it. Here, you really have to be careful—Cross Burning Can Be Dangerous! Since the founding of the Klan, it is estimated that somewhere between thirty-three and seventy-seven cross lighters have been burned to a crisp. Follow these guidelines for the KKK-approved safety ways to light a cross. Use one, or two, or three of the following:

a) Flamethrower

b) Ten-foot wooden match
c) Bow and flaming arrow
d) Trail of gunpowder
e) Special KKK Electronic Cross Lighter
f) Asbestos robe, hood and gloves
g) A really fast Klansman
h) A Klutz (See Glossary for definition.)

3. <u>Klan Humor</u>: We are not without a sense of humor. Other than the humorist, Miss Rosebud Peevy, we have one other funny member, the esteemed Klan Poet Laureate, Dylan J. J. Potts, whose limericks abound with Celtic humor:

The Imperial Wizard named Joe Pete,
Is more than a little off beat,
He belongs to the Klan,
Just so he can
Go buck-naked under his sheet.

The preacher of the Klan is a Kludd,
He believes God shaped man from the mud,
And that W.A.S.P.S. were made better,
After an error, which turned the first batch into a dud.

There was a Klan woman named Gertie,
Who was mean because she was dirty,
But when she was clean, she wasn't so mean
In fact, I thought Gertie was purty.

How to Speak Klanish

The Klan's National Headquarters in Twopeetwopee, Mississippi, is inundated with requests for an official lexicon of Klan words. We are so excited about the following compilation, which will educate new members and provide unity and clarity in our communications with one another. Knowing these words and using them regularly at gatherings will significantly increase your self-confidence and enhance your image with your Klavern's leaders and your family and friends. We suggest you memorize seven a day. In one week you, too, will be Klanishly articulate.

AKIA: a password meaning "A Klansman I Am"; often seen on decals and bumper stickers. These are also the initials for Amalgamated Katzenberger Associates of which the Nathan Bedford Forrest White Bed Sheets Manufacturing Company, Inc. is a subsidiary.

AYAK?: a password meaning "Are You A Klansman?" This is also the Tibetan response to the frequently asked tourist question, "What's 'at big ole, hairy thang over 'ere 'at sorta looks like a cow?"

CABARK: a password meaning "Constantly Applied By All Real Klansmen." Do not confuse with CAMEOW, which is the password for an old men's organization "Curmudgeons Advance For Men's Eminence Over Women."

Exalted Cyclops: the top officer, or president, of a Klavern, usually referred to as the "E.C." It originated with Colonel Faubus Bullthropp who was born with only one eye smack dab in the middle of his forehead.

Genii: the collective name for the national officers who serve as an advisory board to the Imperial Wizard. Genii is a pluralization of genius, meaning an attendant spirit or person who influences another person. Unkind critics are prone to point out that the title has nothing to do with the more common usage of "genius" for people who are intelligent or wise.

Ghouls: the term for rank and file Klansmen, though seldom used because of its ugly association with grave robbing and corpse eating.

Grand Dragon: the top officer, president, of a Realm or state. Old "Triple K's" perverted sense of humor shines through here with his selection of the word "Dragon" to use in the title. His familiarity with the origins of ancient words led him to use this derivative of the Greek word drakon, which came from a remote verb meaning "to look" and "to flash". Until it was removed in the 1950s as a part of the swearing-in ceremony, new Grand Dragons were required "to flash" themselves before the entire assembly.

Grand Wizard: the title conferred on Nathan Bedford Forrest, head of the Reconstruction Klan, is comparable to Imperial Wizard. While Ku Kluxers are not noted for their sense of humor, they dearly love such double entendres as, "At ole Bubba Shrum shore is one Grand Imperial Wizard unduh tha sheet!"

Imperial Konvocation: the national convention, usually held biennially. Rather than being housed in big Republican and Democratic convention halls, the Klan rotates its conventions across the country, holding them in one of the many Katzenberger warehouses.

Imperial Tax: a percentage of the dues sent to national headquarters. The same as with Federal and state taxes the Klan's Imperial Tax goes for such worthwhile causes as salaries for dedicated and selfless officials. While these men love their country they expect to be paid for it.

Imperial Wizard: the overall, or national, head of the Klan, is sometimes compared to the President of the United States. As with all politicians he is a man of great purity of purpose, intelligence, compassion, depth of philosophical understanding and impeccable honor. He is a major recipient of the Imperial Tax.

Inner Circle: a small group of four or five members who plan and carry out "action", such as: cross burnings, bullying, harassment and general mayhem to promote the American Ideal and Christianity; thereby, turning others from their evil ways.

Invisible Empire: a Klan's overall jurisdiction, which compares to the United States, although no Klavern exists in every state. The Klan does not favor one region or state over another. It will set up wherever good people will allow it.

K: Symbol for potassium.

KK: as with all organizations there are those who are an embarrassment to the general membership. In the Klan it is the Klan Kuties, a group of perverts who wear nothing under their unofficial, garishly colored robes and use "see through" hoods, thereby displaying their gold earrings, eye make-up, beauty spots and "stylish" hairdos.

KKK: Kachina Kachine Katzenberger, Triple K's youngest granddaughter, and first female President of Katzenberger Konglomerate, Inc., has not been without criticism for her designer knee robes for women and, more recently, a risqué off-the-shoulder version.

KKKK: Knights of the Ku Klux Klan, the name officially used since the Klan's revival in 1915 at Stone Mountain, Georgia. These are also the initials for Katzenberger Klancraft Kross Kumpany, inventor of the prefabricated cross.

KA KA: the words used by Klan parents when teaching their children bowel control as in, "Does Baby Sister need to go sit on the potty and make KA KA?"

Kalendar: Klan calendar dates events from both its origin and the 1915 rebirth. "Anno Klan" means, in the year of the Klan. The months are called: "Bloody, Gloomy, Hideous, Fearful, Furious, Alarming, Terrible, Horrible, Mournful, Sorrowful, Frightful and Appalling." The weeks are: "Woeful, Weeping, Wailing, Wonderful and Weird." The days are: "Dark, Deadly, Dismal, Doleful, Desolate, Dreadful and Desperate." Now, that's a sense of humor.

Kangaroo: a herbivorous, leaping, boxing marsupial found in Australia and New Guinea. On October 5, 1936, the kangaroo was adopted as the Klan's official animal.

Kardinal Kullors: white, crimson, gold and black. Secondary kullors: gray, green, and blue. The Imperial Wizard's kullor is royal purple. Even the Klan has been influenced by America's sexual revolution in the sixties as seen in the outrageous pastel combinations of some perverts' robes and the increasingly fashionable "see-through" hoods worn by the kinky Klan Kuties.

KBI: Klan Bureau of Investigation. Standards are extremely high for selection into the KBI. They require the ability to:

>find one's own navel.
>
>isochronally pat one's head and rub one's belly.
>
>differentiate between black and white.

KIGY: "Klansman I Greet You!" Should not be confused when seen on Iowa license plates where it stands for "Kalispell Idahoans Grow Yams."

KIWI: a New Zealand bird that walks wherever it's going since it can't fly.

Klavern: a local unit or club, also called a "den". There are also Klan Youth Corps that are comparable to the Cub Scouts and Brownies, thereby evidencing the Klan's contribution to the creation of a better America.

Klectokon: initiation fees and dues. Some ill-tempered Ku Kluxers denounce the Klectokon and Imperial Tax as nothing more than legalized kleptomania.

Klodes: songs sung by Klonvocations. A good example is the ever popular, "The Ku Klux Klan, White Man's Burden Blues" by Unclebrother Littlegeorge. *See Appendix 1.

Klokard: lecturer and teacher of Klankraft, the Klan's practices and beliefs. Foremost among many of exceptional brilliance was the Great Klokard Earl Dee Brightwater who believed that "until you've walked a mile in another man's rubber boots you can't imagine the smell!"

Kloran: Klan Bible. The Kloran makes abundantly clear that much of what passes for theology is a bunch of stuff, explaining in words that simpletons can understand, what God was really thinking and what He really meant when He dictated the Bible.

Kludd: Klan chaplain. These special Christian men are noted for their possession of truth and for their willingness to burn anyone at the stake who disagrees with them.

Klutz: a dumb, dumb Klansman who you can afford to lose. A Klutz is prone to trip on his own robe and go sprawling on the ground. He is usually the one selected to light the cross. (Many thanks to our Jewish friends for their creation of the word.)

Knighthawks: custodians of the fiery cross and of applicants prior to their initiation and, in some Klans, are responsible for carrying out violence; this office is often designated by a black robe. This is one of the Klan's toughest jobs. Knighthawks find it next to impossible to get any form of insurance and when they do the premiums are exorbitant. Job stress results in high rates of "burnout" and psychosis, in the form of pyromania. These guys can really look and act scary, especially when they dress all in black and talk like Darth Vader.

Knockers: the mammary glands of Klanswomen.

Knurd: a Klansman who tries to act like he's smart but is dumb as mud.

Konx: sound made by a pebble striking the bottom of an ancient Eleusinion voting urn.

Kook: a mentally ill Klansman

Kosher: good Jewish food.

Kraken: A Norweigan sea monster of great size.

Krap: KKK body waste production.

Kudos: the fame, fortune, honor and money which Green and Red Pullen (identical twins) hope to receive for their exhaustive research and the time taken away from their families for the creation of this magisterial history.

Kultur: something most Klansmen ain't got.

THANK YOU TO OUR MANY SPONSORERS

Without the generosity of our sponsorers this publication of *Knights of the Ku Klux Klan For Nincompoops* would have been impossible. The products below all have the KKK Seal of Approval. To place an order please contact your local Exalted Cyclops who maintains an up-to-date price list and order blank for each of these fine providers.

Dr. Kinky Sexmund, G.S., H.S., B.A., M.A., Ph.D., KKK, specialist in the treatment of Pyromania, H.R. Phobia (The fear of smothering to death when covered by a hood and robe), The Sin of Onan, obsessive compulsively stroking of matches, fear of the Booger Man, paranoia about everything and everybody and many other disorders that Klan members and their families are prone to have.

Hog Higgins Service Stations, Inc.: Hog Higgins Stations are located at the end of almost every dead-end road in the South. When you go inside put your hand in your pocket and ask the attendant to put his in and when he does, give him the secret handshake which will assure that you receive the low, low KKK price for gas, used crank case oil, Red Man Chewing Tobacco, Moon Pies, RC Colas and Dr. Peppers.

Dr. Funk's Trusty Triboelectric Truss: Dr. Funk's Trusty Truss supports the innards of many of our finest members who have busted their guts trying to lift a cross on their own. If your gut is pooching out, waste no time today in placing your order. "Remember, when you're trussed up in a Funk Truss you'll feel you're all back inside."

Vincent "One Ear" Mullins Stickers: "We have bumper stickers against any and everybody." See a sampling below:

COMMUNISTS FONDLE SOFA-CREVICES

HELP KEEP AMERICA GAY
SUPPORT YOUR LOCAL KKK

SISSY MEN EAT QUICHE ONLY
KLAN MEN EAT RAW BALONEY

IF CALLED BY A BLACK PANTHER
YOU'D BETTER NOT ANTHER

MAY YOUR SOUL BE FOREVER TORMENTED
    BY FIRE
AND YOUR BONES DUG UP BY DOGS AND
    DRAGGED
THROUGH THE STREETS OF MINNEAPOLIS!!!

"Stay Safe with the Flem Snope's Ten Foot Safety Match"

Katzenberger's Klancroft Kross Kumpany, Inc.: Inventor and sole distributor of the KKK prefabricated Cross. If you purchase one of these one-of-a-kind crosses we will—for only an additional $19.95—include with it our KKK Safety Seal of Approval Electronic Cross Lighter.

Hoods and Robes by Kuties

Bo Bo Ledbetter's Lumber Yards: "For a better built cross use Bo Bo wood."

Peeky Poo Nudist Kamp: Members are only allowed to wear see-through robes but otherwise must be barefoot all over.

King Arthur's Round Table, Inc.: A truly "high cotton" experience, one you will never forget. On weekends, from April to October, the sounds of clashing swords, the ring of armor, the twang of bows, the thunder of hooves and whinnying horses and loud Medieval curses can be heard in a remote valley of middle Tennessee where wealthy Ku Kluxers can gather and pretend they are brave and are true knights of chivalry. Accommodations for horses and motor homes are available. For the renaissance experience of your life contact your local Grand Cyclops and make your reservations today.

Appendix 1

THE KU KLUX KLAN WHITE MAN'S BURDEN BLUES

I work like hell to give a fright,
I run around a lot at night,
I get no respect in the news,
Marchin's made holes in all my shoes.
I buy my sheets an' pay my dues,
                    (Refrain)
I wear a pair of worn out shoes,
I got the KKK White Man's Burden Blues.

A Klansman's life is full of shocks,
Folks hit on you with sticks and rocks,
My hands are burnt, my back's a loss,
Ruptured myself liftin' a cross
                    (Refrain)

My wife's sulled up, she's always mad,
Treats me sumpin' turrible bad,
Won't wash my sheets, or shine my shoes,
Talks ugly 'bout tha Wizard's dues.
                    (Refrain)

My kid is big on civil rights,
He dances ballet in flesh-toned tights,
Wears a ring in his right ear lobe
An dresses in a sequined robe.
                    (Refrain)

I'm plumb wore down, I've been abused.
Hot damn, the soles come off my shoes!
Unless, next year, the Klan improves,
They'll suck air, 'fore I'll pay dues.
                    (Refrain)

It ain't fittin' to live this way,
If things don't change, then I just may,
Go sell my sheet an' take my dues,
An' buy myself some brand new shoes.
                    (Refrain)

Epilogue

I joined a new group, just this year,
An' they've rernt my brand new shoes, I fear.
They march a lot an' charge a fee
They call themselves N. Double A. C. P.
I buy no sheets, but still pay dues,
I wear a pair of worn out shoes,
I got the WORN OUT SHOES, WHITE MAN'S
    BURDEN BLUES.

Unclebrother Littlegeorge

DEATH

"Beware, that stern lean man who possesseth truth,
He may burneth thee upon yon stake, forsooth!
Pray, tweaketh his long nose whenever thouest can,
For it helpeth him to recall that he's but a man."

St. Joebobius Tweakius

"I am free of all prejudice. I hate everyone equally."

W. C. Fields

The third bullet was a waste. The first had killed him. The second was to be certain. The fourth and fifth were hatred. The sixth was saved. It was usually always saved when possible.

But then the hammer was clicked all the way back the sixth time. And the trigger was pulled with more hatred.

Now the chambers were empty.

The eyes of the man lying on his back in the dry stubble did not blink. They stared straight up, dead to the vultures circling above.

The sky had not a wisp of cloud as far as could be seen by the man holding the blue-black pistol. His thumb cocked the hammer part way back, clicked aside the loading gate, pulled the empty 45 shell out, put a bullet in, turned the cylinder, pulled another shell out, and put a bullet in. When all six chambers were reloaded he slid the pistol back into the holster on the wide leather belt that hung low against his lean thigh.

He looked around, nodded, walked back to his horse, kneed it in the side, tightened the saddle girth, put his foot in the stirrup and mounted the bay. He looked down at the man on the ground, nodded again, clicked his tongue, slapped the reins and rode away.

He found the next man the next day, another one the following day and the last one four days later. He left all of them for the vultures. After the fourth one he pulled the collar of his sheepskin coat up around his neck and turned the horse's head south. There were three more: two were in Copper Canyon.

Dark clouds were starting to roll across the mountains in the west. The wind was building and there was a bite in the air.

* * * * *

Two days later he crossed the border at El Paso. The air was warmer now. The land had dried hard- beige. The vultures were with him every day. Four days' steady riding, he was in Chihuahua.

He stayed three days to rest the bay and have her reshod, to visit a whore, to confess to a priest and resupply. He killed one of the three there. Done, he moved on.

The mountains, the valleys grew higher and deeper and longer; they angled and twisted on and on. Hawk screams echoed with the clackings of the horse's hooves on the narrow stone trail that wound up and down the cliffs.

He kept seeing her, her gentle beauty. Kept hearing her soft voice calling behind him. So near he looked over his shoulder three times. Each time she was not there. He spurred the horse hard.

At Creel the trail turned down and down. Halfway to Urique, in the side of the cliff, there was the cave and the man and the little Tarahumara woman. As her eyes did not close or look away he killed her. In a little while he cut the right thumb off the man and waited for him to tell him what he asked for, and when the man did not, he cut the left thumb off, then the man told him where the other woman was and he threw the man over the cliff.

* * * * *

He rode southeast it seemed forever. The bay died near Puebla. He bought a strawberry roan from a peasant and rode on. Everyday the shadows and screams from above were there.

He found the woman living with a Mayan family in the jungle at Uxmal. He paid them for her and dragged her to the top of the Pyramid of the Magician where he cut her throat. At dusk he rode into Merida and got a room at the American Hotel. He gorged and whored for five days, then confessed to a drunk priest and boarded a schooner and sailed north.

He sat on the deck listening to the screaming of the gulls, and the clacking of the sails, and the waves slapping against the hull, and to her voice calling.

BENEATH THE STAIRS

JOURNAL OF EVAN WILLIAMS
DYSERTH PLANTATION
HAYWOOD COUNTY, TENNESSEE
DECEMBER 25, 1990

Forgive
Us forgive
Us your death that myselves the believers
May hold it in great flood
Till the blood shall spurt,
And the dust shall sing like a bird
As the grains blow, as your death grows, through our heart

Dylan Thomas

When I was nine, Branwen and I found our mother hanging beneath the stairs.

We are a large and proud family, here for long generations, mixing our Welsh, English, Irish and Cherokee blood into the bones of our faces, our colors, the sizes and shapes of our bodies. The richness of our blood and our land has carried us upward as the depth of the fertile Delta slopes toward us.

My father, "Senator Father", United States Senator William Williams and master of Dyserth, was in Washington, D.C., most of World War II. He came home only to campaign at election time and to vote, and for two days each spring and fall to meet with his overseers. He came once for Christmas in 1942, but on December 25 and 26, 1945, he was not here. He was in Washington.

I am his only son. I was nine years old that Christmas forty-five years ago. My sister, Branwen, was eight. Other than the Negro pickaninnies and the overseers' children, we were the only children for miles in every direction. We were never with white children until we were sent away.

Our cotton, corn and timber stretch outward over seventeen thousand acres of fat, gently rolling land separated into five plantation sections. Through it, like a water moccasin, twists the muddy Hatchie River. The cotton and corn are sold in Memphis, an hour's drive away. Until his death, Senator Father was a member of the board of the Memphis Cotton Exchange. Now, I am its chairman.

Shiny-black African slaves created our fields from swamp and forest. We owned five hundred of them. Now, fewer than four hundred Negro tenants plow and plant, weed, pick, gin and bale the white gold that rises from the black soil. As the generations have passed, their intensity of color has softened from tawny, to hazel, until now you see fewer and fewer of the old shiny, jet-blacks. There are more Negroes than whites in Haywood; they scheme to wrest control from me. They have not. With few exceptions, whites remain as "trash", but still they follow me. Now, I, master of Dyserth, observe these changes and constancies of time and note them in my journal.

* * * * *

Lead bought our land and slaves. Who we are began with my great grandfather Dafydd Williams' lead mine in Denbighshire, Wales. He sold it in 1822, and with its pounds, he booked passage on a clipper to New Orleans. From there, he came up the Mississippi and overland to Haywood. He named his nine hundred acres "Dyserth" after his home village. With him he brought seven slaves, his wife and their only child, my grandfather, Huw Williams.

Six years before the war, Dafydd died from yellow fever contracted while buying slaves in Memphis. He left five thousand acres, one hundred and fifty slaves, two gins, a ferry, mill, hundreds of cattle, horses and oxen and a two-story, six-room brick house with white pillared porches on the front and rear.

Like Abraham, my grandfather, the inheritor of Dyserth, increased our land and wealth. He built the "Big House," the largest and grandest house in West Tennessee. Six great Doric columns span the front portico and verandah. Above the hipped roof rises a cupola, windowed on every side; as far as you can see is Williams land. The house's walls are four spans of red brick made from our own earth. It stands like a Greek temple on a slight rise three-quarters of a mile from the river. To its rear, a long English boxwood garden and walk lead to an octagonal observatory built for parties never held; a little ways beyond is our cemetery, surrounded by an iron fence.

Our fields are our power in Haywood County. From them comes our control of Tennessee and some of

Washington. My father was its king. He created state legislators and governors one after another; despising them all, along with his constituents. He once told me, "Our family rules over the rabble of the earth." From a distance you would have thought him an impeccably dressed boy he was so small. But standing before him, looking into his emotionless black eyes, you saw one you would not oppose. The face in the mirror when he shaved was God's.

* * * * *

Everyone called my mother, "Darlin", and an old schoolmate of hers told me that, even as a young girl, she was "delicate", a word long past, a word once used for genteel ladies given to melancholy. Oh my God, she was beautiful: tall, willowy-slender, with slow languid movements, her face ethereal as Raphael's *Mary*!

She was the Queen of the Cotton Carnival in 1931, the only daughter of the wealthy Episcopal Bishop of Memphis whose riches came from his father's slave market in New Orleans. I believed she was God's final perfection. More than anything in my childhood, I wanted her love.

My father met her the year she was crowned at the Carnival. Mother was seventeen, he twenty-seven. Two months later they married; ten months after that I was born; and the year after came Branwen, my precocious sister. The next year a boy was born dead and seven months later she miscarried. She almost died. The doctor said she would die if she were to become pregnant again. From that time she rarely left the house, except to attend

Holy Day services at Zion Episcopal Church in Brownsville. Once a month, the priest came to Dyserth for lunch with Mother, to deliver a blessing on our family and on our land. Later, when I was grown, I wondered if his deliverance was a curse.

* * * * *

Branwen was a mirror of Mother, very beautiful, and like Mother did when she was agitated, liked to dress in black and swish her skirts.

Her eyes were fox eyes, a vixen's: quick, always watching, their haunting brilliance seeing everything, their shrewdness looking into me, through me, commanding me as though I was naked. I did not know the word preternatural then, but there were times when I believed she was not human.

When she was absorbed in a book—at age five she began taking books from our father's four-thousand-book library—or when she was drawing, or practicing her writing, I would stare at her for long moments until, finally, she raised her eyes—with the same smile she had for me at night—and would motion for me to come close up against her and, when our bodies were touching, she would read to me, or tell me the story of her drawing.

Except for dear old Aunt Rit—the daughter of two of our slaves—who oversaw our house servants and those who kept the yards and gardens, and an ignorant insipid tutor who came twice a week, Branwen and I were left mostly to ourselves to grow up. Within this emptiness of neglect, we created our own world and lived in it most every day and in all of our dreams.

We filled our days with rhymes from *The Real Mother Goose*. Its words were so in our hearts, we came to believe we had written them, most especially those that spoke of death.

The great hallway was our kingdom. On the hottest of summer days, air moved through its large doorways when they were open at both ends. Ten strides in from the front door rose the grand elliptical stairway. Not one home—not even in Memphis—had such a magnificent stairway. Gleaming mahogany, it floated in air as it curved upward, its steps wide enough for four people to walk side-by-side. As Branwen and I sat beneath them our imaginations became reality and the words of Mother Goose told us who we were, and what we were to do.

"The Death and Burial of Poor Cock Robin" was our favorite. Branwen began the chant and I followed,

Branwen & Me:
        "Who killed Cock Robin?"
        "I," said the sparrow,
        "With my little bow and arrow,
        I killed Cock Robin."

Branwen: "Who saw him die?"
Me: "I", said the fly,
           "With my little eye,
           I saw him die."

Branwen: "Who caught his blood?"
Me: "I," said the fish,

"With my little dish,
I caught his blood."

Branwen: "Who'll make his shroud?"
Me: "I," said the beetle,
"With my thread and needle,
I'll make his shroud."

Branwen: "Who'll dig his grave?"
Me: "I," said the owl,
"With my spade and trowel,
I'll dig the grave."

So we passed our long days during the summer of '45. At first we pretended. Then, we began to kill.

Instead of a robin I killed a Rhode Island Red rooster with my bow and arrow. After I pulled the arrow out, Branwen made a coffin from a doll box. We put the coffin into the grave we had dug in the cemetery. We held hands and, with our eyes closed, we chanted together,

"Who'll carry the coffin?"
"I," said the kite,
"If it's not in the night,
I'll carry the coffin."

"Who'll toll the bell?"
"I", said the bull,
"Because I can pull,
I'll toll the bell."

With that, she rang the small bell Mother used to call the servants.

"All the birds of the air
Fell sighing and sobbing,
When they heard the bell toll
For poor Cock Robin."

For a moment we acted sad. Branwen actually cried. It was quiet. Then Branwen began to laugh and I laughed. It was wonderful!

* * * * *

Though we had separate beds we slept together, Branwen and I. At night, as soon as Aunt Rit heard our prayers, tucked us in, gave us a kiss, turned out the light and closed the door behind her, Branwen's feet hit the floor and climbed into my bed, under the covers, pulling herself against me, and we curved our bodies together.

* * * * *

Killing and burying Cock Robin was so much fun we continued to act it out, over and over, for days. We laid flowers on the grave and chanted our lines. But a week later, we were bored.

"I'm tired of doing Cock Robin," I said.
"What do you want to do next?" Branwen asked.
"How about Humpty Dumpty?"

She squnched her nose up, "Stinkweed. That's just an egg."

"Well," and we thought.

"I know what...let's do Ladybird."

And we did.

"Ladybird, ladybird, fly away home!
Your house is on fire, your children
   all gone,
All but one, and her name is Ann,
And she crept under the pudding
   pan

I struck a match to a piece of paper and held the flame beneath a nest in a lilac bush in the cemetery. Branwen slipped a doll's cap over the head of the smallest of the four chirping chicks. It was over in a moment. 'Ann' did not survive.

We would not have survived without Aunt Rit's hugs and kisses.

"You babies come ova heah an give ol' Aunt Rit a big ol hug an I'll tell you a story." And she would pull us to her and begin.

"My great-granddaddy be Gumpa Keeby; he wus bawn across tha big watah an wus always tellin us bout his dreams uv Africa an how he'd see big ol long-neckt animals an ones with hawns an big teeth an claws an he'd get ta makin roarin sounds an hissin an scare us might nigh ta death an we'd scream an run an then he jus laugh an laugh. Ya'll think ol Aunt Rit's black, my granddaddy wus tha blackest human bein God evah made." And all the while she talked she was smiling down on us like sunshine. Finally, she'd let go of us, and with a stern smile say, "You chullin get on now an let ol Aunt Rit git goin cause I knows someuns slackin off their doins."

How could we have stayed alive without the warmth and love of this good woman wrapped around us? We were starved for love and she was our air and food and life. Still, I hear her words, smell her breath of King Leo Peppermint, feel her heavy breasts and arms pressing against my face; I taste her turnip greens, white beans, fried chicken and peach pie. Even now, in my guilt, she brings me some comfort.

But for Branwen and me, her love was not enough to stop us. We continued to kill.

* * * * * *

All with the direction of our rhymes we next killed a crow and a duck and cut off the tails of three baby blind mice with one of Aunt Rit's carving knives.

Then we were ready for "Precious Baby".

Mother's fat, stupid calico cat had green eyes. Mother loved her more than Branwen and me. For long periods of every day that thing lay in the bed beside Mother with its eyes closed. If not there, then, it lay in its loaf-of-bread position, sunning itself on the windowsill in the front parlor. We hated her for every stroke and pat she received from Mother. We decided to kill her.

"Which rhyme shall we use?" asked Branwen.

"I'm thinking."

"I know!"

"What?"

"Ding, Dong, Bell,
Pussy's in the well!
Who put her in?
Little Tommy Lin."

"Oh, gosh, no, not that one 'cause Johnny Stout saves her...here it is...here's the one."

"Hush-a-bye, baby, on the tree top!
When the wind blows the cradle
    will rock;
When the bough breaks the cradle
    will fall;
Down will come baby, bough, cradle
    And all."
"Yes! Yes!"
And that's what we did.

While Mother was gone to Zion for Christmas Holy Day, we put Precious Baby in a doll cradle and carried her up to the cupola. Her eyelids barely lifted once, then twice, then closed.

I opened the front window and stepped out onto the roof. Branwen handed the cradle out to me. Slowly, I eased down the roof above the front portico. A foot from the edge, I stopped and looked back at Branwen. She smiled and whispered, "Down will come baby, bough, cradle and all."

And I pitched the cradle over the edge to the stones below.

The next day, we found Mother hanging beneath the stairs.

Did we do it?

If so, forgive us, Lord!

And from then on, even after we were sent far away to separate boarding schools, we were together again at Dyserth every summer and Christmas. How I felt your love, your body as we hugged, your lips as we kissed.

Oh yes, Branwen, if you had not been my sister, I would have married you. I dream of you, even now I am married with three children, you come to me, and you are in me, and I am in you.

I see your face and body clearly after all these years.
Most especially on Holy Days.
Why did you cut your wrists and leave me?

* * * * *

Yesterday, while reading Thornton Wilder's, *The Bridge of San Luis Rey*, I came upon this quote which brought back all the memories of that summer and winter:

"Some say we shall never know, and that to the gods we are like flies that the boys kill on a summer day, and some say that, on the contrary, the very sparrows do not lose a feather that has not been brushed away by the finger of God."

Oh Branwen, were the lives of Mother, Senator Father, Aunt Rit, you and I only flies of summer, or feathers brushed away?

SISTER BERTHA

Love transcends all differences
Zuba in Madagascar 2

In the spring of 2013 I met a holy woman and fell in love with her - as I choose to believe she did with me.

Long have you and others wondered about the wellbeing and the present life of dear Sister Bertha. Seldom a day goes by that an email or phone call fails to come asking about her. Questions regarding the status of her health and of her present activities are foremost in your communications. Having introduced this gentle little nun and dear friend to you I feel it is incumbent on me to respond to your thoughtful inquiries. But, before I bring you up to date on her exploits since my last email on May 17, 2013, there may be some who read this who do not know about Sister Bertha. For them, and for those who remember this extraordinary child of God, let me take you back to the series of emails written about her in May 2013.

May 8, 2013. Sister Bertha, (she lives with five other nuns three houses down from ours) is little bitty; she is eighty-three, she uses a cane and has a kind, gentle voice as she slowly, slowly walks up and down our street. Ten minutes ago we talked in front of our house. I gave her one of my wife's Siberian Iris. In this fine woman with her smiling face, you see goodness and Jesus. I so love such kind people, no matter their belief as compared to mine. They teach me more good things than do preachers. Three cheers for Sister Bertha!

May 10, 2013. A few days ago I learned that my friend Mohamed Ahmed, the Imam at the Islamic Center, is moving to Washington, D.C., as his wife has been hired there by the Arabic news company, Al Jazeera. I met Mohamed after our son, Adam, was killed in Afghanistan in 2010. Before Mohamed moved I wanted to invite him and Sister Bertha to my house to meet one another. As you may recall, he is a young man and she is eighty-three. Our chocolate Lab, Sally, and I fixed some coffee and key lime pie this rainy morning. When they arrived, as you would expect—if you've heard me talk about them—they and Sally hit it right off just like I knew they would since all three of them are kindhearted.

When it came time for the blessing, I asked who wanted to do it. Mohamed and Sister Bertha looked at one another, paused, and then looked at Sally and me. (I think I detected a slight shaking of their heads when they looked at us.) But then, almost at the same time they said, "We will do it," which was a great relief to me, as I know it was to Sally. Mohamed, being the gentleman he is, let Sister Bertha go first and after she finished he said a few words in Arabic which I thought was a nice touch. They said they liked the pie—each left a bite or two for Sally.

Well, when it came time for them to go, everyone hugged and patted Sally and she licked their hands. Mohamed got his umbrella open and walked Sister Bertha to his car to take her home. I kicked my shoe off at them as they left. That ritual began with an old black woman who worked for my wife's family in Memphis when she was a little girl. Jackie and I continued doing this for fifty-four years before her death. I've kept it up as it assures a safe journey.

You know, having a Muslim Imam, a Catholic Nun and a Labrador Retriever for key lime pie is a right nice way to spend part of a rainy day.

Can any of you introduce me to a nice Rabbi and Hindu in Nashville? If so, let me know, as I'd like to get to know them and invite them and the new Imam and Sister Bertha over for coffee and pecan pie. Mixing different people together is fun and most times you learn things you didn't know.

May 12, 2013. Last night the nuns had me down for homemade vegetable soup and cornbread. I told them that I'd bring the dessert. What I brought was a home run: two bottles of Maryhill Chardonnay and three boxes of Goo Goos: one Original, one Supreme and a Peanut Butter. Sister Bertha's favorite (mine also) is the Supreme. I told the Sisters about coming in second in the National Goo Goo story contest with, *Taking Goo Goos to the Sioux*. It is based on an inspired idea of Jackie's, to take a case of Goo Goos with us when we went to the Pine Ridge Sioux Reservation in South Dakota to experience the Sun Dance ceremonies; we camped with over a hundred Oglala Sioux for a week. The sisters know a lot about these Sioux as the Catholic's Jesuit order established the Holy Rosary Mission there in the late 1800s; their school is called Red Cloud Indian School. We visited the mission and met two of the Jesuits who used to be called "Black Robes" by the Indians; the nuns were "Holy Women".

I want to tell you about the sisters' response to the recent emails I had received about Sister Bertha, which I took to them. They read them after they finished their Goo Goos and were sipping on their second glasses of Chardonnay. They especially enjoyed one, which read, "[I] would never want God to send her [Sister Bertha] to destruction." She was the last to read it. We were all watching her face as she read it the first time, then the second. For a minute you couldn't tell what she was thinking, then a big smile lit her face up and she said, "Whooowecee...that's a relief, he doesn't want God to send me to destruction, 'cause I'd be troubled if he thought God might should destroy me...Mr. Spain, tell your friend the next time you see him, I said, 'God bless him.'"

When it came time to go they all said nice things to me, which I liked. They wanted to know where I got the Chardonnay. Sister Bertha said, "Mr. Spain, be sure and tell the Imam how much I enjoyed meeting him and that I hope he and his wife are well."

May 14, 2013. There have been many exchanges around these emails, some are filled with hurt, which I cannot share in their entirety, only bits and pieces, as in this one, "But I don't mind people, who really love me, thinking I'm going to hell if I'm convinced that they really love me." I cannot grasp the full meaning of this—only its sadness.

Now, to this, Sister Bertha would say, "God bless you." That's the special reason why I like to talk to her;

she always ends our talks with "God bless". I need them, as do both of my friends above.

Long ago, I got these same "blessings" from Father Leo Seinor, a priest who advised me when I counseled devout Catholics. He called me his "Church of Christ friend". When I worked at the mental health center in Columbia, Tennessee, I was a member of the "God Squad" which included an Episcopal priest, a Presbyterian minister and a Methodist minister. At noontime, one day each week, we were available at a table in the cafeteria for counseling students at Columbia State Community College. Sister Bertha and the Imam bring all these people back to me. Indeed, if God is love, He appears in many forms. The next time I see Sister Bertha I must remember to ask her what she thinks about that.

May 17, 2013. I copied all the recent email exchanges about her and the sisters and took them to the nuns' house. She came out on the porch with a tray of oatmeal cookies and lemonade and put it down on a little white wicker table between us. While we sat on the rockers eating and drinking, she read the emails. As before, I watched her face closely for a grimace or tightening of jaw muscles. She read them all through with the same beatific smile she always has and then, without a word, she laid them beside her, picked up another cookie, took two bites, had a sip of lemonade and, with that, she laughed, "Mr. Spain, the Lord has answered my prayers. I've been telling the other sisters that most of the Church of Christ people who live around here are not mean spirited and they have good hearts, even though they do have some awfully peculiar practices and—Ah, ha!—now you've brought me the proof. Tonight at supper, after the blessing, I'm going to read these to them and they'll see that little old Sister Bertha still has the Lord's ear...Mr. Spain, bless you for bringing me these and take the rest of these cookies home for you and Sally."

I didn't realize that this was to be the last time I would be with this Holy Woman. A month later, they were gone, all six of them had moved away. Then, after almost two years, I received the following letter—

February 5, 2015
Red Cloud Indian School
Pine Ridge Reservation, South Dakota
Dear Mr. Spain,
Toh-Neck-too-hch? That means "How are you?" in Sioux. You see, even at eighty-five we can continue to learn. I have a sweet Lakota woman who is teaching me their language and a few written words.

I hope this long overdue expression of appreciation for your many kindnesses to your "Six Sisters" finds you and your family well. I am sorry that there was not time to have you down one last time to make our goodbyes and for more oatmeal cookies and a bit of wine before we left. You were one of our favorite neighbors. You are still named in my nightly prayers.

How is your writing progressing? I read your first book, *Our People*. While I don't care for some of the language, the stories are very believable. I remember your once saying, "Never let a fact stand in the way of a good story."

The land here is so beautiful, the rolling hills, the wind-blown grass, the dark pines. The people have been so kind to me; yet, most have no work, most are poor, many drink their lives away and too many kill themselves, even the young people. If not for God giving me strength, I do not know what I should do for the needs are many.

As you can see from our new address, Sister Louise and I are not terribly far from where you and your wife camped with the Sioux. I love these people and my work with their children. They are so kind to us, especially do they care for their old people and—Ha!—certainly I am one of these.

God gives me energy and life as I look into the brightness in the children's eyes and see the eagerness in their faces and hear the laughter in their voices. They lift me up every morning and all through the day. The Sioux are a great people. They have much to teach us in their beliefs and ways.

I have asked Reverend Father Muller to let me stay here until the Lord calls me home to Him for I love these people and would, if God wills, live out my days among them and be buried here in the Red Cloud Cemetery on the little hill above the Mission. But, as in all things, I bow my head to God's will.

God bless you, Mr. Spain. I *theh-HxEE-lah* you—I cherish you.

Sister Bertha Metzger

* * * * *

I had not heard from Mohamed Ahmed since he and his wife moved to Washington, D.C., where he had become the director of an Islamic program. I emailed him in 2014 but received no reply. Then, as I was doing the final rewrite of "Sister Bertha", I received this email—

Subject: GREETINGS FROM A FRIEND
From: Mohamed Ahmed, Director of Education and Development at Ihsan Foundation for West Africa
To: George Spain
Date: Wednesday, March 11, 2015
Dear George,
I hope all is well. It's been a very, very long time. We [are] all well and miss you a lot.
I love you, George!!!!!!!

My Grandfather and The Heron

My Grandfather always held me on his lap or had me by his side when he told me stories about his life, stories of his boyhood after the Civil War and stories of the years he sailed the seas of the world on the great windjammers. And as he told them, I saw what he saw and I heard what he heard.

"One moment my crewmate was there, the next he was gone. He slipped on the icy footrope, lost his grip and fell backward. I barely heard his last shout, 'DEAR GOD...SAVE...' before it was lost in the shriek of the wind and the flapping of the loose sail.

"Leaning over the yardarm, I saw him falling through the sleet, his arms outstretched to me. He looked straight into my eyes. Then, he disappeared into the sea. And the waves rose higher and higher, all around us, until we were in a valley of water and the waves were higher than the masts of our ship. And I cried, 'Dear God, save me, save me!' And He heard my voice. And He gave my bleeding hands strength and held me tight upon that towering mast, as we smashed onward through the walls of black waves.

"The ship rolled and pitched and fought its way across a sea that would have killed us all if it could have until finally— Praise be to God!—we beat our way around the Horn into the Atlantic. That night, the sky turned red and we rejoiced for we were delivered. The sun rose the next morning upon a clear sky and there in the southern sea with a steady wind against our backs, we unfurled all our sails full wide and sailed north towards home."

Sixty years later, I still hear his voice telling this story. Sitting on his lap, I hear the shrieking of the wind and the flapping of the sails, and as I look down I see the blue anchor tattooed on his left forearm and smell the salty sea all around me.

His stories came alive when he told them. For the moment, they were more real, more alive than the world in which I lived. His words became truths greater than facts; shapes spoke magical beings into flesh and blood, people into giants, and giants into mountains and, even now, if I need them, they return and bring me comfort. After all these years, I cannot fully understand how close my grandfather and I were for often, without a word said, thoughts and feelings passed between us. For me, there is no credible explanation for this since I do not believe in the supernatural. I can only say that it happened, that it was a reality beyond reality. Maybe you will understand what I cannot after I tell you about him and about the last story he told me before he died.

His name was Jeremiah Vann. He was born in 1863, the third year of the Civil War and died in 1945, the last year of World War II. During his long life he was a seaman, a teacher, farmer, scholar, husband, and father of two sons and two daughters, the youngest of whom was my mother. "Granddaddy" wasn't a big man. He was lean but strong, with dark skin and thick hair and mustache that turned snow white when he was old. His mustache was slightly stained at the corner of his mouth where perched the ever-present corncob pipe he smoked. I rolled sheets of newspapers into tapers long enough for him to lean from his chair to reach the fire in the fireplace to light his pipe. He smelled of King Leo Peppermint candy, of tobacco and earth and of a bit of his sweat.

I have an old photograph of him as a young man. His hair is black as coal. His "darkness", so he said of his skin and hair, came from his Cherokee ancestors. I believed him. His Indian blood made me proud. I still brag about it though now I know that what he said was only partly true. It led to my lifelong study of Indians, as his love of books led to my large library. He read right up to his death. On the table beside his chair was, first and foremost, the Bible, then a number of commentaries and collections of sermons. Beside these were the writings of Cicero, Marcus Aurelius, Caesar, Josephus, and Herodotus. The day after his funeral, Grandmother gave most of them to his preacher friend and the rest to my mother. Eleven have come down to me. In the margins of each one are penciled notations of his thoughts and questions.

In every photograph I have of him his expression is solemn, his eyes almost sad. This face, this look, is the one I most remember as I recall how easy tears came to his eyes. Time has taught me how a few words of a song, a few chords, a sudden memory will bring tears, and sometimes they come into our eyes from nothing. So it was with him. Seldom did he laugh out loud; more likely, if something was funny, he would show only the hint of a smile. And, if anger was ever in him it was never on his face or in his voice. Never. With the exception of when he was telling a story he was quiet, often reading. When company came he said little, only occasionally nodding agreement to what was said; if he disagreed you could not tell it.

While his stories were spellbinding, what stays with me the most was the way he talked to me when we were alone; not as though I was a child, but as though I was someone capable of understanding serious things, someone interested in what he really thought and what he really believed, even when it was troubling. For this I love him the more.

When I stayed with them in the summers, Grandmother was the one who saw to it that I got a bath, brushed my teeth and had clean clothes. She fed me like I was always near death from starvation. Without fail three huge meals a day came from her woodstove. The smells of fresh bread and pies, fried chicken, country ham, new corn and squash rose from that old iron stove and spread through the four rooms and out onto the porches, then to the yard beyond. She tucked me in at night and heard my prayers and gave me a last kiss on the cheek before I fell asleep alone in that dark room with its high ceiling. But I wasn't scared, for Grandmother and Grandfather were there.

As I sit here writing and thinking about them, the smells and sounds, the feelings from those summers come to me: mules and hogs, newly turned earth and fresh cut hay, the corn crib, the smoke house and the tobacco barn; the clinking of trace chains and stomping of hooves, the calling of meadowlarks and quail and in the evenings, the lowing of the milk cows as they wend their way slowly from the fields to the barn and the swishing of milk into the bucket; and I feel the warmth of summer rising from the earth and the warmth of their hands holding mine.

As I grew older I was to learn that my grandfather had much passion deep within him, and sometimes in hidden ways, his passion came out and brought pain to my grandmother; but she never gave up on him and, ultimately, she saved him from himself. But I saw none of this as a boy.

What I see are his strong forearms holding me securely against him, his hands gripping the reins to Kate and Beck, the mules pulling the harrow across the plowed ground, crumbling the clods, preparing the soil for the seeds, the rain, the sun and, eventually, the corn. And as the team comes to the end of the row I hear him call out, "Haw" and I see the mules begin their slow and precise turn leftward.

He died in the autumn when I was nine. That summer I saw him the last time. For five straight summers I stayed

with my grandparents on their small tobacco farm near
Schochoh in southern Kentucky.

In those summers he took me everywhere with him: to
the fields; to the mill to grind corn; to the smelly, noisy
and wonderful livestock sales where cows and mules,
saddle horses, hogs and hunting dogs bellowed, brayed,
snorted, squealed, grunted and barked as they were
bought and sold and traded by men, rich and poor, who
shouted their offers, louder and louder, as they sought to
be heard above the voices of beasts and men.

But toward the end of that last summer, everything
changed. For he never left the farm, not even for church.
He sat for hours not saying a word. When Grandmother
asked what he was thinking about, all he might say was,
"Nothin'...just lookin' an' listenin'." And though he might
say, "Nothin's the matter...I'm OK," he ate little and his
pipe, which was most always in his mouth was usually
unlit.

It was then, though I was only a young boy, I somehow
knew he was beginning to die. I would not have said
those words out loud. But I knew. His clothes hung
loosely on him. His body was shriveling; days passed
without him touching his food; more and more he was
forgetful. He began to lose his matches, then his pipe.
And one day he thought someone had stolen his cows
and it took a while for Grandmother to convince him that
they had been sold the week before. His mind would
drift off when we were alone; he would sit there saying
nothing unless I got him started on a story. Now and
then, though it was rare, he would seem to be his old self.
On those days, he sometimes remembered things that

Grandmother and I could not remember. But come the next day it was again as though we were not there.

Then something happened that scared me so, I didn't know what to do. He didn't know who I was. He thought I was him.

That morning we were fishing at the pond next to the tobacco barn. We were sitting on the bank not talking. I was watching for the slightest bob of the cork when he said, "Jeremiah, just then, did you hear that heron calling?" I thought I heard him wrong and was about to ask what he had said, when he spoke again, "Jeremiah, watch the herons, they'll teach you patience."

I glanced at him out of the corner of my eye. There was a strange expression on his face. It frightened me. I reached over and took his hand and said, "Granddaddy, its me, George Edward." He turned and stared at me. His face was troubled. His eyes blinked as though they were trying to focus on what I had just told him.

"George Edward?" He stared for a long moment. Then, his face gradually relaxed, "Yes...yes, I see...I see, you're George Edward. I want to go back to the house now. Help me up."

I dropped my pole and helped him to his feet. With his hand on my shoulder, we walked slowly back to the house.

That night, when I got into bed I lay there for a long time unable to sleep. I felt sad and alone as memories were going over and over in my head. Finally, I cried. I said a prayer and I slept.

At breakfast, he seemed normal again. He ate well and complimented Grandmother's gravy and biscuits. Then,

he looked at me and asked if I was going fishing. "No sir,
I'm going to help Grandmother in the garden." He
nodded. We finished and went outside and sat on the
front porch. He lit his pipe. "Shep", his old farm dog, got
up from where he was lying and came slowly over and
rested his head on Granddaddy's knee.

At midmorning, while Grandmother and I were
hoeing weeds, he came to the garden and said he was
going to take a walk to the long field to "see if everything
is okay". There was really nothing for him to go check on;
there were no crops, no livestock; there was only grass
and sedge.

But Grandmother knew. She knew why he needed to
go "see", And what he was going to do. "Alright," she
said. "But, Jeremiah, I'm tellin' you, don't you get out
there and fall...you go on now an' I'll send George
Edward out in a bit with your lunch." He nodded; with
Shep by his side he headed toward the barn gate that led
to the fields. As we watched him go she said, "It's a
comfort to him; to go out there by himself an' just sit on
his ground, an' feel it, an' smell it, an' remember things."

A little before noon, she called me in and gave me his
lunch pail and said, "Go find him an' do your best to get
him to eat somethin'. An' be sure he drinks some water,
it's hot today."

"Yes, ma'am," I answered and went out the door and
through the gate. I was sure he would be sitting at his
favorite spot, under the large tulip poplar that stood alone
in the middle of the finest field on the farm. From the
foot of the tree, which sat on a slight rise, he could see
most of his land.

That's where he was. Sitting with his back against the tree; his white hair against the gray bark; wisps of smoke rising from his pipe. He smiled, "I'm glad you came. Sit close to me," and patted the ground.

I sat down beside him, unwrapped a sandwich and handed it to him, "Grandmother made your favorite, pork loin with mustard. And she said for you to be sure an' drink some water." He took the sandwich, looked at it for a moment, then raised his eyes and stared across the field as though he were watching something far away, something that if he took his eyes off of it, it might be lost.

I began to eat. Around us was our world: the green fields with tufts of yellow sedge and overgrown fencerows and beyond them, the dark woods and above it all the blue, cloudless sky. Except for the calling of birds and the hum of insects, it was silent.

He was quiet for a long time as he continued to stare into the distance. Then he took his pipe from his mouth and began talking.

"George Edward, I want to tell you a story...

"It's a true story about me when I was nine, the same age you are now." He paused and stared at me for a long moment. In retrospect, I know he was thinking of what he was about to tell and wanted to be certain I was strong enough to hear it. Then he laid his hand on my shoulder, "You and I are so alike; so much so that sometimes I feel we're almost the same person and I get us mixed up. While I can, I want to tell you things about me that you don't know, things nobody knows. This happened a long time ago, but I can still see it all clearly, like it was happening right now. I can see them and hear their voices...my mother...I can see her hair...I can hear her singing...that's where I'll begin...I'll begin with her...I'll begin with my mother...

"Oh my, she was beautiful! I wish you could have seen your great grandmother's long red hair. It hung down to her legs. Her name was Katrine O'Conner. She had great comfort in who she was and, Lord, she was proud of being Irish; she said it's what gave her 'grit'. She was born in 1840 and had just turned five when their English landlord put them off the land. Seldom did I ever hear her talk bad about others, but of the English she said, 'There're good ones among them I am certain, but the great land owners are dung hills.'

"They came to America and used the last of their money to buy land in the mountains not too far from where you live. Their place was at one end of a valley completely surrounded by mountains; at the other end lived a large family, the Pearsons. Mrs. Pearson's grandfather was the first white man to come into the valley. He named it Lost Cove.

"She liked to tell of those days; how hard they worked to get started and about adventures with bears and painters, what people used to call mountain lions. She said they dearly loved to have 'get togethers'. People came from three and four valleys away for the eating and the dancing and singing under the bluff near the Big Sink. Mr. Pearson, he was the best fiddler in the mountains.

"Mama had a beautiful lilting voice. She knew it. She said when she sang they all got quiet to hear her sing one of the old Irish ballads. Many a night she sang me to sleep. This one was her favorite."

And Granddaddy began to sing—

"She is far from the land
Where her young hero sleeps
And lovers are round her, sighing,
But coldly she turns
From their gaze, and weeps,
For her heart in his grave is lying."

"Oh! Make her a grave
Where the sunbeams rest,
When they promise a glorious morrow;
They'll shine o'er her sleep
Like a smile from the West
From her own loved
Island of sorrow."

When he finished, tears were on his cheeks. "George Edward, I wish you could have heard her. It was like a breeze coming through the trees. The words in those old songs brought her childhood back to her, for she'd first heard them sung in Ireland. She dreamed of returning there to meet her people and to see where she had lived. But it wasn't to be.

"Her mother taught her almost everything: to read and write, to sing and dance, to love God, and to make medicines from plants to heal the sick and to bring babies into the world. Though her mother got her started as a healer Mama was gifted far beyond her mother and all the other healers in the mountains. Soon as her parents finished their cabin she went to Mrs. Pearson to learn about the mountain plants; which ones made good medicines, which made poisons.

"She was fifteen when her parents were swept away into the floodwaters that filled the cove's bottomland. They were washed into the Big Sink and drowned. Mama was barely saved from drowning by Mr. Pearson. God love those people, they took her in and raised her as their own.

"They were true mountain people, the Pearsons were. They'd come all the way over the mountains from western North Carolina. They feared God. They were honest. They worked hard and played hard. They loved good whiskey, fiddle playing, fox hunting and hated slavery and despised those that owned them. They helped make Mama a strong woman and taught her to stand up for what she believed and to not worry about what other people thought. My mother had a lot of Pearson in her.

"Not long after she went to live with them she learned that they helped runaway slaves get to the North. The Pearsons must have trusted her from the very first because it wasn't long before they started letting her take food to the slaves who they hid in the cave a little ways beyond the cove. Though I was little, I still remember going into that cave with Mama and Mrs. Pearson after the war. George Edward, you remember last summer, my taking you to that high bluff and that cave's big mouth with the creek coming out of it? That's Buggy Top Cave. That's where they hid the slaves.

"Well, then the war came. When the fever to fight took over, people in the mountains started turning on one another; about half wanted to break away from those they called the Yankees; the other half wanted us to stay together. But it didn't happen. Staying together didn't happen.

"Soon as the war started things got bad quickly: neighbor turned against neighbor; some turned on their own kin. It began with barn burnings and cattle killing, but it wasn't long before people, even women, were being shot and hung. Men called, 'guerillas' or 'bushwhackers' roamed the mountains. No one was safe.

"Then, that second year, a terrible thing happened. Mr. Pearson and his oldest boy were hung by rebel guerillas for helping the runaways. They'd been out on the side of the mountain cutting logs for a new barn, and that night they didn't return to the house. Mrs. Pearson and Mama found them the next morning. They were both scalped and left hanging on opposite sides of a big oak tree."

He stopped. His pipe was out. He turned it, hit the bowl on the palm of his hand, knocked the ashes out, reached into his pocket, got his pocket knife and a twist of tobacco, cut a plug off, pressed it down into the bowl with his thumb, reached back into his pocket, got a match, struck it with his thumb nail, held the flame to the bowl, took three draws, blew the smoke upward and went on—

"A week later, Mama led a slave named Thomas out of the cove. They headed north toward Nashville. They hid during the day and walked at night. She said she was so scared that one night, while he was asleep, she almost snuck off and left him. She knew they'd hang her if they were caught by the guerillas. When they finally got off the mountain, the rebel patrols were so thick they hid for a week in an old, empty cabin on Elk River. Finally, the

Union cavalry crossed the river near the cabin and drove the patrols off. Not long afterward, the infantry arrived and camped near Winchester.

"That night, Mama and Thomas went to the camp hoping to get food and to learn what the safest way was to Nashville. At first, they were treated like they might be spies and were threatened with being shot. But as soon as the officer questioning them learned that Thomas had escaped from his master who was an officer in the rebel army on Lookout Mountain, the soldier asked Thomas to join them and he did. The next day they gave him a uniform and a rifle. It wasn't real long afterward he was killed in the battle to take the mountain.

"George Edward, that runaway slave was my father—Thomas Vann."

He stopped talking. For a moment, neither of us spoke or moved. I was so caught up in the story, in the excitement of the war and the killing, that what he had just said made no sense. He saw I was confused but trying to understand. He saw I was scared.

He reached out and barely touched my hand, just enough to let me know he was there right beside me. It was and is a strange thing but, at that very instant, I knew that he would die soon; that this was the last story he would tell me; that every word he was saying would die with him. And I knew I would not let that happen, that I would remember his words and would one day tell them again.

As we looked out over the land he repeated what he had just told me about his father. He went on, "After he left with the army Mama returned to Lost Cove, got her belongings and went back to the cabin on Elk River. She prayed every night for my father to return safe to her after the war. But that didn't happen. Two years passed before she learned he had been killed and buried on Lookout Mountain.

"I was born in 1863. I grew up on Elk River, not far from the small village of Estill Springs, Tennessee. Everything but my father was there: a river for fishing, for swimming, and for bathing. There was a spring with sweet water, enough cleared ground for a garden and in the river and the woods there were fish and birds and animals of every kind.

"Birds were Mama's favorites. She could whistle, crackle and clatter so good they answered her and, if the windows or doors were open, they'd sometimes fly in and perch for a bit on the back of a chair or a shelf. Most of all she loved the great blue herons. When we'd see one walking in the water across from us she'd say, 'Look there, Jeremiah, watch that one, it'll teach you somethin'. See how it's seein' above the water an' peerin' down at the same time...it's seein' things underneath...things we don't see...but the herons see.'

"For a long while it was like living in heaven. In the woods along the river were plants and roots for Mama to make her medicines. Nobody bothered us. Our place was a ways from others. Sometimes people came for medicine or to get her to come to birth a baby. We were pretty much by ourselves except for the animals. And since we fed them and didn't hurt them some would come right up to us and eat out of our hands and even let us scratch their heads. Animals were my only friends. I loved them and they loved me, most especially, Abe my raccoon and Grant my red fox and Sherman my groundhog that fought any and everything that came near him, except me.

"It wasn't long after we moved there that word spread around that a granny woman and her boy were living in the old cabin not far from the bridge. Soon, people started coming to her with all kinds of hurts and ailments or to get her to come quick to deliver a baby. Things got easier for us. Some gave her money but most paid with chickens and vegetables and fruits and sometimes, even beef and pork. We ate well. Plus, we had our own garden and fish in the river. We only went to the store three or four times a year. We called those years 'our fatnin' time'.

"At the time I wasn't aware of how different Mama was than other people. It was a long while before I realized that she thought differently and many of her ways were different. Not just that she believed colored people were as good as whites, but she believed that fairies and little people really existed and they lived in hollow trees and caves and made music and milked cows at night. But it was religion and what she didn't do that riled up churchgoers. And back then most people were churchgoers. While she loved God and read her Bible every night and used it to teach me to read, we never set foot in a church. Not going to church was almost as bad as her helping colored people when they were sick or having a baby. From time to time preachers came—they always brought their wives—and they tried to use me to make her feel guilty. They'd tell her that if she didn't care about her own soul then she ought to at least care about the soul of her only child. Not a word they said worked.

She'd just smile and say politely, 'Thank you for droppin'
by. That's mighty kind of you. Come again anytime.' It
befuddled them. They'd leave shaking their heads and
thanking her for the fresh herbs she always gave the wives
to take home.

"But then a preacher came for a revival in Estill. He
came all the long way from Charleston. He came with the
reputation of being one of God's great champions against
Satan. The week after he arrived he came with our closest
neighbor, Lucy Taggert, to talk with Mama.

"Lucy Taggert paid the preacher's way to Franklin
County. She was a cruel Christian and a crueler woman, a
woman who wanted to rule under her feet everything and
everyone within her sight. She ruled her husband. She
ruled her children. She ruled her church. She had once
ruled more than a hundred slaves. She was a woman who
never doubted she knew God's will on this earth.
Forgiveness was a word she had no patience for. In the
midst of talking to Mama she said, 'All forgiveness is, is
for giving up to a sinner. It's justice the Lord wants just
like the justice He's going to bring down on every sinner
on that final day which if I had my way would be now!'
The preacher didn't say a word. He just stood there
looking grim and nodding his head. Together, they
thought themselves invincible. And they were certain they
would bring the proud sinner, Katrine O'Conner, to her
knees and save her and her child from eternal
damnation. They would not be bought off with politeness
and herbs.

"Their visit wasn't long. As soon as Mama told them,
'Sir and ma'am, I don't want to offend you, but I don't

believe in belongin' to any church, nor do I believe my soul needs anymore savin.'

"Lucy Taggert's face looked like she had been slapped. It turned red like it was about to bleed. Then, her eyes and voice got hard and cold, 'You an' that bastard of yours are goin' to burn in hell.'

"Well, that was a mistake. A bad one.

"Mama looked like she was bleedin' too she was so angry. She jumped up, grabbed Lucy Taggert by the hair, yanked her out of the chair, dragged her out onto the porch and kicked her in her rear down the steps and yelled, 'Now, you bitch, you an' that so-called man of God get the hell off my property...an' if either of you ever come back I'll sic Katey on you.'"

He paused. There was a slight grin on his face. He went on—

"So the bitch—s'cuse me, George Edward, but that's what she called her—she and the preacher took off for the road where she turned around and screamed one curse word after another and called Mama a 'nigger lover' and a 'witch born of Satan' until, finally, the preacher led her off up the road.

"Mama let out a 'whoof' of air and said, 'Jeremiah, you stay away from the Taggerts' and a moment later, 'Witches aren't born, they're made...like her.' She went back in the cabin and got her Bible and began reading. That Bible is the only thing of hers I still have. When I die it will be yours.

"Not long after that, Lucy Taggert started stirring people up against Mama, especially the churchgoers. She accused her of all kinds of bad things. Some must have believed her or were afraid of her, for fewer and fewer people came to Mama for help. While some already didn't like her because we never went to church, what really upset them was Mama's criticisms of those who mistreated colored people. In those days, lots of people, maybe most, believed if any white person spoke up for a Negro they were a Judas or a Yankee.

"Then, my world was destroyed."

Granddaddy stopped talking. He took a long drink from the fruit jar. We were sitting in the shade but it was burning hot. The sun scalded the air. Heat waves rose from the ground. I squinted my eyes. Mirages glistened like lakes—objects floated upon the waters. Most of the animals stayed back in the shade of the trees. A flock of crows came flying from the woods. They flew in a line to the far side of the field and, one after another, dropped down onto a shimmering lake that was not there. They cawed and cawed and cawed.

As he set the fruit jar back on the ground Granddaddy closed his eyes. His chest rose and fell. I couldn't tell if he was asleep or awake. But then, he resumed talking. His words became more and more vivid. The present faded away. He was back in time, back to when he was a boy—back to when he was my age. As he talked, I felt myself changing. I closed my eyes. Part of me was still sitting under the tree. Another part, the greater part, was with him. We are watching a boy and a river and a heron—

THE HERON STANDS ABSOLUTELY STILL IN THE WATER. It does not move. It peers downward, its spear-like beak ready to strike. Across the river, on the opposite bank, hidden in the cane and brush, the boy watches the heron—it is as tall as he and as beautiful.

The morning sun burns the river's mist away. The boy sees the heron's black eye stripe sweeping backward across its white head. Does it see me watching? Does it hear me? The sun warms the boy like a blanket; he slumps sideways, his eyes droop and close. He dreams what is not a dream.

"Jeremiah, Jeremiah, wake up, wake up, they're outside—hurry—run to the cane—hide—keep quiet, no matter what—I'll find you later—run!"

He hears the high-pitched whinnying of horses and the shouting and cursing of men and over his shoulder, as he runs, he sees three flames dancing in the darkness. He is running through the darkness; he is running through the slashing cane; he is running down and down to the edge of the river and, here, he curls into a ball on the ground with his hands pressed against his mouth to cover his sobbing. The cane is all around him. He sleeps. The heron calls –

'Ack - Ack - Ack - Ack - Ack'

He jerks awake. The sun is straight up. 'Mama...Mama, have you come?' He sits up, looks toward the sound and sees—in one quick, smooth motion a heron lift its head from the water to fling a twisting, shining fish high in the air, catch it and swallow. The heron stands still for only an instant then begins again to stalk its prey, moving without a ripple through the shallow water; its long neck stretching upward and outward; its eyes searching below the water's murky surface. It stops, turns its head quickly and looks straight across the river at Jeremiah.

Through the greenness of the cane the heron's yellow eyes see the light brown skin of the boy and the deep blackness of his hair and eyes. They stare at one another for a long moment. Then the heron gives a deep, raspy call, and leaning forward, takes a few quick steps and unfolds its great wings. It strokes the air powerfully, thrusts itself upward into the air and flies slowly up the river.

The boy is so tired he can barely keep his eyes open. 'Where is she?'

His eyes close. His mind drifts in and out of sleep; fragments of sounds and visions and thoughts, present and past are joined together: 'Jeremiah, watch the herons, they will teach you patience and how to see; look below the surface as they do.' And in the dream comes the clattering, "Rickety, crick, crick, crick," of a Kingfisher's cries mixing with the voice of his mother. He looks across the river. The heron is gone. He reaches into his shirt, touches the feather hanging from the strip of leather around his neck and...she is there.

He smells her, her scent of herbs, of roots and flowers and the smells of her medicines that hang everywhere from the cabin's ceiling and walls. Pottery jars overflow with powders and salves. In a chest beneath the bed are small bundles of feathers.

A man comes from the road to the cabin. He steps up onto the porch. He is alone. He asks to talk to his mother. She says, 'Jeremiah, go outside and play.' He goes out and crawls under the window and listens. The man tells of killing a father, a mother and three children and of his wish to die; he moans and cries.

When men come to see her he studies them carefully. Did his father look like one of them? He doesn't know. He never saw him. He knows little of his father; only that he was killed fighting to free the slaves. One night, while she is teaching him to read, his mother stops and says, 'Your head is full of brightness, just like your daddy. He barely hears her whisper, "Someday, when you are older, I'll tell you all about him."

But she doesn't. She tells him bits and pieces of the war. 'You were just a little boy durin' those terrible times. It seemed everybody was killin' everybody; houses an' crops were burned; food an' animals were taken from women an' children an' old people. People starved. But as awful as it was somethin' good came from it at the end. The colored folks were freed. You and I barely got by. But we did. Times were hard. They're better now in some ways but we've got to be careful. There are still bad men hurtin' people.'

His mother's skin is white as milk. In the fall, he gathers armfuls of red and yellow leaves and places them in her long, red hair. She once said her hair came from her mother's people who lived on a big island called Ireland that was far away across the big ocean. When he looks in a mirror he wonders at their differences. She is tall, slender and fair. He is short and dark, with curly black hair. He once asked why he was so different and not pretty like her, why his skin and hair and nose were different? She smiled, touched his lips with the tips of her fingers and said, 'Shush, Jeremiah, don't say that. You're beautiful.' But she did not explain their differences.

In the night, in the cane above him, a deep voice calls, a voice he has heard before, 'Hey, Jeremiah, where are you? Your mama wants you to come here...boy, if you hear me, you come in now!' He thinks he hears Katey barking and growling. He does not move. He does not make a sound the entire night.

The sun is up. It is quiet but for the calling of birds, the splashing of fish and the hum of insects. From the direction of the cabin there is silence. He listens for Katey. "She must be in the woodshed with her pups." He is so tired he cannot keep his eyes open. He curls up on his side, pillows his head on his arm and falls into a deep sleep.

The sun moves across the sky. Shadows and light shift and move over the sleeping boy.

The sun burns straight down. He wakes. His skin is on fire, red with scratches and mosquito bites. The heat is unbearable. 'Mama,' he calls loudly, 'Where are you? Where are you?' He stands, shadowing his eyes from the sun; looks up the river, down the river, across the river. And listens. He sees little but the cane and the trees and the water and the sky; hears nothing but the river's soft flow and the calling of birds.

Two wood ducks flash by just above the water. There is an odor of decay. From up the river, toward the cabin, comes the raspy call of a heron. 'Why is it calling?

Something is wrong. She should have come by now. Should I go back...I'll go a little ways and look.'

It is hard pushing through cane and brush. He crawls, pulls to the top of the bank and stands upright among the oaks and birch that line the river's banks. There is little underbrush. It is easy walking through the old forest that stretches a fair ways back from the rear of the cabin. He is careful stepping over dead limbs, hiding behind the trunks of trees, stopping, listening. With each step his caution increases. He comes to the tulip poplar at the edge of the clearing behind the cabin. He presses against the trunk. A mockingbird sings.

With one hand on the tree, he eases around the side and stops. Now, a few feet from the woodshed, he whispers, 'Katey...Katey...come.' He breathes a soft whistle...why aren't the puppies whimpering? He shouts, 'MAMA...KATEY!' The only sound is the singing of the mockingbird. With one slow step at a time he moves to the door of the woodshed and eases it open. The puppies' bed is empty. He can barely breathe. He turns, walks to the rear door of the cabin, opens it and enters.

It is dark. A moment passes until his eyes can see the broken furniture; the drawers pulled out, emptied on the floor; clothing and quilts torn, scattered; the floor littered with shards of brown pottery, plants and roots, feathers, powders, flour and dried beans; pictures are torn from the walls and the small stove is battered and on its side. He climbs the ladder to the loft. It is destroyed.

Sobbing and panting, he stumbles through the wreckage and throws open the front door; hesitates, fearing the other side; looking outward onto the yard he sees nothing. He steps onto the porch, slips and falls forward onto his hands and knees; immediately, a thick stickiness is on his hands; he breathes the odor of blood; large green flies swarm up and onto his hands and face.

He sees her. She is stretched out on her side; Katey's gentle face smashed and stuck to the planks in a pool of black blood; her body slashed and punctured; small, white bits are scattered in the blood.

'MAA-MAA...MAA-MAA!' Screaming, he pushes up onto his feet and runs across the yard and jumps down into the sunken road, turns and runs on toward the village, stumbling-falling-rising-running, on and on, until he comes to the entrance of the sprawling plantation of the Taggerts. He slows - stops - vomits – almost falls as he gasps for air.

George Edward, I see the boy. I hear him. I'm not dreaming. He's running down the road. You see him too, don't you? Jeremiah, do you see where he is running to? He's running to the Taggerts. You remember them, don't you? You remember who they were and who they are...

You remember they owned over a hundred slaves and a thousand acres of the best land in Franklin County. Land and cotton and slaves made them rich, but when the end came, when all their slaves were gone, when their money and cotton were worth nothing, Robert Taggert, the master, he gave up. He hanged himself in his barn.

And after it was all over, after all but two of the slaves had gone, the work, when it got done, was done by the twins, Hubert and Sam, and one old colored man and his wife. Those twins were cruel like their mama. They were guerillas during the war. They were killers; they burned and killed anyone who helped Yankees or Negroes. Lucy Taggert's brother, John Gaunt, led them. He was the cruelest of them all.

All they had left after the war was over was the land and that had been taken over by weeds and briars and brush. The fences were down. Only a few of the hogs and cows remained. Nine Taggerts lived in that crumbling big house.

Before he killed himself, Robert Taggert came every few months to talk to Mama. He always came walking through the woods, never by the road. When he was inside the cabin there would be long periods of silence and sometimes broken words, now and then, sobbing. Once he shouted, "All our life together has been nothing but misery, she's killing me...damn her soul to hell!" But when we passed him in the village or on the road he never spoke or looked at either of us.

"Jeremiah, do you see him?"
"Yes, sir."

The boy turns up the lane that leads to the Taggert house. He watches and listens - everyone is dangerous - everything is dangerous. He must have help. He remembers overhearing Lucy Taggert's words to two women in the store, 'If she and that brat don't leave the country, then she's testing the Lord and, someday, His vengeance is going to descend on her.' He hears the whispers.

He prays, 'Please God, let her help me.' Now, near the house, he hears talking and laughter from the backyard. He slows and, just as he starts to ease along the side of the house, he hears a little girl, 'I want that one...that one's mine...that little yellow one's mine.'

Then comes an angry voice, 'Bessie, I've told you already, we can't feed any more dogs on this place...John, why in heaven's name did you bring these pups here...you take 'em home, or give 'em to someone, or drown 'em, but get 'em off this place.'

'Please, Granma, don't drown 'em...please don't!' begged the little girl.

He hears the puppies whimpering.

In the shadow of the house, his hearing concentrates. From the backyard, comes the same deep voice that called him in the night as he lay in the cane, 'Well, Lucy, your boys told me to bring 'em along for the little ones since we had to get rid of the bitch!'

'SHUT YOUR MOUTH, JOHN GAUNT...I told you an' the boys to never again talk about last night, not now, not ever...DO YOU UNDERSTAND!'

The fear is there; so great he cannot breathe. The riders with the torches are there.

We see them and hear them.

'Oh God, Mama! What have they done to you? Oh God, please don't let her be hurt.' He backs slowly away, his eyes on the house until he reaches the road where he begins running back toward home. 'I must get home...I must, I must.' He runs, seeing nothing, hearing nothing. 'I must, I must'...until—

He is there, his strength gone. Barely a breath left to climb the short slope to the yard. He drops to the ground under the oak tree. Sits up. His arms rest on bent knees.

His eyes stare straight down between his legs. He sees the horrors of night and day; they mix with a line of black ants scurrying back and forth beneath his legs; the ants race to and from the entrance hole to their nest.

They hurry through the dust into a shadow where the ground has spots of blackness. Now and then, some pause and touch their antennas together and then dash on.

Everything is there now together: his mother, the flames, the heron, Katey, the ants.

'Dear God, please tell me where my mother is...I am so scared.'

A little breeze from the river rustles the leaves above him—the shadow shifts almost imperceptibly—back and forth—back and forth—across the ants.

He raises his head and looks up into the towering tree and sees sunlight shining through the limbs and leaves.

And, higher up, a shadow shifting—back and forth—back and forth—with bits of light, like stars, glittering in the long red hair—

He brings her down and takes her home.

The sun moves downward, spreading red, orange and yellow across the sky and onto the slow movement of the river.

He leans over the bed to kiss her; straightens, looks at her, leans forward again and, after a few strokes of the comb through her long hair, he takes several blue-gray feathers scattered across the bed and places them in her hair.

He stands and turns in a circle. On the floor, he sees a small bundle of feathers. He bends down, picks it up and puts it in his pack.

Quickly. He shakes coal oil from the lamps onto the walls and the floor and the bed and backs away to the open door.

For a moment, he looks at his mother and whispers, "I love you."

He strikes a match and holds the flame to a page from her Bible. When it is almost engulfed in fire—he pitches it into the room.

He sees her face in the flames.

The day ends. The sun dies. The flames reflect in the heron's eyes.

UNCLE SON

THE STORY OF A MULTIPLE PERSONALITY

Over time I have observed that at the very last second it is easy to die. You can see it in the final flickering of the eyelids. Between lunch and dinner I killed all three of them. They are in the cellar. Waiting. Wash me thoroughly, Lord, from mine iniquity, and cleanse me from my sin.

— Silas

This was written in black ink on a small, blue-lined notebook sheet stuck tightly between pages 580 and 581 of Uncle Son's 1936 first edition copy of Prescott's *History of the Conquest of Mexico and History of the Conquest of Peru*. The sharp, precise, evenly-spaced writing by the nib of his gold pen matched exactly that of his name and address on the upper left-hand corner inside the book's front cover—

Silas S. Singleton
Stone Castle
Hillsboro Road
Nashville, Tennessee
May 1976

I went through the book page by page; there were no other slips of paper or notations. As I was about to close the book, I saw two almost imperceptible penciled brackets at the top and bottom of the second paragraph on page 581, which read:

As the long file of priests and warriors reached the flat summit of the teocalli, the Spaniards saw the figures of several men stripped to their waists, some of whom, by the whiteness of their skins, they recognized as their own countrymen. They were the victims for sacrifice. Their heads were gaudily decorated with coronals of plumes, and they carried fans in their hands. They were urged along by blows, and compelled to take part in the dances in honor of the Aztec war god. The unfortunate captives, then stripped of their sad finery, were stretched, one after another, on the great stone of sacrifice. On its convex surface, their breasts heaved up conveniently for the diabolical purpose of the priestly executioner, who cut asunder the ribs by a strong blow with his sharp razor of itztli, and, thrusting his hand into the wound, tore away the heart, which, hot and reeking, was deposited on the golden censer before the idol. The body of the slaughtered victim was then hurled down the steep steps of the pyramid, which, it may be remembered, were placed at the same angle of the pile, one flight below another; and the mutilated remains were gathered up by the savages beneath, who soon prepared with them the cannibal repast which completed the work of abomination!

I read it and read it again. Then, from the top of the library ladder—twelve feet up—I looked down at his reclining chair by the fireplace. I could see him sitting there though he wasn't. I asked him, "Uncle Son, what'n hell does this mean? It looks just like your handwriting. Is it? If it is why'd you write it? And what'n hell does it have to do with the Aztecs? And what's that about someone being in the cellars? After all these years I've lived here you've never let me see them."

My uncle had left two hours before for a black-tie, fund-raising dinner for the Nashville Symphony. At least, that's where he said he was going. I think.

"Damn my confusion."

"Don't fall, you could break something."

"I won't if I concentrate."

"Then...concentrate...concentrate."

You know how it is when something unexpectedly startling enters your brain about someone you've known a long time, especially if you love them and what you've learned about them is really strange and doesn't fit with what you've always believed; something that when it happens causes a bunch of stuff to confuse your mind. And that's when I may have done something stupid but I'm not sure.

I climbed down from the ladder, went to the desk in the center of the room, took a pen and copied the note and chapter from the book and went back up the ladder and placed the book on the shelf. Just as I was about to take a step down I noticed the book to the right of Prescott's was sticking out slightly. On the spine was, *Psychopathology of Every Day Life* by Sigmund Freud. I hesitated, looked over my shoulder and listened; the house was silent. I pulled it out, opened it and began to flip through the pages; there was another notebook sheet, identical to the first. On it was written:

*People think they know me. They
don't. I remember everything from when
it all began. The terror. We were not
much more than babies when it entered
us.*

—*Silas*

It was between pages 62 and 63. There were
faintly penciled brackets on page 62—

*I believe we accept too indifferently the fact of infantile
amnesia—that is, the failure of memory for the first years
of our lives—and fail to find in it a strange riddle. We
forget what great intellectual accomplishments and what
complicated emotions a child of four years is capable.
We really ought to wonder why the memory of later years
has, as a rule, retained so little of these psychic processes,
especially as we have every reason for assuming that these
same forgotten childhood activities have not glided off
without leaving a trace in the development of the person,
but they have left definite influence for all future time.*

"*Now, what'n the devil does that and the note mean?*"
"It means what Freud meant it to mean."
"And, what's that?"
"If you'll concentrate on it you can figure it out."
"Concentrate...concentrate...concentrate."

* * * * *

Let me tell you about him, about my uncle. Maybe it'll
help you to understand us, I mean him. He's my
mother's eighty-year-old brother. I call him, "Uncle Son".

He calls me, "Nephew". As Mother said, "He's rich enough to barbecue a white elephant." And I guess he is. At thirty-five he founded what is now the largest life insurance company in the southeast and the fourth largest in America. With less than an eighth grade education his brilliant photographic mind conjured all the projections for American life expectancy and death and, how to make money off people dying. He's leaving it all to me so that one day I can barbecue my own white elephant.

His mansion, Stone Castle, is a good ways out Hillsboro Road. It sits on the crest of the tallest hill between Nashville and Franklin. From there you can see Nashville a few miles away and southward toward Franklin—where once there were hills covered with forest and rolling fields of corn and pastures scattered with white-faced cattle and fine-blooded saddle horses—you now see only a sprinkling of horses grazing in the shrunken fields among the subdivisions that are spreading like kudzu.

From the tower that rises sixty feet above the mansion you look out on a land buried in history. When backhoes sink their shovels into this earth, up comes bones and shards of Woodland Indians; the foundations of frontier chimneys; and Minie balls, fragments of cannon balls, uniform buttons from the battle fought here a hundred and fifty years ago, the battle that struck the death knell of the Confederacy—so believed Uncle Son, and so he taught me to believe; as he taught me almost all that is important about the world and about life. With no family of his own, I became his son. I love him more than I loved my own father, a poor shoe salesman whose face I have erased from my memory because of his cruelty.

Uncle Son has told me that my mother—who died in some kind of accident when I was two—was a frail wisp of a woman and that two of her brothers and an uncle were in and out of Central State Hospital for the Insane on Murfreesboro Road. Their mother, my grandmother, died there and is buried there somewhere among the paupers.

All that may have been what influenced me to want to become a child psychiatrist. I did well in medical school at Vanderbilt, but in the third year of my residency, I began having difficulty focusing and, at times, couldn't remember the names of the children I was treating. I started in treatment with a renowned analyst, but after six months, my memory problems were worse, so I dropped out and moved in with Uncle Son and began cataloguing his books. That seemed to help, for my memory improved, yet there are still days when I'm forgetful and have difficulty concentrating. Though I need lots of rest, I think I pay my way by caring for the grounds, cleaning the house, cooking for him when he is home and keeping his Mercedes and Cadillac Deville gleaming. Sometimes when I'm forgetful he'll fuss at me, but never with harshness. I live in a small room in the west wing and never go outside the boundaries of the property.

His brothers and sisters call him "Son," so, of course, we, his nephews and nieces, have always called him "Uncle Son". The second of ten children, the first son, he was the first to rise above the poverty of his family. With intelligence and cold-blooded ambition he acquired wealth far beyond their imaginings.

Not only did he want more, he wanted all he could get; and with it, he wanted to possess power over the police and mayors and governors and congressmen. And he achieved it all.

As a boy, he had watched and listened to the wealthy, the sophisticated and the successful. He saw their trimmed, slick-backed hair, their well-tailored suits and shining shoes, their polished fingernails and white teeth, their expensive watches and cars and smelled their good smells. He took their words; he practiced their pronunciations in front of mirrors, he watched his tongue and lips; and one day he spoke as they did.

Of all his kin I am his favorite. I know this, not just because he's leaving me all his money when he dies. It's more than that. He knows I, beyond any of the others, worship him. I realized he had chosen me over my cousins when I was twelve, when suddenly—at the end of our family Thanksgiving dinner, which he always hosted— he rose from his chair at the end of the table and came to my side, put his hand on my shoulder, and in a voice loud enough for all to hear, said, "Come with me!"

He led me down the hall to the library, his inner sanctum, his world made of books: shelf upon shelf upon shelf were filled with words and words and words that, as I have read them over these many years, have twisted within my brain until, now, there are times their sounds disorder my thinking.

My uncle turned in a circle and pointed upward, "Nephew, one day, all of these and all of Stone Castle and all of my wealth will be yours."

As he turned, I turned, and looked upward and saw the browns and greens and reds and gold and blues of twenty-five thousand books: the evolution of the universe and of man, history from Neanderthals through Greeks and Romans, to the Medievals and those of the Enlightenment, to the founding of our country, especially of the South and slavery. Encircling me were the long wisdoms and stupidities of philosophy and theology, and shelf after shelf on the ways of death: war, murder, suicide, torture, execution, disease, injury, old age, some with graphic accounts and photographs in medical reports, battlefield reports and autopsy reports. In them was every kind of report on death in its many forms, forms you can imagine and forms unimaginable, in one book after another, rising around the walls of the high-ceilinged, walnut-walled library.

I returned Freud's *Psychopathology* to the shelf. I was exhausted and sat down on the desk chair to rest. A second before I closed my eyes, I noticed a large book on the desk I had not seen there before. I sat up and rubbed my eyes. The desk light shone on a large Bible. The black-leather cover, imprinted with gold letters, read—

HOLY BIBLE
Authorized
King James Version
Rembrandt Edition

A red-ribbon bookmarker opened to pages 274 and 275 of Revelation. Tucked into the spine was a note—

Those we create hide our pain.

There is another one waiting.

—*Silas*

Penciled brackets marked verse 8 of Chapter 21—

But the fearful, and unbelieving, and
the abominable, and murderers, and
whoremongers, and sorcerers, and
idolaters, and all liars, shall have their part
in the lake which burneth with fire and
brimstone: which is the second death.
At the end of the verse, in the margin, was written—
All those who have harmed a child
shall burn forever and ever!

* * * * *

"Nephew!"
"Uncle Son?"
"Yes."
"You're home early."
I looked over my shoulder. He was standing in the
doorway so strikingly handsome it took my breath. Even
at eighty his olive skin is still smooth as silk, his gray hair
neatly trimmed, his face sharp-featured with thin lips,
slender and tall with the easy movements of a much
younger man. His manners, speech and appearance are
impeccable; always dressing formally, even at home.
When he is reading, in the evening, he sits upright in his
Gothic-Church chair, dressed in sharply pressed pants,
starched white shirt, blue-black tie and his favorite
cardigan jacket the color of his hair. But it is his dark-

brown Asiatic eyes with their epicanthic folds covering the inner corners that one remembers the most. They watch everything, they do not seem to blink, and when they look directly at you, they fix their emotionless stare like stones on your eyes, as though reading your thoughts and finding you wanting.

"It is time I showed you the cellar...come!"

"Now?"

"Yes! Now!"

He stepped back into the hallway. The hall is thirty yards long; its paneled walls are lined with paintings and statues from around the world. The hall leads to the kitchen in the rear of the house. The cellar door is there, next to the walk-in freezer. The oak door is tightly fitted and always locked.

The hall's candled sconces were dimmed. Uncle Son strode three paces ahead. Neither one of us spoke. Our footfalls were silent on the thick Oriental rug. Empire and Regency furniture are spaced in measured regularity along both sides. There was not a sound in the house.

Halfway down the hall Uncle Son stopped, turned and faced the six-foot tall, gold-framed Regency mirror. He brushed the lapels of his jacket with his fingertips, stared in the mirror for a long moment and slowly with his left hand shifted the knot of his tie back and forth until it was centered exactly over the shirt's top button.

And it was then, just as his hand left his tie, I stepped up beside him and looked in the mirror.

There was no reflection of Uncle Son or of me. Staring out from the mirror was a man I had never seen. He was wearing a white butcher's apron.

THREE WOMEN

The Review Appeal
Franklin, Tennessee, April 18, 1969

Sheriff C. M. Henry reports that yesterday, a little past noon, Mr. Delbert Hawkins was killed with a single shotgun blast allegedly made by his common law wife, Ms. Annie Veach, in Mr. Hawkins' home on Still House Hollow Road, atop Backbone Ridge. Ms. Veach has been charged with first degree murder and is free under $1,000 bond. Trial date has not yet been set.

* * * * *

EXCERPTS FROM THE TRIAL OF MS. ANNIE M. VEACH

Williamson County Circuit Court, Tuesday,
July 21, 1970
The State of Tennessee
Vs.
Annie M. Veach
Charged with First Degree Murder

Henderson Hooper: Attorney for the Defense
Tom Clements: District Attorney

Judge James K. Frank, Presiding

Mr. Hooper:	Now, Ms. Veach, in your own words, please tell the court exactly what transpired in the home of Mr. Delbert Hawkins on, or about, 2:00 PM, of Wednesday, April 17, 1969.
Ms. Veach:	I killed the son-of-a-bitch.
Judge Frank:	Now, hold on there just a minute, Ms. Veach. I don't allow that kind of talk in my court. I don't want to hear any more profanity out of you. Do you understand? And if you do it again, you're going to spend two nights in my jail for contempt. Look up here at me now. Do you understand?
Ms. Veach:	Yes, sir.
Judge Frank:	Mr. Hooper, you may proceed.
Mr. Hooper:	Ms. Veach, please tell the court exactly what happened that led you to shoot Mr. Hawkins.
Ms. Veach:	Because he was messing with my girl, Annie Lee, and she's only thirteen.

Still House Hollow Road
Somewhere around noon, Friday, July 21, 1970

A light early morning rain has settled the dust on the narrow chert road siding a small stream that winds like a snake from a spring at the base of a hill not far back up the road. For July the air is soft as silk. An intermittent breeze ripples the corn leaves in a garden on the other side of the road and continues on down the hollow to the beginning of pastures with black and red and white cattle where the breeze veers right into a side valley with crumbling houses and barns and the one room log jail of the old Poor House Farm.

Looking down from far above the road, the creek, the hollows and hills extend outward like ribs from the highest point, a forested ridge that backbones back and forth for many long miles through the hills and hollows so sparsely inhabited they are called "The Barrens". As the hollows broaden out to cornfields and pastures, ponds and small lakes appear and a little further on beyond the south side of the ridge there is a narrow river.

A sprightly, big-bosomed, wide-hipped, middle-aged woman, who in her face, posture and stride appears to be well satisfied with herself. She is dressed in a low-cut sleeveless mint-green dress patterned with large yellow and black flowers; she saunters down the road, a gold chain and crucifix hang from her neck jiggling between her cleavage. She is twirling a purple sash tied around her waist. Five paces behind her follows Luther Hutchins, a smiling, red-faced, big-shouldered man missing four upper front teeth. He is dressed in overalls and a loose fitting blue serge suit coat, the neck of a whiskey bottle sticks up above the right pocket. The man is having considerable difficulty keeping himself upright and within the confines of the road; he veers back and forth towards the creek on one side and a ditch and wire fence on the other.

Over her shoulder the woman barks an order, "Luther Hutchins, you still owe me for that poke so you keep up now...an if you fall down in a ditch I ain't comin back an pickin you up cept to get my money...you hear me?"

"Okay, Darlene, hon...jes don hurry on so fas."

"Don cha be callin me hon agin or all you'll see's my dust."

Darlene Lovely, for that is the sprightly woman's name, had started life easy; she slid out of her mother—who barely made a whimper—in less than seven minutes after the first contraction. She came out big and whole and healthy and when her cord was cut and tied off she gave a cry that was to stay with her her whole life, a cry that would please many a man.

In the early morning of the next day, just as she was lighting her first cigarette, her mother suddenly gave a gasp and fell forward dead. From that moment Darlene's life turned hard.

Her father was a drunkard who had never done a full day's work in his life, telling everyone he had only one lung and one kidney that worked and that his blood circulated only half of what it should because of a mule kicking him in his chest when he was a boy. Natural affection and concern for his baby daughter was not in him. From the minute she was born he felt God had put a burden on him that he could not bear. So he gave her to the oldest of his five sisters and, from then on, Darlene—who was named after her mother—was passed from one aunt to another, all of whom treated her as though she was a servant with only one ever showing love to her.

But regardless of being born with a dead mother and a worthless father, Darlene had gifts that kept her alive as she grew older. She was a hard worker, quick witted, and, though not beautiful, her coal-black hair and eyes and generous olive-skinned body caused people to notice her. Her father said her darkness came from his blood, for he liked to believe himself to be the descendant of a Cherokee chief. Her teasing laughter and knowing almond-shaped eyes and good heart helped keep her alive; from the time she was twelve she knew how to survive.

Then, when she was sixteen and on her own, she took her unredeemable father into her one-room log cabin so he might survive—though in her heart she did not forgive him.

Now, she was fifty-one and was beginning to tire more easily but her body and her will persevered and her father lived on.

Her cabin had been built long back in time by a French trapper. It was at the bottom of a deep hollow set between two ribs that sloped off the south side of "Backbone Ridge", a long switchback ridge. Atop the ridge ran the Natchez Trace, the road Andrew Jackson and his Tennesseans had marched on from Nashville to New Orleans. Once an animal trail, then an Indian path, the road wound like a tunnel through a forest of oaks, maples, beeches, poplars and hickories. Twenty strides from the back of the cabin a spring rose from beneath a shelf of stone; at first, it was only a rivulet but a ways on down, it became a creek. A steep footpath led from the ridge down to the cabin door. The path was the entranceway for Darlene's callers.

Williamson County Circuit Court

Mr. Hooper: Now, Ms. Veach, if you will, what exactly do you mean by Mr. Hawkins "messing" with Annie Lee? And please explain to the court who Annie Lee is.

Ms. Veach: Well, don't you know what messing is? Well, messing is...you know...messing is...is...you know...screwing...and Annie Lee is my girl...my daughter...not his.

Mr. Hooper: Do you mean Mr. Hawkins was having sexual intercourse with your daughter who was thirteen?

Ms. Veach: Yes, sir.

Mr. Hooper: Ms. Veach, I know this is all terribly hard on you, but if you will please, tell the court what Mr. Hawkins having intercourse with your daughter did to you.

Ms. Veach: Did you just say, "What did it do to me?"

Mr. Hooper: Yes, ma'am.

Ms. Veach:	Well, Mr. Hooper, Fred Hawkins was a worthless piece of...excuse me, Judge, but you see I did catch myself this time. Fred Hawkins was a worthless man. He was making whiskey across the road in the holler. He stayed drunk most of the time. He was a mean drunk. He beat me over and over until I almost couldn't get out of bed in the mornings, and I just couldn't take it no more.

Still House Hollow Road

As Darlene Lovely strides around the bend in the road she sees a young woman bent forward hoeing her garden on the other side of a wire fence that sets back a few yards from the road. The woman is a head shorter and forty pounds lighter than Darlene. She is slim and pretty and young enough to be Darlene's daughter. Sweat streaks the dirt on her face. A black and tan English Shepherd lying near her jumps to its feet and looks up the road. She barks three times. The young woman straightens, wipes the sweat from her eyes with her sleeve, looks up the road, and sees the two figures coming toward her. In the small field, next to the garden, a solid-black saddle horse raises its head from grazing; it turns and faces the road, its ears—almost touching at their tops—twitch.

The young woman lives beyond the pasture, back in the trees, in a two-story, six-bedroom stone house. Two huge stone chimneys rise high above the peak of the house. She is well educated. She and her husband have five children. They are among only a few "outsiders" to move into these remote Barrens.

Seeing she is seen, Darlene picks up her stride and twirls the sash faster. Behind her, Luther weaves forward the best he can on shaky legs. When they reach the woman in the garden they stop. Still twirling the sash with her right hand Darlene hikes her skirt up with her left to avoid the stubble on the side of the road. She steps over the ditch to the fence, lets go of the sash and puts her right foot up on the wire.

The garden is narrow and long. Rows of beans wind around cane poles leaning together in tripods; green and red tomatoes fill the inside of fence wire cylinders; there are high stalks of corn, squash, onions, field peas, lettuce, cucumbers, carrots, radishes and on and on; the garden is filled with food and surrounded by yellow sunflowers. On the far side of the pasture grows a high, thick wild rose hedge. From the hedge comes the, "bob-bob-white" of a quail; in a bit, the call is answered from the trees.

"Well, my Lord have mercy, Mrs. Lynch, I've so long wanted to meet you an here's tha chance done presented itself to me...I'm Ms. Darlene Lovely." She reaches across the top of the wire, points at the garden, "If that id'nt somethin pretty to rest your eyes on."

"Well, thank you, Ms. Lovely."

"I declare, you're such a little thing, did you do all this on your own?"

"Oh, no, ma'am. Our friend, Mr. King, broke the ground up for us and my husband helps on the weekends."

"Well, I see hits prosperin with your tendin. Do you plant by tha signs? I'd plant nothin but by tha signs. I bet you wouldn't either, Mrs. Lynch."

"Well...Ms. Lovely...I'm afraid I pretty much go by the directions on the packages or what the books say."

"Huh, people that write all that got it from tha old people who went by tha signs. Up there in tha holler Daddy an I barely got a place to scratch tha ground but we follow tha signs. All we got's a few taters an a bit of corn an tha varmints have bout taken that away but even with our little we go by tha moon." She looks down and sees a smudge of dirt on the hem of her dress. She takes a clean, white-laced handkerchief from her dress pocket, bends forward, wipes the dirt off, straightens, folds her arms, rises and leans on top of the fence.

"My, my, my, Mrs. Lynch, them pole beans are sure lookin mighty fine."

"Well, yes, they've done nicely this year. Would you like some?"

"Oh, my, yes'um, I'd take some, I'll cook em for Daddy tonight. He dearly loves em."

Williamson County Circuit Court

Mr. Hooper:	Sheriff Henry, have you had reason to go to Mr. Hawkins' home on other occasions?
Sheriff Henry:	Yes, sir. I've been out there nine times in the last three years.
Mr. Hooper:	And why is that?

Sheriff Henry: For four reports he was beating on Ms. Veach, and once because he was running around outside naked and shooting off a shotgun and other times for throwing rocks at neighbors and killing deer out of season and setting the woods on fire. Mr. Hooper, I could go on and on. He's been in and out of jail and she just keeps getting him out. I guess she can't do that this time.

Still House Hollow Road

"My gracious, have mercy, Mrs. Lynch, thank you for fillin that feed bag full of all them good things. You've bout loaded Luther an me down with all tha beans an squash an corn he can carry. We're much obliged."

Luther isn't listening. Though he is standing right beside her he doesn't hear a word she says. Leaning forward with his chin resting on his folded arms on top of a fence post, his ears and eyes are fixed on the black horse.

Darlene turns her head to the left, lifts it and points with her chin toward the hill from where she has come, "Mrs. Lynch, did you know Annie?"

"Who?"

"Ms. Annie Veach, up there on tha hill, who kilt that no-account Delbert Hawkins."

"No, ma'am, I don't believe I've ever met her. But that day, when it happened, I was down here in the garden and saw the sheriff come flying up the road in his

car and a while later he came flying back down as fast as
he could go."

"Well, Annie, tha poor thing's in tha courthouse bein
tried right this minute as we stand here enjoyin one
another an your garden an tha good air...Mrs. Lynch, I'm
feelin for her, for I know her an her child, for she's
always treated me kindly. She's good people; Annie
is...an, oh, my Lord, Mrs. Lynch, if you're of a mind to,
I'm moved to pray for her this minute. Would you be
with me in kneelin down right now an prayin for tha Lord
to save Annie, for there ain't nuthin finer than sunshine
an bein with good people an prayin for one in need?"

For the smallest of moments the young woman
hesitates then, "Yes, ma'am, Ms. Lovely, I'll be glad to
pray with you."

They kneel in the stubble and dirt, only the fence
separates them: the younger woman, smooth skinned,
soft voiced, graced by money and family; the older
woman's face is lined and cracked a thousand times from
a life of hardship, her language and ways are of little
schooling and of poorness. The two women kneel to pray
for the third woman who is not there, a woman whose life
or death is held in the hands of women and men who
know almost nothing about her. Darlene prays—

"Dear Lord God, hear our plea for Annie Veach who
needs Your protectin wings spread wide over her this day
to save her so she can return to her child who needs her
bad. Please, we beg of You, forgive Annie of her wrong-
doin for we know You have told us not to kill one
another, but hit is only You who can see the risin up an
tha goin down of each an every one of us an You know
she were only doin what she believed best to do to save

her baby girl who was havin evil done to her an suffrin mightily. Hear our voice, almighty God, an forgive Annie an save her an set her free! This we pray in tha name of Your Son Jesus Christ, amen."

And Mrs. Lynch's lips move silently, *Amen.*

Williamson County Circuit Court, Summation

Mr. Hooper: Judge Frank and members of the jury, you have heard what kind of man...no, let us not dignify Delbert Hawkins by calling him a man, that would be way too good for him; let us say what kind of thing Delbert Hawkins was. That is more fitting. As you have heard from Sheriff Henry and Ms. Veach, Delbert Hawkins was little more than a predator who roamed the earth seeking whom he might devour—well, you all will remember the one spoken of in the good Book, that greatest of all evildoers who was cast out from heaven and came down to earth to prey upon the innocent and righteous. Delbert Hawkins was a disciple of that evildoer.

Now, will each of you turn your eyes on the defendant seated here before you; see this frail woman, Ms. Annie Veach, who has long suffered at the hands of that...that thing, that thing once called Delbert Hawkins? I ask that you look with understanding and forgiveness upon this gentle woman, Ms. Annie Veach, who has removed this creature who preyed upon the God-fearing people of Williamson County. And as you look upon her, think of your wives, your sisters, your daughters and ask yourself, "What would I have done?" Here before you, you see a loving mother who feared for her dear only begotten child. She feared so greatly that finally, like a vengeful angel of God, she rose up and smote the one who had been sent by Satan to deflower her innocent daughter. Thank the good Lord; Annie Veach had the courage of righteousness to remove the Evil One from this earth before he could do more harm to her dear child, Annie Lee, and to the other precious and defenseless children of our county. For that, it is upon us to be forever grateful to Annie Veach as we are forever in her due. The moment has now come when you good people, who believe we have a sacred duty to protect our children, to fulfill our obligation to Annie Veach by setting her free to go home and care for her only child and into the arms of those who love her, for they are many. I rest my case.

Still House Hollow Road

Luther's eyes are transfixed on the horse. They do not blink.

The horse's eyes are fixed on Luther and the women. Its ears twitch. It paws the ground four times with its right hoof, shakes its head and snorts twice.

A shadow moves over the field and the horse and the dog and the two women and Luther. Far off in the west there is rumbling.

The women rise from their knees shaking the dirt and stubble from their dresses.

"My goodness, do you hear them rumbles? You know what they say, they say that's God rollin His stones up there on tha floor of heaven. Maybe He's letting us know He's heard us. Sure nough fore mornin comes we'll get rain. That garden of yours ull just drink hit up an hit'll git prettier an prettier...now, Mrs. Lynch, I'm embarrassed to say hit but tha Lord's spirit has come over me so strong while we were on our knees prayin together...I've long had a weight on my heart an long needed a good Christian woman to hear me tell hit out so tha weight'll lift off. Your kindness to me this very day causes me to believe you're that woman...Mrs. Lynch, would you mind hearin me confess somethin that's been pressin on me ever since Annie's killin of Delbert?"

As the older woman talks on and on the dog presses sideways tight against the knee of the young woman. She reaches down to its head and strokes it for a moment, then looks up, "Well ...well, Ms. Lovely...well, yes, I suppose you can...well, certainly you can, Ms. Lovely...certainly you can...feel free to say whatever it is you need to say. I'll be honored to hear whatever is heavy on your heart if you're certain you want to say it to me...yes, I'll hear it."

"I do...I do, for today's brought my sinful life to me so I can barely rest. Mrs. Lynch, I fear I've made my way in life with my body on hit's back so long for money I've done sold away my soul...but...but my daddy an I've never starved nor not had a roof over our heads. But though that is a truth I've know'd...I've know'd all tha while what tha Bible says an I've know'd I'm a sinful woman...Oh, Mrs. Lynch, I so feel for Annie, for she must be scairt, for she was livin in sin just like me. But I know'd her these few years, an I've know'd in her heart she was a good woman an she was tryin to save her baby from sin an...oh, oh...my heart breaks for her an for all like we be, for we've all gone astray for whatever reason an we all need tha good Lord who made us to look deep inside us an see our love for Him no matter our doins an to forgive us an save us."

And with her confession, tears roll down Darlene Lovely's cheeks.

Luther finally speaks, "Mrs. Lynch, that's as fine a piece of horse flesh as I've seen in some fair while an I can assure you I've seen a many. Can yer husband handle im?"

"What's that...excuse me, Mr. uh...what did you ask me?"

"Can yer husband handle im?"

At this moment Darlene blows her nose in her handkerchief, wipes her nose, puts the handkerchief back in her pocket and rasps, "Delbert, you just step back there for a moment an shet your mouth. Mrs. Lynch and I'ma talking, you just go on an be quiet."

"No, that's okay, Ms. Lovely, I don't mind. Mr. Delbert, let me tell you about that horse, he's strong, hot-blooded and hard to handle; he's thrown Mr. Lynch three times and Mr. Lynch is an awfully good rider."

The sky's shadow passes over. The sun is warm on the garden and the people and the animals. The quail in the hedgerow calls again to its mate and the mate in the tree calls back.

Luther hacks, spits, raises his chin, turns toward Mrs. Lynch and says, one distinct word at a time, "I...can...gentle...that...horse down for Mr. Lynch so's he won't pitch im no more. You wanta know why I can do hit?"

"Yes, sir, I sure do."

"Well, hits cause I always wanted to be a cowboy."

A long moment passes, a hawk circles high above and screams, the horse snorts and stomps, a line of clouds move out onto the sky. Mrs. Lynch leans over and kisses Lassie's head, she straightens up with a smile, turns to Luther and says, "Well, that's very nice, Mr. Luther, thank you for your offer. Its very kind, very kind of you...I'll be sure an tell Mr. Lynch tonight."

Luther steps back from the fence, his shoulders squared, his face serious, "Yes, ma'am, I'm the man for the job if he's a mind to have that animal gentled. You tell im that if he wants to hire me fer doin hit to jus drop a word with Darlene here. I'm sure he knows where her house is. I come there bout once a week or so when I've got tha money."

At that instant, in one swift motion, Darlene picks up a heavy stick and hits Luther on the back of his left hip.

"Well, damn! S'cuse, Mrs. Lynch, but that hurt like blazes, Darlene. You didn't have to hit me with a stick."

"I should of hit you in tha head for talkin bout me that way!"

"Well, I wadn't talkin ugly bout you. I just said..."

She hit him again, this time on his right ankle. Luther grabbed his ankle and jumped up and down on his left foot. He opened his mouth and was about to yell when she cut him off.

"Luther, just shut up an pick up that bag of generosities an let's git on down tha road. We still got a piece to go fore dark." Darlene turns back to her new friend, "Mrs. Lynch, I don't rightly know how to tell you what your kindness means to me. I've not much schoolin so my words are not pretty, yet I've lived a life that's taught me to see through what's pretend an what's heartfelt an today I've been touched by a great kindness from a kind heart." Tears were in her eyes and on her cheeks, she tried to wipe them away with her handkerchief but they continued. "Mrs. Lynch, I feel a love for your goodness to me this day, an if you'll let me, I'd like to give you a hug across this wire tween us."

Now, the rumbling in the sky is louder, this time it is just a little ways beyond the nearest hills.

The older woman leans over the fence, she reaches toward the younger woman, for a moment their hands clasp and they smile at one another. Then, they release, step back and the older woman hoists her skirt, turns and steps across the ditch onto the road.

"Come on, Luther, you ain't gonna be a cowboy today an not tomorrow an not anytime next year. We gotta get on fore that rain comes...bye, bye, Mrs. Lynch...pray for Annie an me tonight." They start walking away. But before the next bend, Darlene turns, waves, turns back and walks around the bend.

The young woman picks up her hoe and a small sack of tomatoes and squash. She looks down the road. The older woman and man are gone.

"Come on, Lassie, let's go start supper."

Williamson County Circuit Court, July 21, 1970

Judge Frank: Ladies and gentlemen of the jury, you have heard testimony and seen evidence concerning the guilt or innocence of the defendant and it is your duty to weigh all the evidence and facts in this case. You may believe or disbelieve any testimony you have heard. You must decide guilt or innocence.

Charge No. 1 is first degree murder.

Charge No. 2 is manslaughter.

Charge No. 3 is assault with a deadly weapon.

It is necessary that you reach a unanimous decision. If you need any testimony repeated or need to have the meaning of the charges explained, please ask the Bailiff by written note and I will respond. Should your verdict be guilty for any of the charges, I will reconvene you tomorrow to set the punishment according to law.

The rain that night brought a gentle soaking to the earth. When morning came and the sun rose, the clouds were gone and the garden was filled with greens and reds and yellows.

Williamson County Circuit Court, July 22, 1970

Judge Frank: Ladies and gentlemen of the jury, having unanimously found the defendant, Ms. Annie Veach, guilty of manslaughter and having determined in your deliberations that she should serve eleven months and twenty-nine days and that time should be served on probation, the court hereby concurs with the jury's verdict and punishment. This court is adjourned.

The Review Appeal
Franklin, Tennessee, July 23, 1970

ANNIE VEACH GUILTY OF MANSLAUGHTER

IN THE DEATH OF DELBERT HAWKINS.

Yesterday, in Circuit Court, Judge James K. Frank sentenced Ms. Annie Veach to serve eleven months and twenty-nine days on probation.

THE STAFFING OF ABRAHAM REKOTS

1952 DIAGNOSTIC AND STATISTICAL MANUAL OF MENTAL DISORDERS DSM - 1

000-x20 Schizophrenic reactions

These disorders are marked by a strong tendency to retreat from reality, by emotional disharmony, unpredictable disturbances in stream of thought, regressive behavior and, in some, by a tendency to "deterioration".

000-x24 Schizophrenic reactions, paranoid type

This type of reaction is characterized by autistic, unrealistic thinking, with mental content composed chiefly of delusions of persecution and/or grandeur, ideas of reference, and often hallucinations. It is often characterized by unpredictable behavior, with a fairly constant attitude of hostility and aggression. Excessive religiosity may be present with or without delusions of persecution. There may be an expansive delusional system of omnipotence, genius, or special ability.

* * * * *

The hospital's six hundred acres spread in every direction. A major highway and smaller roads formed its borders. The farm's fields, once alive with corn, tobacco, wheat, and pastures for milk cows, lie fallow.

Toward the center of the farm, two hundred yards from the guard's gate and house at the highway, the driveway splits around the broken remnants of a once lush and large magnolia grove. Each division passes staff houses, dormitories and patient buildings and rejoins at the portico that extends from the doorway into the main building of Central State Psychiatric Hospital, once named Tennessee Hospital for the Insane. Built in 1852, its tall, sprawling, red brick and limestone walls are castellated, turreted and spiraled in Gothic hugeness—more English than American—with windows covered in dark iron screens. It is the building where generations of mentally ill Tennesseans have been brought by sheriffs' deputies and, sometimes, by their own families. Here, many would remain for weeks, months or years; some 'til death.

Behind the "Gothic hugeness" are crumbling and empty barns, outbuildings and silos; a hundred yards beyond them, in a weedy and briary cemetery, stands a variety of tilted and broken tombstones under which many mostly forgotten people are buried.

On April 19, 1852, the first patients, thirty-nine men and twenty-one women, were transported to the hospital. From that day the numbers grew steadily; few became well enough to go home. The number of buildings grew and the number of beds grew with them, so that by 1958, a hundred years later, there were two thousand three hundred and forty-six people residing there.

* * * * *

In 1958, I was twenty-two years old, married, and between my first and second year of a Masters Degree in Psychiatric Social Work at the University of Tennessee. I worked for almost two months of that summer at Central State Hospital. I was assigned to the Cooper Building, a rather plain three-story structure with red brick walls and heavily screened windows which housed men and women in separate wings. Many had been there for years; most had little to no contact with their families. My office on the first floor was shared with fellow student, Herren Aho, a bald, strongly built man whose physical resemblance to an SS guard belied his kindness and jolliness.

On my third day, Thursday afternoon, near time for me to leave, a man of average appearance who looked to be in his sixties, wearing a sweat-stained felt hat, no necktie and shirt sleeves rolled to his elbows, suddenly walked into our office and pitched a thick, green, tattered, medical record in front of me. I had never seen him; I would have guessed he was a greenhouse gardener or a maintenance supervisor. Motioning to the medical record on my desk, he said, "Mr. Spain, I'm Dr. Hawk. I run this place, and I want you to see this man every week and write down your observations and thoughts about him in detail in the chart. I'm staffing him next month. He's been here a long time and ain't any better. The question is why not? You're young and don't know a lot, so maybe you can figure it out. After you've seen him tomorrow morning, find me and give me a report." Though he said this politely it was an order. He added, "I'll tell Mr. Hennessey, the head attendant, to be at the nurses' station and expect you at 8:00. He'll show you around the ward and introduce you to Mr. Rekots. Here's a key to the high security ward. Don't lose it." He handed me a large key on a ring and turned to Herren, "And here's a record and a key for you, Mr. Aho...do the same," and walked out the door.

The name on the record's greenish cover was Abraham Rekots. I began to read. An hour later, Herren had gone home; I was still reading and taking notes. It was growing dark so I called my wife and told her I would be home in another hour.

The next morning, I arrived early, read over my notes and double-checked sections of the record, especially the history given by a cousin at the time the patient was admitted. Herren had not come in when I walked to the third-floor ward where the long-term, severely-disturbed male patients were kept under close supervision. At the heavy entrance door I put the key in the lock, turned it, opened the door, stepped inside, closed the door behind me, and turned to look into the ward: a large room with army-green walls; beds separated by side tables; a glassed-in nurses' station on the right; a divider wall at the far end opened in the center to the day room where patients were sitting. There was a slight smell of disinfectant and urine, and also an unidentifiable odor.

The door clicked shut behind me. A flash memory came of when I was eight years old, walking into the "Haunted House" at school on Halloween. I stood for a moment, shook my head and entered the nurses' station. Two white men, both dressed in white shirts and pants, were seated, one with a large nose like a fist, was writing notes in a chart; the other was sorting pills with a spoon handle, scraping them into small paper cups. Neither one looked up.

"Excuse me...is one of you Mr. Hennessy?"

The one writing looked up. "I am."

"I'm George Spain. Dr. Hawk told me to report to you about seeing Mr. Rekots."

He looked at me for a moment. "Well, I'll be damned! He's sent a young'un this time to see the 'bug eater'!" Then he smiled and held out his hand, "I'm Hennessey 'an I was expectin' you...let's go." He stood up and walked slowly down the aisle between the beds.

"As you see, Mr. Spain, we keep this place neat and orderly. Please, while you are here, do the same." The iron beds were white, the pillows and sheets were tight. We went into the day room.

Two men sat like granite statues. Another rocked rapidly back and forth, on and on. A fourth was bent forward looking down at the floor, whispering and giggling. Others sat reading; a few were talking to one another or to themselves. Several paced up and down the hallway; two were reaching out, touching the walls with their fingers. Now and then there were sounds.

"Mr. Hennessey, is one of them Mr. Rekots?"

"Uh, huh."

"Please take me to him."

We stopped in front of a thin, fair-skinned man with almost white hair and a long mustache the same color; he appeared to be about forty years old. With wide leather straps, his arms and legs were held down to a heavy, wooden lock-chair secured to a platform; a wooden tray, like a child's highchair, was secured across his front which protected him from hurting himself and others. His face was long with a square jaw, high cheekbones, a Roman nose and greenish-blue eyes. A dull-gray bruise covered most of his left cheek. He was staring out the window.

Stupidly, I held out my hand to shake his. "Mr. Rekots, my name is George Spain. Dr. Hawk wants me to get to know you and help you if I can." He continued looking out the window. He did not move or speak. His eyes did not blink. Beneath his bound hands, the wood of the armrests was heavily scratched; in the markings were slight streaks of blood from beneath his broken fingernails.

I put my hand down. "Mr. Rekots, may I speak to you for a moment?" Still he did not respond. Why I do not know, but I reached down and touched the fingers on his right hand. "Mr. Rekots, you are hurting yourself; let me get someone to stop the bleeding."

With that, he slowly turned and looked at me with an expression of disdain.

"Sir, who are you addressing? To my knowledge we have never been formally introduced." His voice was so soft it was hard to hear and to understand for he feigned a foreign accent. "And it is apparent in your calling me by some name I do not recognize that you do not know who I am." This last remark was said with a faint growl in his throat.

"Yes, sir. You're Mr. Abraham Rekots."

He snorted and turned away.

"Am I mistaken? Did Mr. Hennessey bring me to the wrong person? I'm sorry."

He snorted again but turned, his eyes widening and staring into mine. "Young man, not only did that fool bring you to the wrong person, he did so in a cruel effort to deny reality as everyone else does here."

"I'm sorry! Forgive me, Mr...uh?" I was embarrassed and extremely confused.

For a long moment he did not speak; his unblinking eyes studied my face. Then, his expression softened. "Sir, what is your name?"

"Uh...uh...George Spain."

"Mr. Spain, I would shake your hand, but as you see I am hampered for the moment." He wiggled his fingers. "Forgive me for not standing and taking your hand." His face muscles tightened. "I am Count R. N. Renfield. My family is an ancient one. The war brought my parents to this country from the Carpathian Mountains in Romania in 1917. My father's lands covered ten thousand acres. His castle had more than a hundred rooms. I was born a year after they arrived in America. Sadly, my parents are dead. The title has now passed to me, though you may address me as Mr. Renfield." He nodded for me to sit in the empty lock-chair next to him.

From that day forward, I visited him at least once a week, sometimes more often. I kept detailed notes in the chart as Dr. Hawk had ordered. The following excerpts capture much of his illness and intelligence, his mixture of kindness and danger, of gloom, of mania, and with a certainty that he was commanding destiny and the beyond.

July 7. Patient has been released from the lock-chair. He is exuberant, smiling and talking almost non-stop. When he saw me he jumped up, came forward and took my hand, "Mr. Spain...Mr. George Spain...Look at me! I'm free!" He pirouetted, bowed, gestured as though removing a hat from his head and pointed to the floor in front of him, "Step forward into my presence and let us speak of life."

I was with him thirty minutes or more. I was seated the entire time as he paced back and forth in front of me. Except for pauses for breath, he never stopped talking. Clearly, he is a man of intelligence, well-read and knowledgable of literature, science and theology; yet it is so jumbled it has no clear meaning. It is gibberish.

Exhausted, he finally stopped and looked at me; his expression was that of a university professor looking down on a student of limited ability who could not grasp the lecture just given. "You may go!" he said. I left.

July 8. After lunch I went to the dayroom. The patient was sitting in a corner sided by windows. He was writing in a small notebook. I reintroduced myself. He nodded but did not look up, "I know who you are," and continued writing.

I leaned over and looked, "What are you writing, Mr. Renfield?

He held the notebook up. The pages were filled with figures and numbers added, subtracted, multiplied and divided into groups and mixed with astrological designs and characters that seemed to be either ancient or created words, words I could not read or understand. It all seemed to begin in the center where the letters RNR were written and from there spiraled outward, the farther rotations breaking apart, finally, into fragments then to nothingness.

"Aha, now, my young friend, you see the runes that tell all that gives life."

He would not let me borrow the notebook to copy. And I did not know what runes meant and was too embarrassed to ask him so I looked it up in a dictionary.

July 11. Today, we were outside with the other patients and attendants on the front lawn under the broken magnolias. Our relationship seems to be improving. He is pleased that I am interested in his notebook in which he continues his obsessive configurations that have no meaning that I can detect. However, for him they are prophetic. My curiosity and questions as to their meaning seem to please him. Even more, there is a hint of a smile when I call him "Mr. Renfield".

His developing trust was evidenced today when I asked for the umpteenth time, "Mr. Renfield, what in the world do these figures and designs mean?"

He was silent for so long I thought I had angered him. Then suddenly, " Can't you see? They are for directing the Master." And with that he went back to his work.

"You mean Jesus?" I asked. But he did not reply. So I left.

July 14. I could hardly wait to see him today, to see if he would tell me more about the "Master". I asked him again if he meant Jesus? For a moment he looked at me with disgust, then he spat on the floor in front of me and was silent as before. What have I done wrong? After ten minutes I left.

July 17. Days pass. Still he will not communicate with me. It is as though I do not exist. Mr. Hennessey says it is the same on the ward. He may nod but never speaks. He lives in his notebook.

July 21-22. For two days Herren and I helped Dr. Millig give electroconvulsive treatments. Mr. Renfield had seven of these last year. One after another, the patients are laid on a mattress on a table. A gag is placed in their mouths so they cannot bite their tongues. The nurse holds the electrodes on each temple. Then, the doctor nods for Herren and me, to stand on each side of the patient to firmly hold their shoulders and hips; with that the doctor turns the switch on and holds for a second then switches it off. Immediately, the patient convulses; their entire body tenses; their hands fist and turn upward, almost to their chin; their arms and legs convulse for about thirty seconds. In less than two minutes they wake and after a brief moment of confusion are helped to their feet and returned to the ward. We held seven patients the first day, six the second.

July 24. For the past week Mr. Renfield has been a model patient of compliant passivity. With me, he has been polite but circumspect in revealing any particulars of his feelings or history. He asked me if I was married and had children. I told him I had a wife but no children. He nodded. I think he is beginning to trust me. I am beginning to like him, at least, to feel for his mental agony. I sense a deep hurt and sadness in him.

August 1. There has been a negative change. Is he regressing? If so, why? He has begun to have outbreaks of violence. While an attendant was handing him medication, Mr. Rekots hit his hand. He stomped the foot of another who continued to call him Mr. Rekots after he demanded to be called Mr. Renfield. Then two evenings ago, he attacked and injured an attendant who was attempting to confiscate a large matchbox filled with live roaches that was partially hidden in the back drawer of Renfield's bedside table. Renfield has been prohibited from continuing his habit of eating insects and small birds when he could catch them. He is again confined to the lock-chair.

August 8. I was sick this past week and did not see him. When I arrived at my office there was a note on the desk, "Mr. Rekots wants urgently to alk with you. Hennessey." I went straight upstairs to him. As soon as I opened the door, Renfield came running down the ward shouting, "George, George, you've finally come!" and took my arm, whispering, "We must get somewhere where no one can hear. There's an empty corner in the dayroom...hurry!" He dragged me along. This was the first time he had ever called me by my given name.

He pulled me close as we sat down and, in a whisper I could barely hear, said, "George, you're the first to know."

"Know what?"

"The sky, the sky, it's aligned with my coordinates. He is following them...He is coming to save me...He is coming."

"Who is coming?"

My Master...my Master...my Master. He is descending through the sky. You and your wife must be ready to join me. Go outside tonight, look upward and you will see."

I patted him on the forearm, "We will, Mr. Renfield, we will. Now remember, I'm not here on the weekend so it will be Monday before I return."

He looked up at me with a sad smile, "You are my only friend."

I could only nod to Hennessey as I passed him. I couldn't speak.

August 11. For the past three mornings I have gotten up just before dawn and gone outside. The sky has been filled with meteors. Slivers of silver streak the sky. What does it mean? Surely, Renfield's foretelling has no connection. Surely, it is only a natural phenomenon. Last Sunday's paper reported that the Perseids Meteor Showers had begun. I feel certain Mr. Renfield knows of this event and has woven it into his delusion.

I have never seen him happier than today. He gave me a hug and kissed me on the cheek. I could not bring myself to question his delusion or confront it with this annual event. How will it help him for me to question or deny his happiness? Someone else might but I could not. All I could say was, "I'm glad you are happy." Probably I should have said something else.

Right before I left work, Mr. Hennessey phoned me. "Mr. Rekots wants you to come see him again before you go home tomorrow."

August 12. Mr. Renfield was waiting inside the doorway. He took my arm and walked hurriedly to the quiet corner where we usually talk. There was no wildness in his eyes, though there was anxiety.

As soon as we were seated he said, "Thank you so much for all your kindnesses. As I'm sure you know they are going to staff me first thing Wednesday morning and they will have me come in to talk with them...I've got something I need to say to you...something I've never said before; it's beyond me or you; something that's had no words until now. I know Dr. Hawk knows who I really am, and tomorrow he won't let anyone say anything mean about me or hurt me. You know, I'm certain he's going to set me free. He knows the time has come. George, you're a good friend, give me a hug. You know when I leave that room tomorrow we may never see each other again...I love you."

I could feel my tears. I couldn't speak. We stood and hugged, and I turned away and left him.

August 13   My last day at work.

* * * * *

Patient: Abraham Rekots   August 13, 1958
Recorder: Bonnie Murray

The staffing began promptly at 9:00 AM. It was held in the small conference room in the Cooper Building, Central State Psychiatric Hospital, Nashville, Tennessee. Chaired by Dr. Seward Hawk, Superintendent and Medical Director. Attended by: Dr. David Millig, Director of the Cooper Building; Dr. Stewart Orr, Vanderbilt Psychiatry Resident; Dr. William Holmwood, Clinical Psychologist; Mrs. Julia Harker, MSW Social Worker; Mr. Kenneth Hennessey, Senior Attendant; Mr. George Spain, Social Work student; and Miss Bonnie Murray, secretary-recorder. Dr. Hawk sat at the head of the table. To his right was the chair reserved for the patient; behind that chair, against the wall, were two empty chairs; the other staff sat around the table. Dr. Hawk specifically requested that the patient's mannerisms, facial expressions and voice tones be included in the recording of this staffing.

Dr. Hawk: "Dr. Millig, please give the patient's medical history and course of treatment."

Dr. Millig: "The patient, Mr. Abraham Rekots, was born in 1918. He was committed to this hospital on December 31, 1936, when he was eighteen years old. At that time he was given the diagnosis of *dementia praecox*. Since 1952, his treatment diagnosis has been Schizophrenic reaction, paranoid type. His physical condition has remained consistently good and well within normal limits. Psychological testing gives him an intelligence quotient of one hundred forty-three. His self-identity has remained fixated on delusions of grandeur and ideas of reference. He has held to his belief that he is Count R. N. Renfield and that his parents were immigrants from Romania. A major aspect of his delusional system is the belief that someone he calls 'Master' is coming to set him free. This is all part of an elaborate autistic fabrication. I will let the social worker give his true history. Throughout his twenty-two years here he has had periods of violence at which times he has attacked the staff and other patients; the most recent was ten days ago. He has made seven attempts to escape, once not being caught for half a day. Unless someone intervenes, the patient continues to eat insects and, on occasion, small birds when he can lure them to him with breadcrumbs. He has had a series of ECT twice, the most recent was last year. Each time there has been a period of a few months of quiescence and then a gradual return of violence and ramblings of the world's relationship to his destiny. His present dosage of thorazine is 400 mg a day. In summation, neither medication, environmental structuring, verbal reasoning, nor ECT has diminished his symptoms sufficiently for him to be considered for discharge. In short, this patient should continue to be treated on the secure unit as his potential for violence against others and flight remain high."

Dr. Hawk: "Mrs. Harker."

Julia Harker, Social Worker: "The patient, Abraham Rekots, was born at St. Thomas hospital in Nashville on October 5, 1918. His parents were Otto and Nancy Rekots. Both were Jewish and second-generation citizens of the United States. They were highly successful jewelers in Nashville; neither had Romanian ancestors. The patient was an only child. Little is known about his parents or early childhood. It appears he was sent to boarding schools until he entered Vanderbilt at sixteen. There, he majored in history and minored in literature and was a straight A student. In the middle of his sophomore year his grades began to decline. He had frequent absences and was placed on probation for fighting with another student. On December 29, 1936, his parents died in a fire in their home. The patient was not there. Two days later, in the early morning, he was picked up by the City Police while sitting on the steps of the Parthenon in Centennial Park. On his lap was a dead cat, which he had apparently killed and sucked the blood from. Blood was on his face, hands and in his mouth. Though his billfold gave his home address and name as Abraham Rekots he insisted that he was R. N. Renfield. No other family members have been found since his admission. He has never had a visitor."

Dr. William Holmwood, Psychologist: "As Mrs. Harker has stated, the patient is highly intelligent. On the Rorschach, with one exception, his responses were a single word. It was only on the last card that he looked up at me and, after staring at the inkblot for a long moment, said, 'Blood.' Then, he smiled and added '...is the life.' On Word Association his words all seemed to have some significance to his delusions.

> 'Happy - Master
> Sad - Here
> Cat - Blood
> Dog - Blood
> Night - Master
> Heart - Blood
> Hate - Here
> Love - Master
> Death - Death
> Life - Blood is the life.'

"On Sentence Completion his responses continued his delusion:

> 'I secretly wish - for my master.
> I would be truly happy if - my Master comes.
> I wish I could forget - this place.
> My father and I - were never.
> I fear - here.
> I get angry when - I am stared at.
> It is hard for me - to be without blood.
> My mother and I - were never.
> I feel like - my Master will come.
> My dream - is to be with my Master.'

"In summary, the patient remains firmly entrenched in his psychosis. His fixations on blood, a master who will come and take him away, and that he is Count R. N.

Renfield have not changed during the twenty-two years he has been in this hospital. These delusions and his periodic violent outbursts evidence his continuing danger to others."

Dr. Hawk: "Now, Mr. Hennessey, give us a report on his behavior on the ward."

Mr. Hennessey: "Except for showing some interest in Mr. Spain, with whom he sometimes talks, Mr. Rekots' behavior hasn't changed since the last staffing six months ago. He spends most of his time either writing and drawing in one of his notebooks or sitting in the dayroom staring out the window. He doesn't participate in social or recreational activities, seldom communicates with other patients, and with the staff only when absolutely necessary. While usually quiet and compliant there are still outbursts of anger, some so violent he must be constrained in the lock-chair until he calms. His appetite is good and he is rarely ill. At night he becomes restless, often pacing back and forth, mumbling to himself, occasionally making references to a 'master' coming. He becomes irritated if questioned about who this master is and when he is coming."

Dr. Hawk: "Now, Mr. Spain, according to Mr. Hennessey you have formed some kind of connection with Mr. Rekots. Please give us your observations and any suggestions you might have."

Mr. Spain: "Thank you, Dr. Hawk, for asking me to see this unusual man. He is, as everyone has said, very ill. Everything said about him is true. As I have slowly come to know him, I have come to believe he is suffering from a great loss. From this has arisen his need to create a master who is coming to take him to a world where he will be safe and live in grandness forever. I believe he can be brought back from this. I believe his illness can be reversed. Dr. Hawk, I recommend Mr. Rekots receive at least twice weekly psychotherapy sessions by a skilled therapist."

Dr Hawk: "Thank you, Mr. Spain. Now, Mr. Hennessey, will you please go out and bring the patient in."

Mr. Hennessey left the room and in a moment brought the patient in with two attendants. The patient was stiffly erect as he entered. His face showed no emotion. His eyes were fixed on Dr. Hawk who motioned him to the chair next to his. When everyone was seated Dr. Hawk resumed.

Dr. Hawk: "Mr. Rekots, thank you for coming. You've been here before and, as you know, we are reviewing your progress to determine your future treatment goals. Before we begin to make our decisions we want to ask a few questions and hear how you believe you are doing and if you have any suggestions to make. We are here to help you so please speak freely."

There was a long silence. The patient continued to look at Dr. Hawk, then turned and looked at George

Spain. He said nothing. His expression was sullen and angry.

Dr. Hawk: "Mr. Rekots, are you willing to talk to us? We hope you will."

The patient did not speak or make any motion with his head.

Dr. Hawk: "Mr. Rekots, I understand you believe your name is R. N. Renfield. Is that true?"

There was no response from the patient.

Dr. Hawk: "Well, Mr. Rekots, apparently you do not wish to speak to us today. I must tell you that your continuing acts of violence, the unchanging delusion of who you are and fictitious creations of a master who is coming to save you, all indicate that your present course of treatment is not helping you and therefore we will be considering certain changes which might help. Dr. Millig will see you later today and let you know about your future course of treatment. Thank you for coming, Mr. Rekots. I wish you well."

Dr. Hawk stood and held out his hand, which the patient did not shake, but turned to the door and the attendants took him out and returned him to the ward.

Dr. Hawk: "This patient is clearly unresponsive to existing treatment. Therefore, my recommendations are to double his thorazine to 800 mg a day and next week start him on another series of shock treatments which should be increased from seven to twelve. Dr. Millig, Dr. Orr, do you agree?"

Drs. Millig and Orr voiced their agreements. Dr. Hawk wrote a brief note in the chart, wished everyone a pleasant day, and left the room. The staffing ended.

Bonnie Murray, Secretary-Recorder

An hour after the staffing I received a phone call that my wife was in labor. I left immediately for Vanderbilt where our first child, a son, was born early the next morning. The following week I returned to school. I never saw Abraham Rekots again.

* * * * *

Two years later, when I was working as a child therapist in the Vanderbilt Department of Psychiatry, Dr. Orr approached me in the hallway and said that Abraham Rekots had died at Central State from an unknown cause.

WIND BIRD

What is written here is as it was, though some of it may be imagined, it is as true as memory makes it.

We will always carry each other around in
our hearts forever.
                                                                Wind Bird

So I have carried you in my heart all these fifty plus years; even now, at seventy-nine, I see you standing in the open doorway of my office in your canary-yellow dress; your eyes and hair black as crows' wings, your skin dark honey. You say these words, turn away into the hallway and are gone —forever.

She was wild. Not feral. Not autistic. Not retarded. Wild. Unpredictable. Sometimes making animal sounds. She was short and strong, at times dangerous. Her mother, full blood Cherokee. Father unknown. She was eleven when she came all those hundreds of miles from Wears Valley, from the foothills of the Smokies, to the Children's Psychiatric Hospital in Nashville.

Three days after her arrival, she leapt onto an attendant's back, grabbing him around his neck, pulling him backwards, twisting him to the floor, all the while grunting deep in her throat. The third week, she tripped a nurse with a broom handle, spraining her wrist. The fourth week she disappeared. The doors to the ward were locked. No one saw her run out. In an instant she had disappeared. Searching, and looking and looking; she was not there.

And then, a tiny, mouse-like, fair-skinned eight-year-old boy, who had smothered his baby sister to death, pointed to a corner pillar jutting out from the wall where a low wooden cabinet was built against it. We got down on our knees, opened the cabinet door and saw an opening into the pillar. She was there just above us, just a bit inside the pillar.

She came out kicking, scratching and growling.

* * * * *

Born in freezing winter, the girl baby came quickly out of her squatting mother onto a gunnysack that lay on the dirt floor of a tarpaper shack at the bottom of a steep-sided hollow. The mother tied a leather shoestring around the cord and cut it with a dull knife, then laid the screeching baby on the cold, dirty gunnysack. The mother grimaced. She looked down at the wet, flailing baby, "I'll be damn, she's gotta lotta wind in er...I think I'm gonna call er Wind."

An old man watched all of this with his watery, half-shut eyes. He was sitting in a ladder-back chair beside a tilted iron pot-bellied stove that was growing cold. He barely nodded through his blurred vision, then drank a long swallow from the fruit jar always beside him; his eyelids flickered; his shoulders slumped and he slept.

"Goddamnit, Daddy; hit's freezing in yair, git up an git some wood an git tha far a-goin. I need ta heat up some water an clean that little un an me." The old man didn't open his eyes or move. She picked up a piece of kindling, threw it and hit his knee. "You'uns go git some wood an build this far back up."

"Damn! That done hurt like hell!" He rubbed his knee for a moment then staggered to his feet and out the door. Even through the log wall he could hear the screeching of the baby.

* * * * *

Among the many men who came to her, Wind's mother had no idea who was the father; for they never seemed to stop coming down the steep, narrow footpath that led from the ridge road. Down and up the hill they came and went, Indians and whites and even an occasional black man; most brought money, some whisky, a few came with chickens or a shoat.

And year after year, as she grew older, more and more, her mother would send Wind out of the house when the men came. But there were times, if the weather was bad, when she was kept inside. Then she would curl herself into a ball under a filthy scrap of blanket in the corner farthest from the only bed in the room. With her fingers in her ears she tried not to even breathe, she was so frightened of her mother and the man. It was then that she began to run away into her mind, disappearing into the woods, listening to the animals and birds panting and groaning and crying and calling to her.

While most of the men paid no attention to her, a few spoke kindly, but there was one who pulled the scrappy blanket off and began to fondle her until her mother broke a crock jar on his back and threatened to cut his throat. Her grandfather did nothing but drink and sleep, and stare into the fire until his daughter threw something at him. Then, he would stagger out and cut more wood or bring a bucket of water from the spring.

She was eight the first time she ran away into the woods and stayed gone for three days and nights until hunger and the cold drove her back to the cabin. But, as time went on, she ran away again and again. And, as she grew older, she stayed away longer and longer, eating wild plants, fruits, nuts, roots; sleeping in the hollows of trees; speaking to animals.

She told me these things. She drew them on paper. She made their sounds and drew pictures of the animals and of herself with them. Slowly, she taught me to understand.

I began to read about feral and wild children, most especially, I was taken by a small book by Jean-Marc-Gaspard Itard, French physician and educator of the deaf. Published in 1801 his *An Historical Account of the Discovery and Education of a Savage Man, or of the First Developments of the Young Savage Caught in the Woods Near Aveyron, in the Year 1798*. Victor, the "Wild Boy of Aveyron", was brought to the National Institute for the Deaf in 1800. There he met Itard who affectively adopted Victor and began to attempt to teach him to speak and communicate with others and "to develop him physically and morally".

* * * * *

A child of eleven or twelve, who some years before had been seen completely naked in the Caune Woods seeking acorns and roots to eat, was met in the same place toward the end of September 1799 by three sportsmen who seized him as he was climbing into a tree to escape their pursuit. Conducted to a neighboring hamlet and confined to the care of a widow, he broke loose at the end of a week and gained the mountains, where he wandered during the most rigorous winter weather, draped rather than covered with a tattered shirt. At night he retired to solitary places but during the day he approached the neighborhood villages where of his own accord he entered an inhabited house...

Jean-Marc-Gaspard Itard

* * * * *

A small bit of me was as she was—Cherokee—my father's father, olive skinned; high, rounded cheekbones; great, great, grandson of James Vann, leader of the Upper Villages; hunter; whisky maker; lover of wild things; so was my father. So am I.

I was drawn to her – to our shared blood.

She came all those hundreds of miles from the mountains of East Tennessee to Nashville without family, without a friend, with only a social worker who did not know her, a woman whose eyes were scared, whose eyes said, 'I want to get this over with and go home,' who, as soon as she put the records on my desk and signed the admission papers, fled without a glance or a word of good-bye to Wind. As the door of the ward closed behind her there was nothing in Wind's eyes. I put my hand on her shoulder and she jerked away.

* * * * *

The records were in two tattered, gray folders marked #1 and #2; together they were three inches thick. I opened the first one and began to read:

Referring Provider: Smoky Mountain Mental Health Center

Date: May 10, 1966

Patient: Wind Bird. **Age:** 11. **Born:** July 7, 1954. **Place of Birth:** At home in: Wears Valley, Tennessee. **Parents: Father:** Unknown **Mother:** Storm Bird, full blood Cherokee. **Education:** Possibly, Grade 2. **Religion:** Unknown. **Race:** Cherokee. **Health History:** Old scars are on her legs, arms and hands; otherwise, no health problems. Though there are times she will not communicate, her hearing, speech and vision are unimpaired. After removal from her home in March, she was taken to the Sevier County Public Health Department for physical examination, at which time she received all immunizations.

Behavior History: From early childhood patient has had serious behavior problems in the home, school and community. Becomes angry at the slightest provocation, during which she may scratch, bite or strike others. She has destroyed eggs of setting hens, pulled blossoms from fruit trees, opened gates and let livestock out, poured the contents of slop-jars into cisterns, and prevented postmen from continuing their route by refusing to move from in front of their car. She has been dismissed from school five times for fighting classmates, teachers and school bus drivers. When enraged, she makes guttural and screeching sounds like animals. But, by far the most potentially dangerous behaviors for herself are her frequent runaways into the forest, where bear, wild boar and poisonous snakes abound. She may stay gone for several days and nights; twice for more than a week. During this time she lives off wild plants, nuts and fruits and vegetables she steals from gardens. At the time of her removal her mother no longer notified the authorities but allowed her to remain gone until she returned home.

Removal From Home: As a result of complaints from school authorities and members of the community, the patient was removed from her home by the Sevier County Public Welfare Department on March 1, 1966, and placed in a Child Detention Home. Subsequently, by order of Sevier County Juvenile Judge Jack Stanley, the Mental Health Center saw the patient twice: March 14 and April 12.

Evaluation: Though the patient was resistant to testing and interviewing, she is in no way psychotic, intellectually limited, deaf, mute or autistic. Rather, she appears to be highly observant and reactive to others in a manner that suggests her driving force is to avoid being controlled by others and, failing this, her aggressive impulses are to combat them and, that failing, to flee from them.

Due to the abuses she has experienced, it might well be surmised that beneath her aggressive behavior is a great

254

amount of fear and need for security, acceptance and affection.

It is our belief that this patient will benefit from a period of hospitalization followed by prolonged residential care during which time she should receive schooling and regular psychotherapy. Her mother is agreeable with this recommendation and does not oppose the Tennessee Department of Public Welfare having custody of her daughter.

Payment: Payment for the patient's hospitalization will be made by the Tennessee Department of Mental Illness and Mental Retardation.

* * * * *

[The boy was] a disgustingly dirty child affected with spasmodic movements, and often convulsions, who swayed back and forth ceaselessly like certain animals in a zoo, who bit and scratched those who opposed him, who showed no affection for those who took care of him; and who was, in short, indifferent to everything and attentive to nothing...

[Escape was his obsession,] when observed in his room...his eyes [turned] constantly toward the window, gazing sadly into space. If a stormy wind then chanced to blow, if the sun suddenly came from behind the clouds brilliantly illuminating the skies, he expressed an almost convulsive joy with clamorous peals of laughter, during which all his movements backward and forward very much resembled a kind of leap he would like to take, in order to break through the window and dash into the

garden. Sometimes instead of these joyful emotions, he exhibited a kind of frantic rage, wrung his hands, pressed closed fists to his eyes, gnashed his teeth audibly and became dangerous to those who were near him.

* * * * *

I was Wind's therapist. I saw her twice a week in my office during the year she was in the hospital and, afterwards, once a week during the three years she was in the Christian Children's Home in Nashville.

I was never afraid of her. She never attacked me. At the beginning, I was intellectually fascinated by her being Cherokee and by her past life and behavior, then over time I began to like her, and toward the end we came to love one another. She was special.

At first, she did not want to come. But when she understood we would leave the ward, she came readily. I knew she saw this as a chance to escape. My hand stayed near her. She knew it. So she never lunged away. She said nothing. She walked beside me down the hallway and turned into my office. I closed the door behind us. So we began.

That first time, for twenty minutes or so, she roamed around the office carefully studying photographs and pictures on the walls, most especially, the etchings of a Gyrfalcon and a Red-tailed Hawk. I could see her eyes fix on the hawk's eyes; slowly she raised her right arm, reached out with her fingers and gently stroked the hawk's head as she made faint, high-pitched sucking sounds between her closed lips. She turned and looked at me. There was no expression on her face. "I help hawks that have been hurt. I'm a falconer," I said.

She continued around the office, now and then picking up objects and smelling them, once putting a small bronze deer to her mouth and touching it with the tip of her tongue. From across my desk, she saw a green vase filled with hawk feathers. She could not reach the vase from her side so she came around until she was by my chair. She took three feathers out and rubbed them across her face, again making sucking sounds.

The office had a large window. The blinds were raised. It looked out into a manicured, grassed courtyard with two large oaks. The air was crystal clear with the sun's brightness. She stood in front of the window; for a long while she stared at the grass and trees and sky. And then, suddenly, she sprang upward onto the windowsill and began to pound with her fists on the glass panes, making little sounds and crying, "Please...Please...Please!" until I grabbed her around the waist and pulled her down. She growled and cursed, and kicked and scratched.

* * * * *

[These are my aims:]

I^st To interest [the wild boy] in social life by rendering it more pleasant for him than the one he was then leading, and above all more unlike the life he had just left.

257

2^d To awaken his nervous sensibility by the most energetic stimulation and, occasionally, by intense emotion.

3^d To extend the range of his ideas by giving him new needs and by increasing his social contacts.

4th To lead him to the use of speech by subjecting him to the necessity of imitation.

5th To make him exercise the simplest mental operations, first, concerning objects of his physical needs, and later, objects of instruction.

* * * * *

All I sought at the first was her trust.

The next day, I gave her a Red-tail feather.

She took it and turned away.

The next day she was waiting at the ward's door.

That day, in my office, she drew a picture filled with trees and birds and animals. They were highly detailed and realistic. Above them was something that resembled a face, part animal, part human. She would not tell me what it was or explain what it meant. She handed the picture to me. I thanked her. She said nothing. She made no sounds.

The next day, when I unlocked the door and stepped inside, she was hunkered down next to the wall; she looked up at me, straight into my eyes. Without a word she stood up and took my hand. When we entered my office she immediately saw her picture taped to the wall next to my desk. Her mouth opened slightly as though she was about to speak. But she did not. From that day on she was always waiting at the door when I came.

I learned from the head nurse that she loved fruits and nuts and raw eggs, so I began to keep them in my office as treats. Slowly she began to make quick smiles and talk with me in her mountain language.

Then, three months along, I knew Wind trusted me as I trusted her. I began to take her out of the hospital onto the grounds. And, it was that first day, as we went out into the courtyard, I saw her cry. Then, she dried her eyes, looked straight into the sun and smiled and began to whistle like a quail.

As the months passed, our walks lengthened, taking us beyond the courtyard to the larger campus with its wide yards, trimmed hedges, oaks, maples, magnolias and elms. Whether a burning hot or freezing cold day, as we left the building she had the habit of stopping and raising her face to the sky with her mouth opened wide and flicking her tongue out to, "taste tha ire, fer hit feeds me." And then, she would run ahead skipping, leaping, twirling, whistling, cawing, chirping and, now and then, when she came to her special maple with its low limbs, she would spring up onto its trunk and climb fast as a squirrel and scoot out onto a limb from where she would gesture for me to join her, laughing, "Mr. Spain, yer a big ole sissy."

How could I not love her?

* * * * *

[Once in an attempt to teach Victor vowel sounds Itard rapped Victor's fingers with a small stick when he erred in the task.] *I cannot describe how unhappy he looked with his eyes thus closed and with tears escaping from them every now and then. Oh! How ready I was on this occasion, as on many others, to give up my self-imposed task and regard as wasted the time I had already given to it! How many times did I regret ever having known this child, and freely condemn the sterile and inhuman curiosity of the men who first tore him from his innocent and happy life.*

[And later, as his despair for Victor making any significant improvement increased, Itard wrote,] *Unhappy creature, I cried as if he could hear me, and with real anguish of heart...since my labors are wasted and yours [Victor's] fruitless, take again the road to your forests and the taste for your primitive life. Or if your new needs make you depend on a society in which you have no place, go, expiate your misfortune, die of misery and boredom at Bicetre [the asylum].*

* * * * *

Wind lived in the hospital for a year. Gradually, outwardly, she became domesticated. Her outbursts of rage became fewer and fewer, her attacks on others stopped; she no longer attempted to flee. She began to read and write and sit at a desk, to use a knife and fork instead of her hands; most special to me, she began to laugh at funny things and look sad when she heard something that was sad. Yet, she still did not participate in games and play with the other children. Other than me and a motherly nurse and a young woman teacher, she showed little feeling toward the other adults and often scowled at them when she was told to do something she did not like.

It was only when I received permission to take her and two other children and an aide off the ward to a remote lake within a hilly forest that stretched for miles and miles did I see that the wildness was still in her. For, as soon as we were out of the car, she ran ahead making her animal sounds and leapt into the lake and swam out, dipping under water, then springing up and shouting, "Come on...come on...come on!" And I did. And we did. And it was as if at that moment, she was my daughter.

* * * * *

When the severity of the season drove every other person out of the garden, he delighted in taking many turns around it; after which he used to seat himself on the edge of a basin of water. I have often stopped for whole hours together, and with unspeakable pleasure, to examine him in this situation; to observe all of his convulsive motions, and that continual balancing of his whole body diminished, and by degrees subsided to give place to a more tranquil attitude; and how insensibly his face, insignificant or distorted as it might be, took the well-defined character of sorrow, or melancholy reverie, in proportion as his eyes were steadily fixed on the surface of the water, and when he threw into it, from time to time, some remains of withered leaves. When in a moon-light, the rays of that luminary penetrated into his room he seldom failed to awake out of his sleep, and to place himself before the window. There he remained, during a part of the night, staring motionless, his neck extended, his eyes fixed towards the country illuminated by the moon, and, carried away in a sort of contemplative ecstacy, the silence of which was only interrupted by deep-

drawn inspirations, after considerable intervals, and which were always accompanied by a feeble and plaintive sound.

* * * * *

A few days after her twelfth birthday Wind was discharged to a Christian children's home in Nashville. I continued to see her twice a month for three years. With patience, love and firmness her house parents and teachers transformed her into a well spoken, courteous and considerate person. And, with their help, she reached her appropriate grade level in school in two and a half years. How we celebrated! I gave her copies of the *Audubon Field Guide to the Southeastern States* and a collection of Wordsworth's poetry. Not only had she caught up in school but her pronunciation was, but for an occasional lapse, free of mountain dialect.

On July 7, 1970, Wind's fifteenth birthday, I received the phone call I knew would one day come. She was returning home. Her mother, Storm Bird, had reformed her own life. She was no longer a prostitute. She had stopped drinking and joined the Wears Valley Pentecostal Church. Her father was dead. She had a full time job as a housekeeper at a resort hotel at the edge of the Great Smoky Mountains National Park. She had moved into the small town and rented a house trailer. She wanted her daughter back. After verifying the mother's stability to properly care for Wind, the Home's social worker was taking her home.

I saw her the last time on July 14, 1970. We held hands walking across the campus; neither of us spoke. She stopped before her favorite climbing tree, let go of my hand, walked over to the tree, reached around the trunk, pressed her cheek against it and hugged it.

We returned to my office where we both cried. Then the time came; she turned away into the hallway and was gone forever.

Later on, months later on, I attempted to contact her. I was not successful. I never heard from Wind again.

We will always carry each other around in our hearts forever.

* * * * *

Finally, however, seeing that the continuation of my efforts and the passing of time brought about no change, I resigned my efforts to the necessity of giving up any attempts to produce speech, and abandoned my pupil to incurable dumbness...I was obliged to restrain myself and once more to see with resignation [my] hopes, like so many others, vanish before an unforeseen obstacle.

In 1828, Victor died in the home of Madame Guerin, his caretaker. He was forty. Itard died ten years later.

* * * * *

Dear Wind,

How are you? Did you marry? Do you have children? Are you still alive? I pray that you are and that you are happy. You are still in my heart. Am I in yours?

Love, George Spain
January 2016

RUNES

When I left my mother's womb I entered hell.

I touch the tip of my right forefinger to my tongue then slowly skim my finger across my face. In the bathroom mirror I watch it trace the carvings in my flesh, the crumbling eyelids and lips, the gray skin, the thinning hair and the sockets deepening into darkness. I see the mortification and necrotizing from the bacteria feeding within. It stinks of death. I no longer leave the house. I am consumed by despair and hate.

My wife argues with me to the point I want to choke her. She says that these are just the lines and wastings of old age. She begs for me to stop constantly staring into mirrors and feeling my face. Her fussing and begging make me hate her more than I already do. Damn it to hell, I am contaminated by some disease or curse that her stupid doctor's tests are incapable of detecting. I'd kill her before ever returning to see him.

Nothing slows its progress: the salves, heat lamps, the Epsom soakings and prayers might as well be piss. Every food preached to be good for skin is useless: salmon, eggs, blueberries, spinach, gallons of orange juice and those pathetic avocados pass through my body and the decay continues. Nothing removes the poison that entered me through my mother's blood and milk.

She carved these runes into my soul if I have one. She was incapable of mothering. Oh yes, she fed me and kept my clothes clean but she never kissed me or hugged me, never said, "I love you." The only time she ever used the word "love" was when she was speaking of God. How then was I conceived by someone barren of any affection except for the lover who lived in her mind? Did my father rape her? Or am I a child of an immaculate conception?

The Bible's air filled our house. It was my teacher. Its words were the whips that struck my hands and back. Only fear of hell stopped me from killing her. I should have done it when I first thought of it. I was six. She had whipped me with a telephone cord until I bled because I couldn't name all the books in the Old Testament. God should have killed her for me. But He did not.

Surely, I was not created for the suffering I have endured. Or was I? I have read and reread the lamentations of David. Why? I do not know. What little comfort they bring passes as soon as I look into a mirror and see and smell the deterioration; the deeply cut characters in my face and brain.

Beneath my right eye, just a fingernail's length below the lid, there is a tiny crack shaped like a cross leaning sideways in the earth. It can only be seen with a high-resolution magnifying glass capable of exposing truths hidden beneath cryptic designs. My flesh is filled with fallen crosses. I've tried to show them to my wife. She only turns her back, shrugs and says she has them all over her body. She is lying. I am certain. Though I haven't seen her naked in thirty years. As I ponder her deprecations, quick flashes of my mother's face appears. More and more, they are the same.

I am not sure I ever loved her—my wife that is. I may not have been capable. We haven't slept together for years. Now, I cannot bear the thought of her lying beside me, smelling the stench that comes from my pores at night. I can barely stand it myself. It would only give her another reason to berate me. Every morning, I shower and spray deodorant over my entire body.

The only thing I thank God for is that we have no children who might perpetuate this horror to their children. I thank Him for nothing else.

Tonight, before I fall asleep, my last thought will be of killing her.

References

Rune (roon)

Noun 1. Any of the letters of the earliest Germanic alphabet, used esp. by the Scandinavians and Anglo Saxons from around the 3^d cent. AD, and formed by modifying Roman or Greek characters to facilitate carving on wood or stone: a similar character or mark believed to have some magical power of significance. Also a character of a non-Germanic or esp. ancient alphabet. 2. an incantation, a charm esp. one denoted by magic or cryptic signs; a magical word.

Oxford English Dictionary

300.7 – Body Dysmorphic Disorder

The essential feature of Body Dysmorphic Disorder is a preoccupation with a defect in appearance. The defect is either imagined, or, a slight physical anomaly is present, the individual's concern is markedly excessive...most individuals experience marked distress over their supposed deformity, often describing their preoccupations as "intensely painful", or "devastating". As a result, they often spend hours a day thinking about their "defect", to the point where their thoughts may dominate their lives. Significant impairment in many areas of functioning generally occurs. Feelings of self-consciousness about their "defect" may lead to avoidance of work or public situations.

Desk Reference to The Diagnostic Criteria From DSM-IV

ONE LITTLE BOY

THE MOUNTAINS – THE BOY – THE TRACKER –
THE SEARCH – THE YEARS AFTER

*Until you have lost your own little girl or boy and never
found them, how can you ever know the suffering of
losing a child who has touched your face with their
fingers, and smiled at your smile and called you,
"Mama...Daddy"?*

*Though it never leaves you, the sharp pain of seeing
your dead child may dull with time. But if your child is
lost and never found and you're never certain they are
dead, how then, can they ever be dead within your heart?*

*Over time, the meanderings of memories create new
stories from the old ones.*

Since it occurred forty-six years ago, I cannot separate
in my mind if what I remember is actually as it was or if I
have created bits and pieces that are inaccurate. While
letters, books, newspaper articles and websites have
helped in telling this story, it is possible some of my
memories recall other truths not yet told.

June 14, 1969. Six-year-old Dennis Martin is lost in
the Great Smoky Mountains National Park. This is a
story of that little boy, and of a tracker who helped lead

the search, and of the week I spent with him and two other trackers.

The Mountains

At first the earth was flat and very soft and wet...[Then] the Great Buzzard, the father of all the buzzards we see now...flew all over the earth, low down near the ground and it was still soft. When he reached the Cherokee country, he was very tired, and his wings began to flap and strike the ground, and whenever they struck the earth there was a valley, and when they turned up again there was a mountain. When the animals above saw this, they were afraid that the whole world would be mountains, so they called him back, but the Cherokee country remains full of mountains to this day.

Myths of the Cherokee and Sacred Formulas of the Cherokees, 1992
James Mooney

Spence Field, on the crest of Bote Mountain, is four thousand nine hundred twenty feet high; a grassy bald, covering two hundred acres, herds of cattle and flocks of sheep grazed there in the 1800s. In the first week of July 1969, I lay in the oat grass in Spence Field, resting in the sun. Propped on their elbows, their radios on, J. R. Buchanan and Arthur and Grady Whitehead, rangers and trackers for the National Park Service, lay nearby. We looked for circling buzzards that might lead us to the remains of a little boy named Dennis Martin.

In the distance, the Smokies rolled on and on like a graveyard of ancient giants. For a billion years they had formed and reformed. Then, two hundred fifty million years ago, ice and rain and wind began to steadily shape the flowing curves of the mountains we see today. Spence Field lies atop a stretch of the long Appalachian backbone that stretches fifteen hundred miles from Southeastern Canada to Central Alabama. Toward its southern end lies the land of the Cherokee, *Shaconage* ("the place of blue smoke"), the Great Smoky Mountain National Park. Three thousand to six thousand six hundred feet high, the mountains spread outward over five hundred twenty-two thousand four hundred nineteen acres, as far as the eye can see; their colors always changing: deep greens to black, variations of blues, some to deep purple; but in the farthest distance they fade away to ash and pearl-gray mists - then disappear.

The Boy

Dennis Lloyd Martin. He is handsome. Look at his photograph on the website, *The Charley Project: Dennis Lloyd Martin.* You see the smiling face of a little boy who might have been your son or grandson or one of your family. He is beautiful.

Vital Statistics at Time of Disappearance

Missing Since: June 14, 1969, from The Great Smoky Mountains National Park, Tennessee
Classification: Lost/Injured/Missing
Date of Birth: June 20, 1962
Age: 6 years
Height and Weight: 4'0" – 4'1", 55 pounds

Distinguishing Characteristics: Caucasian male. Dark brown hair, brown eyes. Dennis's hair is wavy and he has long, thick eyelashes. He was missing one of his upper front teeth at the time he disappeared.

Clothing/Jewelry Description: A red tee-shirt, dark green hiking shorts, white socks and black low-cut oxford shoes with a simple heel.

Medical Conditions: Dennis had learning disabilities in 1969. At the time of his disappearance, his mental age was about half a year behind his chronological age.

Disappearance

Friday, June 13, 1969, Dennis climbed the trail up Bote Mountain to Russell Field—a long way for a little boy with short legs. Here is the story as told by Ranger Dwight McCarter on the website of *Porchlight International for the Missing and Unidentified:*

The 1969 search for Dennis Martin is a tale with a beginning and a middle. Yet, the story still has no end [46] years later.

On Father's Day weekend in 1969, the men in the Martin family from Knoxville went on an annual hiking and camping trip in the Great Smoky Mountains. Six-year-old Dennis was just a few days shy of his seventh birthday when he made the trip with his father, grandfather, older brother and another family who had a couple of young boys.

At around four thirty in the afternoon on June 14, the group played in the grassy area of Spence Field along the

Tennessee and North Carolina state line. The boys huddled up and planned a playful prank on the adults.

The boys were going to sneak up and scare their family. The three older boys went one way and Dennis went the other way. The plan was for them to jump out of the woods on both sides and scare the adults. The older boys jumped out and everyone laughed and had a lot of fun. Then they asked where Dennis was. When it came time for Dennis to show up and scare the family, Dennis never showed up.

At that point, official reports say it had only been between three to five minutes since the group last saw Dennis. Nonetheless, his father, Knoxville architect, Bill Martin, wasted no time and immediately started searching for his son.

"They hollered for him but couldn't find him. For anyone, it is very easy to get turned around in the thick rhododendron and rugged terrain up there. But, especially, a little boy," said McCarter. "Another problem at Spence Field is there seems to be an incessant wind that comes out of Tennessee and whips over the mountain. You could blow and whistle up there and the wind drowns it out."

Bill Martin hiked the paths in several directions searching for Dennis. The grandfather, Clyde Martin, hiked down to Cades Cove and back. Park rangers and other people in the park were notified and a search began.

As darkness started to fall, so did extremely heavy rain. It came in buckets at the worst possible time. The storm dumped an estimated two and a half inches of rain on the mountain that night.

The storm was so vicious, the people there at the shelter had trouble even lighting a fire. You have lightning and thunder and all that rain. You can imagine the people there in the shelter just imaging what the little boy was going through. That's all you could possibly be thinking. Where was he? Where could he be?

In the following days, crews started searching the trails and swollen creeks for any sign of Dennis Martin. Special Forces were in the area performing exercises and were made available to assist in the search. The search party now included the Green Berets with experience in fighting and navigating the jungles of Vietnam...

On June 20 the road to Cades Cove was closed as more than four hundred volunteers took to the mountains. If he was found alive, a helicopter was standing by to fly him to the Marine Corps Base on Alcoa Highway and from there an ambulance would take him to the University of Tennessee hospital.

The search and hoped-for rescue was getting national attention. Clairvoyant Jeane Dixon, who gained nationwide recognition for predicting the assassination of President John Kennedy, told the News Sentinel she "sensed" Martin was still alive. Seven days after he disappeared she told the paper "the boy was still breathing last night."

[My response to the previous comment by Jeane Dixon: I feel that such "seers" are either delusional due to their own mental problems, or are religious fanatics who prey on mentally ill and emotionally disturbed people. Through my work in mental health, I have seen the damage such people can do to those who are mentally ill, and to their families.]

"It went from hundreds of people to where you eventually had fourteen hundred people saturating the area. And when you've got fourteen hundred people, they've stomped on everything. It just doesn't work. Every broken branch or 'piece of white' an experienced tracker looks for has been trampled. You've got search dogs that cannot sniff out any clues because there were fourteen hundred people there. We did searches back then like they were forest fires. You surrounded it and drowned it."

Any clues not washed away by the rain were drowned by the flood of good-hearted people trying their best to help. The search dragged on. People claiming to have psychic powers started sending messages to the Park and then showing up to influence the search...

People across East Tennessee and the nation desperately searched for Dennis Martin. How could a young boy wearing a bright red shirt disappear so quickly? How could fourteen hundred people not find a single trace of him?

Theories ran rampant but were mostly based on rumor or speculation. Some thought he may have been killed by a bear or wild boar. The shorelines of Fontana Lake were searched in case he was washed away in the heavy rains. The family offered a reward for their son's return for fear the total disappearance meant Dennis had been kidnapped...

After weeks went by, survival grew unlikely for Dennis if he was still in the Park. With the strong possibility of death in the air, that's when many searchers turned their attention. They searched the air for any decaying odors in the woods. They watched for vultures and buzzards circling overhead. The searchers found lots of small animals, a dog carcass and a dead bobcat. Still, no sign of Dennis....

As for what happened to Dennis Martin, the question has no answer. The story has no ending.

The Tracker

J. R. Buchanan was ten years older than me. He stood five-foot-four and in his prime weighed one hundred twenty-eight pounds. As my grandmother use to say, "There wasn't an extra slice of pie anywhere on him." He was an ordinary looking man. But everything else about him was way bigger and much smarter than most any man I've known! He once told me, "J. R. stands for just plain J. R." Like his name, he spoke his thoughts straight, without twists or hidings. Tough as the mountains where he was born and where he would die, he was a man who spoke truth, as he believed it. And yet, there was a great kindness and tenderness in him as you will see in his letters to me. He was good to me and good to my family, most especially, our son Brad who he trained to track.

The FBI nicknamed him "Walking Small." In World War II he served as a demolition technician under General George S. Patton. In 1986 he went to Washington for the ceremonies where the Secretary of the Interior presented him with the Medal of Valor, the highest award the Department of Interior gives.

On December 2, 2001, the *Nashville Tennessean* had a long article on him, in which he was called: "The bloodhound of the Smokies". As he sat in his living room during the interview he pointed to his walking cane that waited within easy reach near the door. It was made from North Carolina Bellwood. He spoke to the journalist in a raspy, slow voice. He pointed to his cane. Listen to his seventy-five-year old voice –

"You can take that stick and whup the biggest bear there ever was...I done tracking. Some of them called me 'the bloodhound'. I tracked everything from the wild boar to ginseng diggers, poachers, pot growers and killers...

"It was a lot of pleasure to track down a person that was lost to bring them in alive...I enjoyed my work, except for the times I'd have to go tell somebody that their brother or sister or whoever it was that you had found them dead. A lot of times, it was plane crashes or falls or drownings that would kill 'em. I believe I brought out and had to bring out 25 people – dead."

He learned the craft of following tracks from his grandpa and his great uncle when he was a teenager in the 1930s...

As a tracker, he was on call 24 hours a day. When he entered the woods, he always carried a gun, radio, daypack (with candy bars), flare gun, map and compass...but his eyes and ears were his most valuable tools.

"I've tracked all over this park...I never did get lost. I got turned around two or three times, but I'd just sit down. If you'll just sit down, start to thinking, then you can get up and get on, or I could have always backtracked myself.

"There's two things makes a good [tracker]. It takes somebody who has spent quite a bit of time in the mountains and a good deer hunter...

"As far as I am concerned, there's never been an expert. I still think that...the only thing I would say would be an expert would be a fellow who don't do nothing. You're gonna make a mistake. I still make mistakes and a lot of 'em. Especially up in the Smokies.

"You may be tracking a person and all at once, it may be two sets of tracks. You may take one of 'em and may wind up after a quarter of a mile find out it's a bear you're tracking...I've tracked a lot of bear..."

End of the trail

Buchanan and Phyllis, his wife, live in the house they built in 1988 in Cades Cove; as the crow flies, it is about four miles away.

He has a flower garden thriving in a one-acre patch of sunlight in the back yard. Blueberry bushes, 50-foot-tall cane, trees of every sort, pokeberry, Mexican sunflowers grow here. All types of wildlife – boar, bears, coyotes, snakes, birds and butterflies – pass through his yard.

Unless they do damage, he leaves them alone. J. R. Buchanan has a peace treaty worked out with nature, and after seventy-five years together, they get along just fine.

The Search

The intensive search ended on June 29, 1969. But the very next day three rangers were assigned to continue looking.

I could not get out of my mind the horror that Dennis's parents must have felt knowing the larger search had been called off and their son might still be out there.

I read every article written in the *Nashville Tennessean* and the *Nashville Banner* about the search. In his face in the newspaper, I saw the faces of my own children. Having a daughter about his age, I think I was obsessed.

I decided to go look for him even if he was dead. My wife approved and the psychiatrist who directed our clinic said okay. So I went.

I am not certain I remember it exactly but I believe most of what I remember is as it was.

On Saturday, July 5, 1969, I drove from Williamson County to Townsend, Tennessee, in our powder blue Volkswagen station wagon with a sleeping bag in the back, a kerosene lantern, a stove, some extra clothes, a backpack, canteen, a sack of food and a couple of books.

I arrived in Townsend at dusk and found a small campground on the bank of the Little River. A restaurant was a few hundred feet away. It turned out to be a good location as every evening when I came back from a day of intensive searching, I was dirty and so my first action was to bathe in the river, put on clean clothes and go to the restaurant for a good meal.

Early the next morning I drove into Cades Cove Visitor Center where I was directed to the Ranger Station. I was anxious and a little scared that they might reject me.

But "lo, and behold!" the opposite occurred. The ranger who greeted me seemed genuinely appreciative of my coming. He filled in a form with information about me and told me to report the next morning at seven forty-five and bring a backpack with my lunch and water.

On Monday, July 7, at eight o'clock I arrived at the ranger station and was introduced to rangers J. R. Buchanan, Arthur Whitehead and Grady Whitehead, three mountain men, one short and the others tall, each dressed in neatly creased, mildly starched khakis. They had lean, raw-boned faces with intelligence and confidence in their eyes: men I came to admire and have affection for. They loved their world of mountains and valleys where they had been born and would die. There was much kindness in their hearts.

And so, for the next five days I met them every morning, climbed into a jeep and bounced up Bote Mountain on a narrow fire road to Spence Field. What do I remember of those days? Disjointed bits and pieces - they may have been in different sequences, yet these I'll tell are photographed in my brain filled with obsession and some caution of danger –

It is the first day. We are spread out on a slight slope not far from the crest of the mountain. I can't see the others. We are crawling on our bellies beneath a "laurel hell". The entwined laurel branches inches above my head, are so thick they are impassable walking upright; the earth, inches beneath my face – initially firm – suddenly becomes broken as though plowed by a sharp blade; the air is thick with the rank odor of animal. The next moment, immediately in front of me, though I cannot see them, I hear a herd of wild boar leaping to their feet, squealing, grunting and crashing away through the laurel and a shout from someone below me, "Hogs, don't move!"

Another day comes. We are on a steep pitch of a mountainside, joggling and bouncing in the jeep up a narrow, rutted fire road. Arthur is driving. Gears grind. The jeep jerks forward into a rut and tilts downward and sideways. With every gripper on my body I grip everything I can to not be pitched out, while behind me I am smothered by the sloshing, souring smell of corn mash in an oil drum, that J.R had picked up earlier that morning from a still. We ground to a halt. J. R. and Grady jump out, lift the drum down to the ground, take the lid off, tip the drum sideways and walk down a narrow trail, spilling the thick liquid mash onto the trail behind them and then I see, not far ahead of them a large cage trap. Arthur says, "George, tha hogs dearly love tha mash."

I am the first one up from the rest break and lead off on the narrow foot trail that twists along the side of a steep stone pitch walled by laurel. The others file close behind. It's the first time they've let me lead off, and I don't want to do anything dumb, like tripping and falling off the side. We walk for fifteen minutes. My balance is good, my eyes and ears sharp. I am aware of everything. Just ahead there is a sharp, quick-cornered right turn around a stone pitch. With my right hand I brace myself and carefully step around the corner and there...barely six feet away...is a bear...the biggest bear God ever made. One quick sucking of air and I cannot breathe. I cannot speak. I cannot move. I am about to be eaten alive. Then, as I suck in a lung full of air, I push backward. I push against a human being behind me who curses. I push backward hard again and there is another curse. And I hear what seems to be my voice whimper, "Bear." Sound and sight blur. Someone pushes from behind and I shove back hard. My eyes fix on the bear. It seems to have grown a hundred pounds larger and turned to me with its mouth stretched wide. Then, in a blur I see a leap of sheer blackness as it disappears from the trail and crashes downward into the wall of laurel as though it is made of tissue paper. And it is gone and there is laughter—but not from me.

We lie under the sun on the soft grass of Spence Field eating baloney and cheese sandwiches looking out onto a clear day and the far distance of the mountains. We are tired and happy. We've searched for three hours, now we are resting and eating and looking for circling buzzards—buzzards looking for the dead. The rangers' radios were on...suddenly, there's a report of someone firing a gun from a car coming up Newfound Gap Road. We listen to the chatter as pursuit begins and higher up a roadblock is set. It is a beautiful day, a breeze waves across the grass and as the sun shines on my face, J. R., who tends to stammer and curse a bit when he is excited and there are no women and children around, says, "I hope they catch tha...tha...son-uv-a bitch on tha North Carolina side 'cause that Judge ul put his ass under tha...tha jail." Arthur stands up, hoists his pack onto his back, puts his radio on his belt and says, "Okay, it's time to go." And we start on down the slope into the forest and downward.

We are walking along a fire road where the ground is level. Beneath the trees it is fairly open and we can see a fair distance ahead. I am in the rear. J. R. and the Whiteheads are dressed in clean, pressed khakis. Walking behind them, I see how little they sweat, not a thimble-full of stain is between their shoulder blades or under their armpits; only a gnat or two flies around their faces. Their movements are easy as though they are walking from one room to another in their homes. At the same time, I look and feel like I have been dragged by mules through these mountains; drenched in sweat, swarmed by a million gnats, filthy and wandering in a world not my own.

We come over a slight rise and see a little ways ahead a station wagon parked in the middle of the road. A bear is standing on its hind legs leaning into the driver's open window. No one is in the car. The trackers shout; the bear jerks out and runs off into the forest. The car is Dennis Martin's father's. He is there searching. We do not see him. We move on.

The slope is steep and pummeled with boulders; a rivulet runs through the sharpest cut. I am careful. A fall here could break a leg or arm or worse. We go to a large "den tree" where a bear has had her cubs high up in a cavity. They show me the tree to teach me as they have tried to from the first. They love these mountains. I can tell they like me and want to share what they love. They try to teach me the signs of tracks. "George, look there, see them prints. You know what they are?" (I never know. As a mental health therapist I am pretty good at reading people. As a reader of animal tracks and signs I am dumb as mud.) "That's where a bar wus walkin' on its hind legs." And, "See them scrapings on that tree, that's where a bar was markin' its territory." And, leaning down Grady gently put two fingers around a small flower, "George, the deer dearly love these."

The next day, or was it the next, I left them and the Smokies. Forty-six years later, I cannot forget J. R. and Arthur and Grady. Rare it is in life to know people of such intelligence and wisdom and strength of body and goodness of mind. We shook hands as I left the ranger station. They asked me to return to visit them and their families. Our friendship was born in tragedy.

As I drove away from the mountains and headed south toward home my mind went back to Dennis, the forest, the bears, the hogs, my new friends, but then they began to gradually fade away and all I could think about was seeing and hugging and kissing Jackie and our children.

The Years After

After that year my family and I maintained contact with J. R. and his family. They came to stay with us for a few days at our home in Williamson County. We took them to the Ryman Auditorium to see the Grand Ole Opry where we saw Dolly Parton perform. And once we took our pop-up camper to Abram's Creek campground in the Smokies and fished; and J. R. and the Whiteheads came and ate with us and told tall tales of their adventures with bears and boar and humans. One evening we went to the homes of Grady and J. R. in Happy Valley and shot our muzzle-loading pistols in their backyards.

For several years J. R. and I wrote to one another. I still have four of his letters to me and one brief one to Brad who took J. R.'s tracking course in 1985 for park rangers and the F.B.I.

J. R. wrote in pencil on lined notebook paper with his unique spelling, capitalizations and punctuation. His work as a ranger is scattered throughout. He always concludes with words of affection. His first letter was written six months after my week with him in the mountains. It begins formally with, "Dear Mr. Spain." In all of the following letters he calls me, "George". The letters are given in full, exactly as structured, spelled and punctuated.

12 - 17 - 69

Dear Mr. Spain
I am sending you a Map you
may get to use it some day

(Two aerial photographs showing the area we searched were rolled up in a tube. I still have them.)

I sure would like to be back
up on the Mounting with you
again. We stayed on the Mounting
until Nov 25ʰ and we Found nothing
but we got a lot of Hogs.
if you do get back down here
we may get to go back up on
the Mounting We have had a

good Fall but the hunters gave
us a hard time to I am off now
For 2.65 hours so I am goind to
Hunt and Fish sume Me and
Grady went Fishing to day We got
11 good Fish if you come Down
about June or July or Aug I may
get to Fishing with you.
Well Pall I hope that you and
Your Family has a good Xmas
And tell all the Kids Hello
For Me.

good night
With Love J. R. Buchanan

2 – 23 - 70

Hello George
I was glad to here From
you.
but sorry to here that you
all had the Flu I hope that
you all are over the Flu by
now.
We are all ok I am about
wore out. I sure would have Liked
to have had you with me I
had to walk in the Snow
day after day up to my belt
and I sure got Cold

(He is referring to a search in February 1970, for
Geoff Hague, a boy scout, who wandered away from his

troop. Eleven days later, on February 18, he was found frozen to death beneath a tree.)

We had 2 Choppers but they had
to stay on the ground a Lot
of the time but it is over
now and I am glade.
Well old Boy you said that you
was goind to come down and
go fishing Well if you have
a camper or a Tent you can
Stay at Abrams Creek Camp
ground and I will be
glad to go fishing with
you and your Boys and I will take my Boy
along

#

he Likes to go with me
and we go out a lot
and when you get Ready to
Come Let me know and I
will be Ready I don't know
what days I will be off but
we can get to good days Fishing
in and Grady will have 2 days
so you can get 4 days Fishing
and the Best time is June
July and Aug but you can come any
Time and we will get in
Some good Fishing.

Well old Pal I am goind to
Stop For now I have go company
so I will stop.

Love J.R.

5 - 22- 70

Hello George
and all.
And how are you all by now
Fine I hope.
Well as far as we are ok
I am sorry that I haven't
Wrote you sooner but I have
been working pretty hard and
I was on a fire this week
on the 20th and I got home
the next day I was on the Fire
241/2 and I sure was all in when
I got home and we got the
Fire out and I went back
On pt in the Cove to day and
In the Morning I will be
On the Creek and that is
My Last in the Rangers
Force for a while I will be
in the campground and it will
be 8 hours and I will be off.
and George I sure was glade
to get the Book I have n
my wife and Kids has
I may get time to Read
In the Summer I have had

To haul 2 bears out of the
Campground one of them went
500. LPS. and one 300 LPS. and
the Big one we Shot for 500 LPS
and he went on he would go
a lot over 500 – but we did not
get him but if he comes back
we will.
I have been Fishing some and
I have had good Luck
and if you get to come up
and Camp we will go and
have a time I am off
Thursday and Friday and we will
Stay all night if you want
to. I don't guess you can
make this out but I am almost
a sleep and I have got to
be in the Cove by 6 AM.
I will stop for now so
Write me Soon
With Love

J R.
Over DS

the wife and Kids said think
you for the Book and I think
you. So good Night

I

2 - 4 - 72

Hi George and all.
I hope this will find you all ok
We are all ok I think I am Still
Frozen and I have been all day I
have been out all day in the snow
and ice and I had Plenty of
ice on the Parkway and sume
snow and We have got a lot
of snow on Smokey and I wish
that you and the Boys were here
We could Find Plenty <u>Hogs</u> they
are coming Down it is to cold
up on the Big Mounting I May
go out and see if I can Find
sume in the Morning.
I forgot to tell you that we are at
the Chilhowee Ranger Station now we
have
been here For about 4 weeks I don't know
how Long I will be here I am goind
to Move over to Abrams Creek Ranger
Station I hope it may be 6 weeks or
more I don't yet but I hope soon
and we will be Looking for you
all to come Down and spend sume

II

time with us and we can do sume
Fishing I helped the State Stock tuesday

We put 3700 [trout] in and this was one
More truck load come in and it
had about 3700 in it and they
Closed the Lake until March
15th so this will be a lot of trout
I chicked one man before the Lake
Closed he had (3) Rainbows – 21½ 20 19
½

so when you come we will have a
Lot of Fun and I hope you will get
to come Down this summer and tell My
Buddy (our son Brad) that me and him
will go hog
hunting he can carry my new gun
I have got a 22 Ruger Single (6) 22 or 22
mag
it sure is a good one.
I can walk for 3 or 4 weeks and I still
want get over half of my Dist.
We got 3 men For killing a doe deer
but they keep on hunting and we
keep on goind out after him I have got
(5) Bear Traps so they want use them
any more. Well I am goind to stop
For now so Let us hear from you all
soon and I hope to see you
all this summer at Abrams Creek
I have got sume papper work
to do so I will say good Night

With Love the Buchanans

The following letter was sent to Brad, who was twenty-six, after he had been certified as having, "Satisfactorily Completed The Visual Tracking School" for The F.B.I., National Park Rangers, and Rescue Workers" directed by J. R. in the Smokies in the early summer of 1985.

6 - 3 - 85

Hi you all
and how are you all By now
ok I hope. Well as For us We are
all ok I have had a cold For
two weeks and I have still got it
and worked in the Rain about
all week I have been doing sume
work in Cades Cove on a case you
may have heard about it the Bones of
a Lady that was found I have been
working with the F. B. I. We do [not]
know
who she is But we don't know how she
died.

Well Brad I will stop For now
Write soon
J. R.

In August, 2000, J. R. wrote a last brief letter to me -

To one of my Best Friends
We walked in the Big Mounting
And the Little one and I

Loved Every day You are a good
Friend so stop By and we talk
About the good old times.

Love JR Buchanan

* * * * *

How could you not love this man?

* * * * *

J. R. Buchanan

October 13, 1926 – August 3, 2004

Visitation:...August 6, 2004
Service:......August 6, 2004

J. R. Buchanan – age 77 of Happy Valley passed away Tuesday August 3, 2004 at his home. He was a member of Happy Valley Missionary Baptist Church and was a retired Park Ranger from the Great Smoky Mountain National Park Service. He was a veteran serving in the U. S. Army serving during WWII.

Funeral services will be 8:00 p.m. Friday in McCammon-Ammons-Click Funeral Home Chapel with Rev. Steve Whitehead and Rev. Beecher Whitehead officiating. Family and friends will meet 12:00 noon Saturday at Happy Valley Missionary Baptist Cemetery for the interment service.

On-line Memorial Program by "FuneralNet"

And so...

What more can be said about the loss of Dennis Martin, the little boy lost in the Smokies in 1969 who was never found? Was he killed and eaten by an animal? Was he abducted? Did he fall into a pit or wander so deep into a laurel thicket he was overlooked by the searchers?

There is no answer.

Why am I writing about him forty-six years later? It is simply this: he has never left me; J. R. Buchanan has never left me; and the Smokies where I hiked the Appalachian Trail when I graduated from high school, and searched for Dennis for five days in 1969, and afterward camped there with my family; all these years this little boy and these mountain people have never left me. But more than all this, Jackie and I had five children, one near Dennis's age at the time he disappeared and the questions at the beginning have never left me –

Until you have lost your own little girl or boy and cannot find them, how can you ever know the fear and pain of losing a child who has touched your face with their fingers and smiled at your smile and called you, "Mama...Daddy?"

If your child is lost and never found and you are never certain they are dead, how can they ever be dead within your heart?

CPSIA information can be obtained at www.ICGtesting.com
Printed in the USA
LVOW08*2046060416

482482LV00001B/1/P